The man's eyes were all over Ivy

Taylor stifled a groan as Don pulled an empty chair up to the table.

"Ivy, how come I haven't seen you around? Where are you from?"

"Baksra. It's an island in Indonesia," she explained. "I'm here for a month, and Taylor is kindly showing me around."

"I'll bet it's no trouble for old Taylor." Don smirked. "However, if he finds himself tied up and there's somewhere you'd like to go, just give me a call. I'm at your service night and day."

Fortunately, just then the hostess signaled that their table was ready. Taylor jumped to his feet. "Be seeing you, Don."

As Taylor spirited Ivy away, he muttered to her, "Don't ever call him, for anything, nothing, ever. Understand?"

Ivy shook her head in bewilderment. She'd never ever understand Americans.

ABOUT THE AUTHOR

For the Love of Ivy is Barbara Kaye's fifteenth Superromance novel. Set in part on the fictional Indonesian island of Baksra, the story will transport readers to a romantic, exotic location they are sure to enjoy.

Barbara has also contributed to Harlequin's CRYSTAL CREEK saga, which begins this month. Barbara is a natural for these set-in-Texas stories. Although she lives in Oklahoma with her husband, she is a native Texan who combines her intimate knowledge of the Lone Star State and its people with her considerable talent in the first CRYSTAL CREEK book. Be sure to look for *Deep in the Heart* by Barbara Kaye this month.

Books by Barbara Kaye

HARLEQUIN SUPERROMANCE
433–CHALLENGE OF A LIFETIME (HAMILTON HOUSE: BOOK 2)
449–CHANCE OF A LIFETIME (HAMILTON HOUSE: BOOK 3)
495–LOVE ME TENDER

HARLEQUIN AMERICAN ROMANCE
19–CALL OF EDEN

Barbara
Kaye

FOR THE LOVE OF IVY

Harlequin Books

TORONTO • NEW YORK • LONDON
AMSTERDAM • PARIS • SYDNEY • HAMBURG
STOCKHOLM • ATHENS • TOKYO • MILAN
MADRID • WARSAW • BUDAPEST • AUCKLAND

Published March 1993

ISBN 0-373-70540-9

FOR THE LOVE OF IVY

CHAPTER ONE

THE CALL CAME shortly after Taylor Edwards returned to his Fort Worth office after lunch, and a summons from Eleanor Cameron was not something anyone took lightly. Least of all Taylor. Eleanor was more than a dear friend and mentor; she was a large part of the reason the prestigious law firm of Sheldon and Ernst had offered him a junior partnership. He owed her a lot.

Taylor left his office and stepped out into the blinding afternoon sun. It was as stupefyingly hot as only Texas in July could be. The interior of his car was an inferno, even though he had left the windows slightly opened. He whipped off the white towel that covered the steering wheel—without the towel he would have been unable to touch the wheel without running the air-conditioning for several minutes—rolled down all four windows and was on his way.

It only took a few minutes to cover the distance between his office on Camp Bowie Boulevard and the large, imposing Cameron home in Rivercrest. The neighborhood was the recognized bastion of first-generation oilmen. It lay to the west of the city and swept along the edge of the country club. Mature trees protected the half-timbered English-style homes from the cruel heat. It was a sedate, solid neighborhood, representing old money—by Texas standards—and plenty of it. A white-uniformed servant named Wilma answered the door. "Good afternoon, Mr. Edwards. Mrs. Cameron is waiting for you in the library."

"Thanks, Wilma." Taylor strode down the darkly paneled hallway to double doors that opened into a massive room filled with antiques and books. Everything about the house had a museumlike elegance; one half expected to encounter rooms roped off with red velvet and Authorized Personnel Only signs. Taylor had heard it said that from the day Ben Cameron had brought in the well that had opened up the highly lucrative Wheeler Field in West Texas, he and Eleanor had devoted themselves to the acquisition of fine things from all over the world. He supposed that had been an attempt to shake off all vestiges of their rural Oklahoma roots, an attempt that had been only partially successful. Eleanor would have been at home in any drawing room in the world; Ben never lost his biscuits-and-gravy farm-boy demeanor.

Ben's down-home persona was certainly reflected in his choice of a pet, Taylor thought, as he came across the large dog lying in the entrance to the library. Jethro, honey colored and of questionable parentage—larger than a spaniel but not as large as, say, a boxer—had been Ben's constant companion. So far as anyone knew, the dog hadn't had anything to do with anyone since Ben's death. He received food, water and periodic visits to the veterinarian and the groomer, but beyond that, his attitude toward the human race could best be described as indifferent. He usually greeted Taylor with an annoyed growl, and this afternoon was no exception.

"Pleased to see you, too, Jethro," Taylor said as he stepped around the dog and entered the library. Jethro slunk behind him and took his customary spot near the hearth.

Eleanor was waiting, seated in a high-backed brocade chair near the fireplace. Taylor thought it had the effect of making her look dainty and delicate, a deceiving impression. Though she stood something less than five-four, she was so dynamic and forceful that no one thought of her as small for long. As usual, she was dressed as though she were on her way to afternoon tea, and her silver hair was immaculately coifed. Diamonds gleamed from her lobes and fingers.

Taylor never stepped into the matriarch's presence without feeling a trifle nervous—like a schoolboy called before the principal. She only had to look at him and he experienced the urge to wash his hands, comb his hair and straighten his tie. It helped to know that the woman had the same effect on just about everyone. Even senior partner David Ernst, himself a rather formidable old gentleman, seemed humble when confronted by Eleanor.

It was almost impossible to believe she had ever been submissive and respectful, the archetypical silent helpmate, but Taylor had heard stories. When old Ben had been strong and powerful and energetic, it was said that Eleanor had stayed in the background, devoting her energies to him, their children and grandchildren. But today, whether from desire or duty, she had her fingers on the pulse of every facet of Cameron Oil Corporation. When she spoke, her sons and grandsons listened.

Taylor crossed the room and briefly took her hand. "Hello, Eleanor."

"Hello, Taylor. Thank you for coming so quickly. Would you like something to drink?"

"No, thanks," he said, stepping back to take a chair across from her. "Eleanor, when you called you said you had something important to discuss with me."

"Yes," Eleanor replied. "Very important." She picked up an envelope from the table at her elbow. "I received this in the morning mail. It's taken me some time to collect my wits and decide what it is I want to do about it. I'd like you to read it." She leaned forward and stretched out her arm.

Taylor partially rose and took the envelope, then sat back down. Inside was a letter written on an ancient manual typewriter.

Dear Mrs. Cameron,
It is with deep regret that I inform you of the

deaths of Drs. Gordon and Claire Loving three days ago. They were the victims of a boating accident off the coast of Baksra during a sudden squall. They were buried with much ceremony this morning, for they were greatly loved and admired by our island's residents. I myself have lost two of my dearest friends.

I apologize for having to inform you of the tragedy in such an impersonal way, but Baksra has no telephone service, and our only contacts with the outside world are radios and a plane from Djakarta that arrives on the island every five days. It may take some time for this to reach you.

May I extend to you my deepest sympathy. Ivy is doing as well as can be expected under the circumstances. Please be assured that she has friends here and is well taken care of. She has asked me to convey to you her warmest regards.

Sincerely,
Erik Soewadji

Taylor glanced at the top of the page. The letter had been dated two weeks ago. He frowned, trying to think who the Drs. Loving could be. Then the name Claire rang a bell. Eleanor's daughter, the anthropologist? It had to be. He looked at the elderly woman seated across from him. He didn't expect to see tears, and there were none. There had been none at Ben's funeral, either. If Eleanor needed to cry, she would do it privately.

But the news had affected her, he could tell. She didn't seem quite as formidable as she usually did. "Your daughter?" he asked quietly.

"Yes, my daughter."

"I'm very sorry, Eleanor."

"Thank you. I'm sorry, too. But it's been so long since I last saw Claire that reading the letter was almost like being informed of the death of a stranger, and I really never got to know Gordon at all." Her incisive eyes grew distant, but only for the briefest second. She turned back to Taylor. "Tell me, how much do you know about our family?"

The question took him by surprise. "Well, I...I'm not sure I know what you mean."

"Oh, come, come, I know we're gossiped about incessantly. Why that's so, I can't imagine. Except possibly for Claire, I think we're a pretty ordinary family. Perhaps we're a bit heavily populated with males, but there's really nothing unusual about us."

Taylor wondered if she honestly believed that. Having many millions of dollars might be considered unusual to a lot of people. But in spite of all that money, the Camerons were a pretty good bunch. Not one of them had been content to sit around the Petroleum Club and watch their real estate appreciate. They'd all done something. Ben and Eleanor had two sons, Robert and Michael, who now ran Cameron Oil Corporation. Both of them had the chic, lovely wives that custom seemed to decree men of their stature should have. Each also had two sons. Robert's were actively involved in the family business, while Michael's had taken different paths. One was a Dallas physician; the other was a Houston architect. Except for being a lot better off than most people in their thirties, the grandsons were a normal group—not a flamboyant, free-spending airhead in the lot.

"Well, Eleanor, I imagine you know what I know about your family," Taylor hedged. "I'm acquainted with your sons and their families, and I like all of them."

Eleanor nodded. "Yes, they've turned out well. I think I have Ben to thank for that. There was no nonsense in his own upbringing, and he allowed none in Robert's and Michael's. The boys in turn have passed that along to their own sons." She paused to sigh. "Claire, however, was a different matter."

Taylor had never met Eleanor's only daughter, and he knew very little about her. Claire and her husband were renowned anthropologists who had written several scholarly books on remote cultures and societies. One, he had heard, was almost a bible in the field. But Claire and Gordon Loving had all but completely divorced themselves from the Camerons and Texas long ago. Claire was never spoken of, and there were no photographs of her in any of the rooms he was familiar with.

"As the youngest child and only girl," Eleanor went on, "she was horribly spoiled, I'm afraid, not only by her father but by her brothers as well. No one could tell her what to do. She was a young woman in her twenties when the decade of the sixties rolled around. Do you remember the sixties, Taylor?''

He smiled. ''I wasn't born until 1956. I was just a kid during those years.''

''Dreadful decade, absolutely terrible. It couldn't have been a worse time for Claire to be reaching womanhood. She was headstrong but also idealistic and impressionable. I noticed such a change in her after she went away to college. She seemed almost embarrassed by the family's wealth. She fell in with a group of young people who were turning their backs on their parents' way of life, who somehow equated poverty with all that was right and good in the world. She kept lecturing me, *me!* about excessiveness and overconsumption.'' Eleanor made a derisive sound. ''I reminded her that I had begun married life in a dog-run cabin. I told her I was on quite familiar terms with making do and doing without, thank you. I also told her that her father's lease payments to ranchers and farmers had built more schools and roads than she could count. It did no good. This was all she'd ever known...'' Eleanor's hand made a sweep to indicate the house as a whole ''...and she'd come to the conclusion that it was somehow wrong to live this way. It always puzzled me that she never admired or appreciated the sheer hard work that enabled us to live this way.'' She sighed again.

It occurred to Taylor that those occasional sighs were the nearest thing to a slip in composure Eleanor ever displayed. And he had no earthly idea why she had chosen to tell him all this, but when it came to Eleanor, his was not to reason why. "So," he said, "how did she come to take up anthropology, of all things?"

"She met Gordon, and that was his field. She had been studying art, but that was abandoned after he entered the picture. He convinced her it was their mission in life to go out into the world and find the perfect unmaterialistic society where people were wondrously content living without 'things.' Then to write about it and supposedly show the rest of us the error of our ways." Eleanor made another derisive sound. "Sounds idyllic, doesn't it? And utterly non-sensical. Anyway, Claire got her degree in anthropology, then a master's, eventually her Ph.D. She and Gordon were married by then, or said they were. And the next thing I knew, the two scholars were on their way to South America."

She paused. Taylor could tell she was having some difficulty relating the story. He felt a sense of personal satisfaction that she had made him her confidant, but he still wondered what the point of it all was.

"I suppose they were gloriously happy in their snake-infested jungle," Eleanor continued, "but then something happened that not even two brilliant Ph.D.s were able to prevent. They had a child, a daughter. I fully expected that to bring them back to the States, but a few months after the child was born, I received a letter from Claire. She and Gordon simply couldn't abandon their 'important' work at such a 'crucial' stage, but a jungle was no place for a child. It was the first completely intelligent thing I had heard my daughter say in years. I immediately flew to Belém, met Claire and brought the baby back here. And except for a few sporadic visits from her parents as they were on their way to this village or that island, Ivy saw little of them until she was nine.''

Taylor had wondered who the Ivy in the letter was. "What happened when she was nine?''

Again the distant look came to Eleanor's eyes, but again only for a second. "Claire and Gordon came to see us. They were on their way to northern India to live with and study a Hindu family. They professed to be horrified at the way Ivy was living.''

"How was she living?''

Now Eleanor's eyes flashed. "The same way her cousins were living, of course. She had a lovely room of her own and servants to watch her. She had lots of nice clothes, plenty of good food, playmates and a shiny new bicycle. It was Christmas, and she was very excited about what she might get. What child isn't at Christmas? She was a healthy, happy, well-adjusted child, but her parents declared that we were teaching her all the wrong values. They insisted she leave with them.''

Taylor's breath escaped in a hiss. "What did you do?"

"What do you think I did? I called David Ernst and told him I wanted custody of the girl. Sadly, he told me I was wasting my time. The courts would never let me have Ivy if her natural parents wanted her. Claire and Gordon weren't unfit parents, David told me. Just unconventional ones. The more I looked into it, the more I realized he was right. I didn't have a chance. But it was Ben who finally gave me the strength to let go. 'She'll be back,' he said. 'She's had nine years of this. She'll come back.'"

"But she never did?" Taylor prompted.

Eleanor shook her head. "No. She couldn't as a minor, and by the time she was of age, I suppose she had forgotten what it was like here or had been seduced to her parents' way of life. I wrote to her every week the first year they were in India, but gradually her letters became less and less frequent. Eventually I contented myself with cards to her at Christmas and on her birthday. Originally I put money inside them, but then I got a rather testy letter from Claire saying the money was difficult to exchange and of little use to Ivy. That was absolute nonsense, of course. I've done a bit of traveling around this world, and never once did I have any trouble exchanging an American dollar. They simply didn't want Ivy to remember all she had here."

She paused again, looked down at her hands, then went on. "They had placed her in an exclusive and very straitlaced English-speaking academy by that time. Then she entered the University of Singapore, and her parents left for that godforsaken island. Apparently at some point Ivy decided to join them. I'm very vague on a lot of this. Ivy seldom contacted me. The last time was...oh, two years ago, I guess. I imagine she barely remembers me."

"Where in the devil is Baksra, anyway?" Taylor asked.

"Somewhere in the East Indies, the Spice Islands, I think. I've never been able to find it on any map, but when you consider there are seventy-nine thousand of those islands, I suppose that's not surprising."

"Seventy-nine *thousand?*"

"So the books say. However, we now know the island has plane service every five days, so it isn't inaccessible. It can be reached, though God knows how long it will take. We know that Ivy is still there, and we know there is someone on the island who can be communicated with—the man who wrote that letter."

An alarm went off inside Taylor's head. "Eleanor, surely, *surely* you aren't thinking of going to a remote island in the East Indies, because if you are—"

"Oh, good heavens, no!" Eleanor exclaimed with a little laugh. "At my age? A trip to Dallas for lunch exhausts me. There's no earthly way I could consider making such a journey."

"Thank God for that," Taylor said, relieved. If Eleanor had actually decided to undertake a trip like that, nothing on earth would dissuade her, and at eighty-six she had no business even thinking of such a thing.

"I want you to go for me," she said calmly.

"Me?"

"You."

"Wouldn't...wouldn't one of her uncles or cousins be a more logical messenger?"

"No, you're the perfect choice, a third party. I want you to see Ivy and persuade her to come back here where she belongs."

Oh, Lord, he thought, totally taken aback. So that was it. "Are you absolutely sure you want that, Eleanor? It's been a very long time...for both of you."

"Eighteen years, I know. But that letter alarms me more than I can tell you. There's no mention of what Ivy intends doing now. I think she would have let me know if she had gotten married, and who is she going to find to marry in the back of beyond? I can't believe a young woman would consider staying in that remote outpost alone, but no telling what foolish ideas her parents instilled in her head. They may have broadened her cultural horizons with that insane life of theirs, but they didn't give her what I believe everyone is entitled to—roots and a home. It only makes sense to me that she should come back here, but convincing her of that might take some doing. A letter won't do. Letters are too conveniently ignored. And the island has no phone service, though a phone call probably wouldn't be any more effective than a letter. So that's where you come in. I'm counting on your considerable powers of persuasion to convince her she should at least come back and see what's available to her here.''

Taylor couldn't have been more dismayed by the request. He thought fast. He owed the Camerons a lot. He had been a very junior member of a San Angelo law firm only eight years ago, performing all the most menial tasks. Naturally he had dealt with the firm's least important clients. One of those clients, a crusty old sheep rancher, had been approached by Cameron Oil about taking out some leases on his property. The rancher had asked Taylor to hie on up to Fort Worth and find out if the deal was a solid one.

Like every other business, the oil industry had its share of shady operators, but Taylor discovered that not only was the deal a good one for his client, Ben Cameron was one of the most scrupulously honest businessmen he had ever met. The man himself had been a tough, canny old bird, a man of action and few words. To a certain extent, Ben had reminded Taylor of his own father. The two of them had hit it off right away, so much so that Ben had invited him home for dinner, where he'd first met Eleanor. The three of them had spent a wonderfully companionable evening together. Only a week later, Taylor was surprised by an invitation from Sheldon and Ernst to come for an interview. He hadn't wondered why for long, not after discovering that Ben, Eleanor and all their offspring, to say nothing of Cameron Oil Corporation itself, were clients of the firm.

His career had taken off and today he was a junior partner. But it was the Camerons' friendship he most cherished. Since Ben's death four years ago, Eleanor had turned to him more and more frequently—for legal advice, financial advice, sometimes simply for company and conversation. There was nothing he wouldn't do for her.

But then, she'd never before asked him to travel halfway around the world on her behalf. Taylor shifted uneasily in his chair. "Well, Eleanor, there's the small matter of Messrs. Sheldon and Ernst."

"That won't be a problem, I assure you," she said, and he knew it wouldn't be. All she had to do was call David Ernst, and Taylor would be packing his bags.

She offered him a sad smile. "I'd always wanted a daughter, and when Claire was born I was ecstatic. We had a wonderful time together when she was a child, but somewhere along the way I lost her. Now I'm eighty-six. How many more years can I reasonably hope to have? It would be so wonderful to have a second chance with Ivy. Beyond that, she needs to know she isn't alone, that she has a family who would like to know her better. I want to see her so badly, so badly."

Taylor uttered an inner sigh of resignation. Eleanor had a way about her, a way that could be utterly impossible to resist. She had meant to touch him, and she had succeeded. He knew he wouldn't refuse her this. He would go to Baksra and do his damnedest. And he further determined that short of physically abducting the woman, he would not return to Texas without Ivy Loving in tow.

CHAPTER TWO

IVY STEPPED out of the bungalow and raised her eyes to the blue-green mountains that separated the village from the sea. A thin mist hung over their tops, as it did most of the year. The lushness around her was always enchanting—riots of wildflowers grew almost of their own free will. The front yard sloped down to the dirt road that led to the center of the village some five miles away. A carabao cart with a banana-leaved roof lumbered down the road. A farmer was returning home after a day at market. He peered from beneath his coolie hat and waved; she waved back.

Brushing at an errant strand of ash-blond hair, she scanned the sky to estimate the time. It had been years since she'd worn a watch, for watches had no place on Baksra. Things happened when they happened and were almost always timed by the sun. The island straddled the equator, so the sun rose at the same time year-round, and the temperature was a constant.

It was nearing five. Soon the damp heat of the day would give way to cooling darkness. Ivy frowned. If Erik was going to stop by today, he would have to hurry. Not many people on the island moved around much after dark, mostly because there was little electricity. The Lovings' bungalow, the homes of the large planters, and some of the buildings in the village were equipped with generators, but most of the islanders got by with candles and kerosene lanterns.

She sniffed the air that was fragrant with the smell of nutmeg and clove, the island's principal crops. Erik Soewadji and a few others like him had become wealthy from those two crops alone. There also were abundant groves of coconut and banana trees and acres upon acres of flooded rice paddies. These crops were exported, too, but the lion's share was for the locals' own consumption.

She gave one last hopeful look down the road before returning inside. The bungalow was luxurious by Baksrani standards, not as grand as Erik's plantation, of course, but it contained many amenities that were beyond the scope of most of the islanders. Though her parents had maintained a contempt for luxuries, they definitely had insisted on certain creature comforts—something other than dirt floors, some sort of workable kitchen, real beds and, if possible, indoor plumbing. After many, many boat trips and shopping excursions to some of the larger islands, all had been installed in the bungalow.

Ivy felt as though it were the only home she'd ever had, though she did remember quite a bit about India, mostly things she didn't care to dwell on, and a little about her grandmother's house in Texas. Her parents had always spoken so disdainfully of the

Camerons and their life-style, but all Ivy remembered were pleasant things, like a brick schoolhouse, playmates, huge family gatherings in a big house. Of course, she had only been a child and hadn't realized, as her parents had told her time and time again, that her grandparents led meaningless lives full of extravagance and conspicuous consumption.

She glanced around the comfortable, cheerful parlor. Even the humblest homes on the island looked pleasant because everyone had flowers, indoors and out. She idly plucked a blossom from a vase and held it to her nose. Her gaze wandered on to the study located just off the parlor, and the aching sadness came back. How many countless hours had her parents spent there at the double desk, typing, studying, talking? Though Gordon and Claire Loving had been far too caught up in their work and each other to be doting parents, she did miss them so.

Just then she heard the toot of a horn. Going back to the door, she saw Erik's blue Japanese-made sedan coming up the dirt path that served as a driveway. The automobile had caused quite a stir in the village the day it had arrived by ship. Most of the motorized vehicles on the island were either ancient or virtually homemade, put together from parts of broken trucks and buses. The shiny blue sedan still caused people to literally stop in their tracks and stare in admiration.

Erik stepped out of the car and started up the rise toward the house. He was a man in his mid-sixties, three years older than Gordon Loving had been, very distinguished even in planter's khakis. Part Dutch, part English, part Malay, his handsomeness was arresting. Well-read and well traveled, he was an interesting conversationalist and a never-boring companion. And he had been nothing short of a godsend during those first difficult days after her parents' deaths.

"Hello," Ivy called. "I'm so glad you came."

A broad smile creased his face. "I almost didn't, but then I received an interesting letter in the mail. You simply have to see it."

"Oh?" Ivy opened the screen door, then stepped back to allow Erik to enter the house.

"You remember I told you I wrote to your grandmother in Texas?"

"Yes."

"Well, it seems that one of her attorneys wants to talk to you and will be paying a visit to the island soon. He asked if I would be available as an interpreter." Erik chuckled. "Perhaps he thinks you no longer speak English."

"Little does he know that's all I speak well. I wonder why he needs to talk to me," Ivy murmured with a frown.

"I have no idea, but it must be important for this fellow to make such a journey. I must say I don't envy him it. He's leaving…well, it would be today, so that means he'll doubtless be on the next plane, five days from now." Erik handed the letter to her; she took it but didn't look at its contents.

So strange, Ivy thought. *Someone from the United States.* It had been a very long time since she'd talked to an American. "Mysterious," she said with a little laugh. "Will you meet the plane?"

"If you'd like."

"I'd like." Ivy glanced at the envelope, noting the Fort Worth return address. It had been ages... another lifetime ago, or so it seemed. "Please stay for dinner, Erik?" she asked hopefully.

"Oh, my dear, I would so love to, but my place is teeming with import-export people from Sydney. I left my overseer in charge of them, but I really must get back."

Ivy swallowed her disappointment. "Tomorrow, perhaps."

"Perhaps. I'll try." He bent to give her an affectionate kiss on the cheek. "Take care, dear. Is there anything you need?"

"No. I have everything."

"Then I'll be off. Ta-ta."

"Goodbye, Erik."

Ivy stared after the car until it was out of sight. Then she closed the door. Of course there was plenty she needed, she thought sadly. Company, something to do, a goal of some sort. When her parents had been alive she had been so busy—sorting, cataloging, typing, filing, keeping the house and garden. Studying, too, for they had attempted to make up for her lack of a university degree by teaching her themselves. Now she awoke each morning with a pressing need to *do* something.

Except for the first nine years of her life, she had always been alone. At least it seemed that way. But the aloneness had never been as difficult as it was now. She had hoped that Erik would already have followed through on her parents' plans for her future. But then she chided herself. She couldn't, *wouldn't* rely on someone else for her emotional security. She wouldn't allow herself to be devastated if Erik's own plans did not coincide with those of her parents.

Suddenly she remembered the letter in her hand. Opening it, she read it quickly. It was short and to the point. One Mr. Taylor Edwards was coming halfway round the world to see her, and though no reason was given for the trip, his business with her obviously had something to do with the grandmother she barely remembered.

What could it be after all these years? An inheritance perhaps? How would she handle that? Her parents had been so against her having anything to do with Cameron money. They had been so adamant about it that they even had confiscated the small amount her grandmother had sent on her birthdays and at Christmas.

Ivy refolded the letter, stuffed it into the envelope and laid it on an end table on her way into the kitchen to begin dinner preparations.

THE EVENING WAS A REPLAY of all the evenings she had spent since her parents died. Unless Erik or another of the Lovings' friends came to call, her routine was unvarying. She ate a solitary meal, usually one consisting of fish, rice and whatever vegetables the garden yielded, everything but the rice heavily spiced. After cleaning the kitchen, she spent hours reading or listening to the radio. She was almost numb to the sameness of it.

Tonight, however, her mind was too preoccupied for reading. Images flashed in and out of it in no particular order, some distorted, some sharply clear. After a while one stood out from the rest.

She saw her grandmother's house, at least as she remembered it. There was a big front porch and a swing, and she was there with some boys, three or four. They all seemed to look alike; in fact, two of them were carbon copies of each other. "Are they twins, Grandma?" Ivy could hear her childish voice asking. And an older woman replied, "Kevin and Jeffrey? Oh, goodness, no, darling. But they're alike as two peas in a pod, aren't they?"

Ivy smiled now, amazed at being able to recall a conversation held nineteen or twenty years ago. It was amazing, too, to realize that across a vast ocean and many miles into the interior of a big country there were people who were her family. She wished Mr. Edwards had given them prior notice about his impending arrival. She would have written to ask him to bring photographs of her grandmother and her cousins.

She shook away the images and tried to concentrate on the book, but it was useless. She put it aside, picked up a magazine, glanced through it idly, then gave up altogether. Rather than stare at the walls, she went up a short flight of stairs and began getting ready for bed.

Surprisingly, she slept, and that night her sleep was filled with dreams. Out of the mists of memory, long-forgotten details filled her mind.

"BUT WHY DO I HAVE TO GO, Grandma? I want to stay here with you."

"Oh, darling, how I wish it could be. But you have to go with your parents."

"Who says?"

"The law, I'm afraid."

The child threw her arms around her grandmother and buried her face in the woman's soft bosom. "Will I never see Kevin and Kirk and Jeffrey and David again?"

"Listen to me, Ivy, and listen well. You are nine years old now, and the law says you have to go live with your parents. But you won't be nine forever. In a few years—and they'll pass more quickly than you can imagine—you will be able to do what you decide to do. I want you to promise you'll come back here when that day arrives. I'll be waiting for you."

"I promise."

"HONESTLY, IVY, you've got to stop this moping. It's depressing your father and myself, and we won't have it. You are on your way to a great adventure, child. I insist that you regard it that way."

JUST BEFORE DAWN, the old grandmother of the simple house summoned the child into her presence. "I have noticed that you take proper care with cleanliness, so from now on you will help me in my kitchen. But you must bathe and put on clean clothes before being allowed inside. You have to do something around here."

"I should be in school," the child said.

"Perhaps your parents will find a suitable one for you. In the meantime, you will assist me. I will start by teaching you to properly prepare the kitchen floor every morning."

IVY WOKE WITH A START, instantly realizing it wasn't yet close to dawn. The dreams, her first in years, puzzled her. Why was she remembering such things now?

Then she recalled the letter from the American attorney. That had to have prompted them. She lay there, thinking of dozens of possible reasons for the visit, but it was useless to speculate. If nothing else, Mr. Edwards's visit would be a novelty, a change from the unrelieved monotony of her days.

CHAPTER THREE

DURING THE PAST FOUR DAYS, Taylor had been on and off more planes than he could remember. First the flight from Texas to Los Angeles, on to Honolulu, then to Sydney and to Djakarta. At last he was on the final leg, aboard a vintage DC-9 island-hopper that crisscrossed the Banda Sea, its ultimate destination the island of Baksra. The pilot, a Dutchman who spoke good English, had informed him that even in the Spice Islands, Baksra was considered "the end of the earth."

Splendid, Taylor thought. He wasn't even sure what day it was. Monday, he thought. Sunday back home. And how he wished he were there. Only for Eleanor Cameron would he put himself through such an exhausting ordeal.

And he could add a good dose of uneasiness to his exhaustion. The DC-9 looked barely airworthy. His nervousness hadn't been eased a bit when the passengers broke into applause as the plane actually left the ground.

His fellow travelers were an odd assortment of people. It seemed to Taylor they represented every nationality on earth. It amused him to speculate on what sort of business had them going to places with names like Makasar, Ambon and Baksra.

By the time the plane reached Baksra, only Taylor and four other passengers remained on board. He glanced down when the pilot announced their approach. From the air the island looked primeval, nothing but a thick carpet of green forest going down to the water's edge. The airstrip where they touched down was hard surfaced, but the terminal was little more than a bamboo hut on stilts. "Remember," the pilot said as Taylor started to leave the plane, "we're on the ground here three hours, no more. Then we start the return trip to Djakarta. If you don't make the flight, you're here for five days, like it or not."

A tall, silver-haired man in khakis, obviously not Indonesian, stood in front of the terminal. When his eyes met Taylor's, he stepped forward. "Mr. Edwards?" he inquired in an impeccable British accent.

"Yes, and you must be Mr. Soewadji. I hope I pronounced that correctly."

Erik nodded. "It's pronounced the way it's spelled. My name is Erik. I'm very glad to meet you."

The two men shook hands. "I'm Taylor, Erik. I do want to thank you for meeting me."

"Don't mention it. If you're ready, we can be off to Ivy's straight away."

"That's fine. The sooner the better."

"Capital!" Erik led the way to the blue sedan and deposited Taylor's suitcase in the back seat. In less than a minute he wheeled the car around, and they drove through a busy village where chickens and cows wandered the streets and the townspeople moved with unhurried grace. The majority of the buildings were frame and bamboo structures, but there was one masonry building standing in the center of town, solid and large. When Taylor inquired about it, Erik told him it was a government building. The village's only other masonry structure was the schoolhouse.

The town's busiest citizens seemed to be the street vendors, who squatted on reed mats under thatch roofs and displayed their wares in large round baskets. Most of the young people he saw wore Western-style clothes, with shorts, slacks and T-shirts being much in evidence. The older women favored saronglike skirts and blouses, most of them in vivid colors. Bicycles and motorcycles of every description darted in and out of the throngs. Taylor noticed that Erik drove with one hand on the horn, and people, animals and vehicles made way for him.

They soon left the village behind them and drove down a narrow road that snaked through lush vegetation. Thatch huts and bamboo houses peppered the landscape. Erik kept up a running commentary, explaining some of the history of the island. There was a pungent, pervasive smell in the air that Taylor couldn't identify. When he asked his companion about it, Erik said, "Nutmeg and clove, this island's wealth. It was while looking for them that Columbus stumbled onto your world, I believe."

Suddenly he braked and turned off the road onto an even narrower trail that led up a rise to a house, a much larger house than any Taylor had previously seen. It was surrounded by trees and had a large front porch. Erik gave two toots on the horn, and the front door opened. A young woman stepped out onto the veranda and waved. Taylor's breath caught in his throat. He had become vastly curious about Ivy Loving during the past two weeks, and now at last his curiosity was about to be satisfied.

Ivy moved across the yard to meet them. She was medium height, slender and had long, shiny ash-blond hair that had a smoky hue to it. It had been tied at the nape with a fuchsia ribbon. She wore an ankle-length, saronglike skirt of a bright print, and a green T-shirt had been tucked into its waistband. As she neared, Taylor could see that her skin was a golden tan, but only when she was almost upon them could he fully appreciate what a beautiful woman Eleanor's granddaughter was.

She had almond-shaped green eyes and a beautiful mouth. She wore no makeup—or if she did, she had applied it so artfully there seemed to be none. The green shirt hugged curves that were admirable by anyone's standard. Beneath the skirt's hem, her dainty bare feet were hardly covered by the sandals she wore.

She stood and waited while Erik stopped the car and got out. "Hello, dear. I've brought your visitor." Taylor emerged from the passenger side.

"Ivy," Erik said, "this is Taylor Edwards."

"How do you do, Mr. Edwards," she said, her voice soft and warm, without a trace of a discernible accent. "Welcome to Baksra."

"Thank you, Ivy. And please call me Taylor. Your grandmother sends her love."

"Is she well?"

"Eleanor is amazingly well for a woman her age."

"You've had a lengthy trip."

"You can say that again!" Taylor exclaimed. Her eyes had him all but mesmerized.

"Then please come into the house, both of you. I have refreshments waiting."

Erik retrieved the suitcase from the back seat, then slipped his free hand beneath Ivy's elbow. The three of them crossed the yard and entered the house. The interior was perhaps ten degrees cooler than it was outside; the result of all the trees shading the roof, plus ceiling fans whirring overhead. Glancing around, Taylor took in the big main room, a parlor. A dining room opened off it and a see-through window gave him a glimpse of the kitchen beyond. On the other side of the parlor was another room dominated by a massive two-sided desk. Books and stacks of papers were everywhere. He assumed that had been the study used by Claire and Gordon Loving.

"Please sit down," Ivy said. "I'll be right back." She moved out of the room, oblivious to Taylor's eyes staring after her. In the kitchen she took a tall pitcher of lime punch from the icebox, along with three tall, chilled glasses. As she poured, she thought of the American.

He was about thirty-five, she guessed, which was a surprise. She had been expecting someone much older. Tall like Erik, Taylor Edwards had thick, sun-streaked brown hair that was conservatively cut. She feared she might have stared at him too openly, perhaps even rudely, when they were introduced, but she had become very curious about him during the past five days. Not only was he the first American she had seen in years, he was the first man of her own generation she had encountered in some time. All the adults she knew were much older than herself.

Ivy thought he might have the nicest masculine smile she could imagine—open and warm. Weren't Texans supposed to be among the friendliest people on earth? She could hardly wait to find out why he had come to Baksra. Placing the pitcher and glasses on a tray, she went back into the parlor in time to hear Erik say, "You must know that Ivy and I have been alive with curiosity over the reason for your visit."

"Yes, I can imagine," Taylor said idly, his eyes riveted on Ivy. She placed the tray on the coffee table, removed a glass and handed it to him, then another to Erik. She took the final one and sat in a chair near the older man. Taylor sipped the beverage, which turned out to be a sweetish punch that was surprisingly refreshing on the sultry afternoon. After the three of them exchanged some small talk, Taylor got down to business. "The reason I'm here, Ivy," he said, "is because your grandmother would like to see you. And I'm sure you realize she can not make a journey like the one I just made, not at her age. She would like nothing better than to have you return to Texas with me."

Ivy looked at Erik. Some sort of silent, private communication seemed to pass between them. Taylor wondered just what Erik's relationship with the Lovings had been. Dear friends, he had said in the letter to Eleanor, yet Taylor sensed an even closer bond.

Ivy turned to him. "Why does she want to see me after all these years?"

The question took Taylor aback. "Well . . . she *always* wanted to see you. She would have liked to have you visit her often. She would have liked you to get to know your uncles and aunts, your cousins. And . . ." He hesitated, considering what he wanted to say next. "I think she wants you to see firsthand that there's really nothing so terrible about the way the Camerons live. You have quite a family back in Texas. I know all of them and like them very much."

Ivy studied her hands a minute before saying, "I suppose I would like to see her, too, but I don't want to have to travel all the way to the United States to do it."

"Why not?"

"My parents told me it was a terrible place—big, crowded, noisy, dirty and, most of all, corrupt."

Taylor smiled. "Well, I wouldn't be honest if I said there aren't places like that in the States, but it's not all like that, not by any means. If that's the image you have, I think you would be very surprised by the reality."

Ivy cocked her head and eyed him speculatively. "I can't believe you traveled halfway across the world just to ask me to visit my grandmother."

"I'm afraid I did. That's my mission...my only mission. And of course Eleanor would never ask you to make such a trip alone. That's why she sent me to accompany you. And I'll be glad to accompany you back here if..." he hesitated.

"If?"

"If you decide you do indeed want to return."

Ivy and Erik exchanged amused glances before she said, "But of course I would want to return, Mr. Ed...er, Taylor. This is my home."

Erik had remained silent throughout the conversation between Taylor and Ivy, but now he leaned forward and said, "I know it's sometimes difficult for outsiders to understand the island's hold on some of us. My Dutch ancestors lived in Indonesia for generations, but only as colonists. They never lost the desire to return to the Netherlands. As for the British side of the family, they find it impossible to understand why I remain here by choice."

"And why do you?" Taylor asked with interest.

"Because it's quite simply the nicest place on earth to live. I believe Ivy feels the same way."

Taylor turned to Ivy, who nodded. "I've been here such a long time, you see," she said. "I would never be able to live in a fast-moving, industrialized society. If you stayed here and got to know the Baksrani people and their customs, you might understand."

Taylor doubted that. The island might seem like Shangri-la to Ivy and Erik, but he was more inclined to share the pilot's view of it as the end of the earth. He realized they were digressing from the main reason he had come to the island. "What do you remember about Fort Worth, if anything?"

Ivy gave it some thought. Bits and pieces of memories had been returning almost daily. "I think I remember the house most of all. It was huge, and it had a wonderful shaded front porch where I played in the summer. Often there were some boys there, too. They must have been my cousins."

"Yes, you have four of them. Two still live in Fort Worth and have their own families now. I've been fortunate to have been invited to join some of the Camerons' family get-togethers, and they are wonderful affairs. Aren't you curious about them? Wouldn't you like to see them again?"

"I don't know," Ivy said. "I've never thought about it. But...I suppose it would be nice for a week or two. Are they curious about me?"

"Well, Ivy, I didn't get a chance to speak to any of them before leaving town, but your grandmother certainly is. A few weeks is all I'm asking for. It would mean so much to Eleanor."

Actually, Taylor was fully aware of Eleanor's intentions. If he could get Ivy to come back to Texas with him, she planned to launch a full-scale campaign to convince her granddaughter to stay. But that was between the two women. His only task was to get them reunited. Whatever occurred after that was none of his business.

"Just what is my grandmother to you?" Ivy asked. "Are you only her attorney, or do you work for her in some other capacity?"

"I'm also her friend. I've always felt close to both your grandmother and your grandfather."

"He died a few years ago, didn't he?"

Taylor nodded. "Yes. Four to be exact."

"I remember that my mother received a letter. Of course, by the time it reached her, the funeral had been held weeks earlier."

"Eleanor still misses him terribly. They were together such a long time. I think seeing you again would be wonderful medicine for her."

Ivy frowned and looked at Erik. "What do you think, Erik? Should I go?"

"I think, my dear, that you should do what you want to do. Or what you feel you should do. Naturally I would prefer your not being gone so long, but Taylor here seems like a responsible chap. I don't think I would have to worry about your well-being." He offered Taylor a smile of acceptance.

Taylor noticed that Ivy seemed to rely on the older man considerably. Perhaps considering the deaths of her parents, that was understandable. And that led him to momentarily dwell on Ivy and the rather strange life she seemed to lead. What sort of future could she possibly have on Baksra?

"I just don't know," Ivy finally said. "I'll have to think about it."

At least she hadn't given him a flat no. Taylor supposed he should be thankful for that. But giving her time to think about it meant he would be at loose ends for five days. It occurred to him that by hurrying he might catch the plane back to Djakarta, certainly a more appealing place to cool one's heels. But he wouldn't have any influence with Ivy if he was fifteen hundred miles away, so he guessed he would have to stay on the island. And that prompted him to wonder if either Erik or Ivy had made any arrangement for his lodging.

"I hope you'll think about it, Ivy. Eleanor will be awfully disappointed if you choose not to return with me." He glanced from her to Erik. "So I suppose I'll spend five days as a tourist. Does the island have a hotel?"

"Not in the accepted sense of the word," Erik told him, "though several establishments rent rooms. However, Ivy and I thought you would be far more comfortable staying at my plantation."

"Well, that's nice of you, Erik. Are you sure it's no imposition?"

"None whatsoever. I'll more than enjoy the company. Unfortunately, my guest quarters are presently occupied by some Australian gentlemen, but they'll be leaving tomorrow. Tonight I think it would be perfectly acceptable if you stayed here with Ivy. I'm quite sure she will enjoy the company, too."

The suggestion startled Taylor. He quickly looked at Ivy, expecting to hear some vehement protest from her, but none was forthcoming. On the contrary, she clapped her hands together. "Oh, how nice!" she said. "I haven't had a visitor in ever so long."

Taylor had to collect his wits. Did these people actually see nothing unorthodox about a man and a woman who had just been introduced spending the night together in this house? He would be a perfect gentleman, of course, but how did they know that? He could be an ax murderer for all they knew. "Well, I..." he stammered.

"It's a sensible arrangement," Erik declared, getting to his feet. "I'm sure Ivy has dozens of questions about her American family, and your stay might help her make up her mind about the trip."

Taylor also stood, still amazed by this display of blind trust. Erik bent and placed a light kiss on Ivy's cheek. "I really must run. Have a nice time tonight, dear." Straightening, he offered his hand to Taylor. "Tomorrow you must come to the plantation. I think you'll find it interesting. Most people do."

"I'm looking forward to it."

Once Erik had left, Ivy jumped to her feet. "Oh, this is going to be so much fun. Someone to cook for again. Come, Taylor, I'll show you to your room."

Dazed, he followed his hostess through the house. It was a maze of rooms on different levels as though it had been built in stages, with little thought to the flow of traffic. But he was greatly relieved to notice real beds and indoor plumbing.

The room Ivy took him to was sparsely furnished with a bed, a chest of drawers and a chair. The absence of extra furnishing, he realized, gave the room a light, airy feeling, a real plus in the tropical climate.

"I hope you'll be comfortable, Taylor. I'm sure it seems rather spartan compared with what you're accustomed to."

"It looks very comfortable, thanks." He set his suitcase at the foot of the bed. "Tell me something, Ivy. Do you have servants, someone else who lives here with you?"

"No, there's only me."

Taylor shook his head in disbelief. "Are you usually so trusting of complete strangers?"

"What do you mean?" she asked, her fascinating eyes wide and guileless.

"You don't know me from Adam, yet you invite me into your home to spend the night. I'm sure you know there are places in the world where that would be unthinkable."

"Not Baksra."

"I'm not a Baksrani. I might be a very dangerous man."

She smiled, unconcerned. "I don't think so. First of all, Erik is a good judge of character. He would never allow you to stay here if he was at all worried. Secondly, my grandmother wouldn't send a man whom she didn't trust implicitly to accompany me to Texas. And thirdly, there is no crime on Baksra, none, so there's little law enforcement. If you were to harm me, Erik would have you killed. He could do it, too. The men who work for him obey him without question."

Taylor blanched slightly, then chuckled. "I guess that would tend to keep me on the straight and narrow."

Pivoting, Ivy turned toward the door. "Now I'll begin preparations for dinner. Once the sun goes down in an hour or so, the night becomes quite lovely. We'll eat on the back porch, if that's all right."

"It sounds wonderful." Taylor followed the beguiling woman through the maze and into the kitchen.

The room was simplicity itself and a marvel of ingenuity, though most Westerners would wonder how one ever put a meal together in it. A huge wooden chopping block dominated the center of the room. There was one counter with a sink. Shelves lined the walls, holding all sorts of vessels and utensils, many of them unfamiliar to him. There was a large brazier that appeared to be the only cooking device. An appliance that looked like an old-fashioned icebox stood in one corner, and a wooden table and four chairs in another. Ivy invited him to have a seat so they could talk while she worked.

She was no novice at cooking, he could see that. She worked efficiently and with economy of movement, chopping vegetables with a cleaver.

"Are you an important attorney?" she asked.

He smiled at the question, asked so seriously. "I'm not sure what you mean by 'important.'"

"Do you prosecute criminals?"

"No, the firm I'm associated with specializes in corporate law, estate planning, living wills and things like that. Why do you ask?"

"I just assumed that because there is so much crime in America, all lawyers are busy with the criminal element."

Good God, Taylor thought. What kind of garbage had her parents fed her? "Ivy, there is crime in America, I'm not going to deny that. But you have the wrong impression entirely. Most Americans go about their business and never have any trouble at all. I just wish you could experience firsthand the way your grandmother and her family live. Haven't you ever once wanted to go back?"

"Oh... I think I did in the beginning. My grandmother's house was all I had ever known, and I was very confused about why I'd had to leave. But Mom and Dad did such exciting work that I soon forgot that."

"India must have been interesting," Taylor said, his eyes drawn to the movement of her hands. They were very graceful, like a dancer's. He wondered if she had ever taken dancing. In fact, he wondered a lot about her.

"Almost everyone I meet for the first time says that, and, yes, I suppose it was interesting . . . if different is interesting. In the first place, the family we lived with was Hindu, which meant they were strict vegetarians. We couldn't even have eggs because they represented potential life. It was quite a shock to come from my grandmother's house where we sometimes ate meat twice a day to that." She laughed lightly. "I complained about it a lot at first, but that made my mother very angry, so I accepted it. In fact, it was a long time after I came to the island before I could make myself eat fish. Longer still before I'd eat pork, and that's what the islanders serve on festive occasions."

"Did you have any Indian chums?"

"Oh, no. The family we lived with only had sons, and I wasn't allowed to play with them. Also, I was non-Hindu, therefore suspicious and capable of being a corrupting influence."

Though she spoke matter-of-factly, Taylor suspected her childhood in India had not been particularly happy. "What about here on Baksra? Any religious or dietary taboos?"

"Depends on what corner of the island you're on. Religion here is such a mishmash of different sects that food taboos have all but disappeared. You have to remember that Baksra was under European rule for centuries, and that diluted the pure Indonesian customs. A few of them are slowly coming back, but most are gone for good." She put down the cleaver and curled a long strand of hair behind her ear.

"Is there any industry on the island?"

"Some copper mining. The real money comes from the spices. But most of the residents are self-sufficient farmers who can live nicely on . . . oh, the equivalent of forty dollars a month. Fortunately, they can easily make that by selling their crops at market. Some of the more ambitious people take theirs by boat to a larger island where they can get more money. Others are content to make do with what they get here."

"I guess commerce is commerce the world over," he said with a smile. "Erik doesn't strike me as the kind who lives on forty dollars a month."

She uttered another lilting laugh, a delightful sound. "Hardly. Erik is a wealthy planter who does business all over the world. He's forever flying off to Sydney, and he even sometimes goes to San Francisco." She spoke the city's name as if it were as distant and exotic as Baksra was to him. Distant, anyway.

"He's a nice man," Taylor remarked. "A good friend of your father's?"

"Yes, a very good friend. He was interested in my parents' work. We all used to have great discussions. I learned far more from him than I ever learned in school. He's so well traveled and has done so many interesting things that one never tires of his tales."

"It's nice he's here to help you, but I'm curious about something, Ivy."

She looked at him, raising an inquisitive eyebrow. "Yes?"

"What are you going to do now?"

"Do?"

"Yes. Now that your parents are gone, will you work, travel, what? If you work, what will you do, where will you go? It doesn't seem to me that the island offers much in the way of opportunities for a woman your age."

"Not for women of any age," she said with a smile. "But I hope I'll do what any planter's wife does. Oversee a house and servants. Have children. Those are very big responsibilities, you know, and taken very seriously here."

Taylor didn't understand. "I beg your pardon?"

"It should have happened long ago, but due to circumstances, it just wasn't possible. But now I rather imagine Erik will ask me to marry him."

CHAPTER FOUR

TAYLOR'S MOUTH DROPPED, and he stared at her for a full minute. His silence caused Ivy to glance over her shoulder with a smile. "I can see that surprised you."

"I ... well, Ivy ... he's old enough to be your father. I realize that's not the most uncommon thing in the world, but ..." Of course Taylor knew that older men married young wives. It happened all the time. But in this case the age difference was pretty dramatic, possibly over thirty years. One could never fault Erik for wanting to marry a beautiful young woman like Ivy, but why on earth would Ivy want it?

"Not only is it not uncommon here on Baksra, it's actually the custom. Everyone has two spouses in a lifetime, one much older and one much younger."

"Everyone?"

"Yes. It's one reason the island culture is so unique. One learns from the older spouse, then in turn teaches the younger one. The custom fascinated my parents. They had reached the opinion that it should be followed all over the world. It all started hundreds of years ago when the island was ruled by a sultan. When he was in his twenties, he fell in love with an older woman and married her. When she died, he married a very young woman, not much more than a girl really. He was so pleased with the arrangement that he strongly suggested all Baksranis follow the custom from then on. I guess when a sultan suggests something, it becomes law."

Taylor digested it all, then uttered a grunt. "That's the damnedest thing I've ever heard!"

Ivy smiled. "That's the reaction of all foreigners, but the custom works well. Divorce is unknown here. There isn't even any legal apparatus for obtaining such a thing."

Taylor shook his head in amazement. "Be realistic. You and I know that not all those marriages can be happy ones."

Ivy shrugged. "I guess it all depends on what one expects out of marriage. I read Western magazines and books. It seems to me that Western women want everything—a husband, children, a job, utter and complete happiness at all times, and all the 'good things' in life. To me, that's unrealistic. I wish you could have known the grandmother in the house in India. She did all the cooking, and she cooked all day every day. Yet she wasn't allowed to eat until all the men, first, then the children, then the women in the household had, and she ate alone in the kitchen. And she was probably the most contented person I've ever known."

Taylor tried to envision an American housewife putting up with not being allowed to eat until after the rest of the family had. "How did your parents fit into that life-style?"

"Oh, it was understood that they were foreigners and non-Hindu, so they weren't expected to follow the customs so stringently. But my mother pretty much stayed with the women of the household in order to learn the way of life from their viewpoint. My parents were very serious researchers, and they more or less followed the 'when in Rome' kind of thinking. It was the same when they came to the island. They fit in the best they could, and the islanders accepted them as best *they* could."

Taylor wasn't going to get into a debate over the desirability of one society over another, but he did have some questions. "Tell me something else about the island's marriage customs, Ivy. What happens if someone comes along and messes everything up?"

She frowned. "I don't understand."

"What if every once in a while the older spouse lives an unusually long time? Or what if two people the same age fall in love? What then?"

She gave it some thought. "In the case of two people the same age...well, I doubt it would happen. People the same age don't mix socially, and what could two people the same age teach each other? But if it did...I suppose they would leave the island. But the other is what actually happened to Erik and myself. We should have been married years ago, but his wife lived a very long life. She was such a wonderful woman. It was she who first suggested to my father

that I would make a perfect second wife for Erik."
Ivy placed a coconut on the work surface, took the
cleaver and, with one expert stroke, split open the
fruit.

Taylor watched her, taken in by her unusual beauty.
It pained him to think of her spending her life on this
remote island with a man older than her father had
been. It shouldn't have made the slightest difference
to him . . . but it did. "You know, it's really a pretty
rotten custom when you think about it. If a young
man marries a woman past childbearing age, he
doesn't become a father until he marries a younger
woman, and by then he's not so young himself. And
he never gets to know his grandchildren."

"That's true," Ivy said casually. "It's extremely
rare for a child to have a grandfather. But children
have grandmothers, and those relationships are wonderful to see."

Taylor still thought it was the damnedest thing he'd
ever heard and that the men got the bad end of the
deal. "Has Erik actually proposed? Have you actually accepted?"

"No, of course not. That would have been in bad
taste. His wife, you see, died less than a year ago, and
custom demands at least a year must elapse before
remarriage. But I know he and my father discussed it
many times."

"I'm surprised the two of you go along with the
Baksrani customs. Erik is European, and you're
American."

"Erik has lived in Indonesia almost all his life, and I haven't lived in America in eighteen years," she said simply, as though that explained everything. And Taylor supposed it did.

It also explained a lot of other things. Why she was still single and living with her parents at twenty-seven. Why she still radiated innocence. It especially explained why she still lived on this godforsaken island. She planned to marry its wealthiest inhabitant. Now he understood why Erik had so blithely invited him to stay in this house. He knew Ivy would never look upon a man her own age with any sexual interest.

Wait until Eleanor heard this!

THE MEAL IVY SERVED that evening was one of the most delicious Taylor had ever eaten. He had expected to be served all manner of unidentifiable food, but he discovered to his surprise that, save for one leafy green that looked like spinach but didn't taste the least like it, everything on his plate was familiar—rice, fresh fish, four different stir-fried vegetables. In every dish there was the faint, pleasant taste of coconut; Ivy cooked in coconut oil and made sauces with coconut milk. Also in every dish was the burn of chili peppers, and there was nothing faint about that. He loved Mexican food, but it was pabulum compared to these chilies.

In his honor, the table on the porch had been set Western-style with knife and fork, but she could and usually did, she told him, eat Indonesian-style with the fingers of her right hand. "Show me," he said, then watched in wonder as she picked up a small cube of fish, two pieces of vegetables and encased them in a small ball of rice, and then popped the whole into her mouth. Taylor tried it and made an embarrassing mess, sending her into a fit of giggles.

And throughout the meal they talked. He was curious about the island's marriage customs even though he thought them absurd. "What kind of wedding ceremony is held here?"

"Oh, they're very exciting. They go on for days and days. Pot after pot of incense is burned. A certain amount is required before the couple is considered married. Then whole pigs are slaughtered and cooked in pits. The feasting goes on and on."

Mostly, however, Ivy quizzed him. She might have been unsure about traveling to the United States, but she was vastly curious about the place, especially about the grandmother she barely remembered.

"I do seem to recall that she was very fond of me and wrote to me quite often when we went to India," Ivy said rather wistfully. "I suppose she and my mother didn't get along very well. Mom was very opinionated. And idealistic. And she had a lot of strange ideas about money. She really thought that having it was the worst thing that could happen to a person, that it corrupted people. I suppose my parents made a lot of money... well, some anyway... but they kept only what they considered necessary and gave the rest of it away."

Which meant Ivy herself probably hadn't been left much, Taylor thought. "And you, Ivy?" he asked. "How do you feel about money?"

"I'm not sure since I've never had any to speak of. In fact, I really don't know much about myself."

"That's a strange thing to say."

"It's true."

"You must know how you feel about certain things, what you like and don't like."

"I wonder. You see, I've had a lot of schooling, first at the academy and then at the University of Singapore for a while. And traveling and working with my parents was educational, but I'm smart enough to know there are some things about growing to adulthood that escaped me completely. For instance, what the Westerners refer to as 'dating' is unknown to me."

That one really took Taylor aback. "It is? You've never had a date, not one?"

She shook her head. "In India the sexes were totally segregated, and the school I went to was all-female. I'm afraid it made me 'different,' too different for the university, that was certain. Then my parents came here to Baksra. I visited them, liked it, and... well, you know the relationship between men and women here. The next time you're in the village take a look around. Except for little schoolchildren, you'll rarely see a man and woman the same age together. That's one reason I think I'll probably stay here. I'm unsuited for life anywhere else.''

Maybe she was right, Taylor mused. What kind of people would raise a daughter that way, knowing she would live most of her life in the twenty-first century? "You know, that could be remedied, Ivy. You could learn to live in the mainstream world. It might be different at first, but . . .''

"I'm not sure I want to. It doesn't seem to me it's a very pretty world, and life here is so safe and simple.''

"And that's what you want—safety and simplicity?''

"Is there anything wrong with that?''

"Well, I . . .'' The whole thing was so weird to Taylor that he didn't know what to say. Now that he knew more about her, he tried to envision her living in Texas. Fort Worth was an American city with all the problems of other American cities. Virtually all the women of Taylor's generation—at least the ones he knew—were well educated, had worked for a number of years and knew all about modern relationships between men and women. He'd never before thought to use the word *sophisticated* to describe them, but now that he'd met Ivy, those women seemed Park Avenue sleek. She, he imagined, would have a hard time relating to them, and they would find it impossible to relate to her.

A warning bell sounded inside his head. *Give it up. She doesn't belong back in Texas. She'll probably be very unhappy there, even for a few weeks. Just forget it.*

But, of course, he couldn't do that. There was Eleanor to consider. He had to do his damnedest, for her sake.

Ivy glanced at his face. "Oh, Taylor, I know life here on Baksra is hard for outsiders to understand. I read English and American magazines. We have a radio, and there's an English-language station from Djakarta. The reception is sometimes awful, but the point is—I don't live in a complete vacuum. I'm not entirely ignorant of the rest of the world, but most of it sounds so terrible. Once you've known the serenity of island living, it's almost impossible to imagine living anywhere else."

What could he say? He decided not to press the issue further, not tonight. After all, he had five days. "Tell me what you do all day."

The light in her eyes dimmed a bit. "It's been very lonely since my parents died. They were writing a book, you see, and I was their assistant. I don't know how much you know about their work, but they wrote a book called *Coming of Age in Allahabad* after our stay in India. It's a classic."

"So I understand."

Ivy seemed impressed that he'd heard of it. "Oh, I don't mean it was a bestselling novel or anything, but for a book of its kind, it was very popular. They were working on a similar project, calling it 'Growing Up on Baksra.' My mission was to bicycle around the island, asking questions and taking notes. And I steeped myself in the island's history. It was very interesting, and I enjoyed it. But now..." Her voice trailed off.

"You have little to do," Taylor finished for her, absolutely touched by the woman's plight in spite of himself.

She refused to admit it. "I've spent the past week getting what they've done so far into some kind of order. Their American publisher has expressed great interest in it. I'm hoping that with what's already been written and all the research notes, someone somewhere can finish the book. It would be such a shame if it never was finished."

"Can't you do it?" Taylor asked. "You were closest to them, most involved in their work."

"Oh, Taylor, I'm not a writer. Just having the facts isn't enough. You have to know how to put them together in a way that makes them interesting to others." She smiled sadly. "I wish I could do that, but I'm afraid if I tried to finish the book, it would come across like, 'See the monkey on the fence. See the monkey peel the banana.'"

He laughed, but the wheels in his brain were turning. He might be able to use her desire to see the book finished to his advantage. He wasn't sure just how, but he'd think about it.

Ivy got to her feet and began clearing the table. Taylor stood to give her a hand, but when he picked up his plate and utensils she looked at him as though he had gone mad. "What are you doing?"

"I'm going to help with the dishes."

"You do dishes?"

"Of course I do dishes. I live alone." He carried his dishes inside to the sink.

Ivy followed with a most puzzled look on her face. "No man I've ever known in my entire life would be caught dead doing dishes."

"Oh, I'm the handiest guy you ever saw. I do dishes and can cook after a fashion. I do my own laundry when I have to, and I've even been known to mop a floor."

"Do all American men do such things?"

"Not all of them, but those of us who live alone have to be self-reliant. And most husbands today are a little better about helping out at home than they were in my dad's time."

Taylor reached to turn on the faucet, but Ivy intercepted him. "Please . . . go sit down. You're making me uncomfortable."

He laughed, and with a shrug he turned and did as she asked. Ivy filled a basin with soapy water and talked to him over her shoulder. "Why aren't you married?"

Taylor couldn't hold back a grin. It was curiously refreshing to be with someone who'd never learned the fine art of subtlety. "I almost got married once," he said, which didn't exactly answer her question.

"What happened?"

"I was in law school and poor. Then I was starting out and poor. I guess I was waiting until I thought I could afford marriage, and I guess she got tired of waiting. She married someone else."

"Were you devastated?"

"I think *stunned* would be a better word. In my enormously self-centered way, I thought she'd wait forever."

"Isn't it odd that you never found anyone else?"

"Well, we had been together a long time, and I was thirty when she got married. Obviously, it took me a while to accept that, and . . . I don't know. Marriage just hasn't happened yet, but I certainly haven't given up."

Ivy didn't say anything for a minute. Then, "Tell me more about my grandmother."

To the best of his ability, Taylor described Eleanor, leaving out words like *formidable* and *willful*, choosing instead to paint a picture of a sweet, elderly woman who desperately wanted to see her only granddaughter before she died. "I know for a fact Eleanor deeply regrets the estrangement with your mother. And she's never gotten over missing you. You know, Ivy, it's occurred to me that you and I might strike a bargain."

"Bargain?"

"Yes, Eleanor is a favorite client of mine, and I like to do what I can for her. She wants to see you. If you'll come back to the United States with me and visit her for a while, I'll do whatever I can to help you get your parents' book finished. I know for a fact there are writers' organizations all over the Dallas-Fort Worth area. I might start there ... or at Texas Christian. I'll think of something.''

She considered that for several minutes, her brow furrowed in thought. She finished the dishes and had stacked them in a drying rack. Turning and wiping her hands on a towel, she said, ''It's tempting.''

''Then let's do it. We'll both get what we want.''

''I'll talk to Erik about it tomorrow. How's that?''

''It will have to do, I suppose.'' Apparently the man's influence with her was total. He looked at Ivy, at her delicate face and guileless eyes. The thought of her being married to a man in his sixties filled him with absolute dismay, and that was absurd. Thinking about it realistically, he could see she belonged here on the island. She'd probably be gloriously happy with Erik, having been brought up with these crazy customs. She knew nothing else except a Hindu caste where the sexes were segregated. And she certainly displayed no signs of independence or feistiness. There was, in fact, something of a child in her. An older man who would look after her was probably exactly what she wanted and needed.

What you should be thinking about, he reminded himself, *is getting Ivy back with her grandmother. Nothing else.*

DARKNESS DRAINED the heat from the island. For an hour or more after dinner, Taylor and Ivy sat on the bungalow's front porch, talking about everything under the sun. She was not knowledgeable about the ways of the world or its men and women, but she was well-read and could converse intelligently about any number of subjects his contemporaries would know little about. Because of her travels, she knew something about the politics of countries most Americans would be hard-pressed to find on a map. She had seen the Ganges River, the Taj Mahal, Bombay, Calcutta, places he had only read about. Beyond that, her smooth, melodious voice mesmerized him, and her beautiful face filled him with admiration. It was a memorable evening, one Taylor was sure he would recall many, many times in the future.

Finally, the days of travel catching up with him, he pleaded exhaustion and went to the room she had shown him earlier. He was sound asleep within minutes of hitting his pillow.

Ivy, however, remained on the porch long after Taylor had gone upstairs. This was her favorite time of day. Actually, it was her favorite time of year, when their weather was influenced by dry air from Australia instead of moist air from Asia. Tucking her hair behind her ears, she propped her feet on the chair Taylor had vacated and closed her eyes.

It had been a glorious day, such fun to have someone to cook for and talk to. She guessed she had talked more that day than she had in her entire life. There had been times during the course of the evening when saying all those words had felt strange on her tongue, but Taylor had a way of just pulling them out of her.

She liked him, she really did, and she thought what she liked best were his eyes. They were kind. Ivy couldn't remember seeing eyes like that on many men—maybe on none. He looked trustworthy; even Erik had seen that.

Thinking of going to America with him was frightening. The fact she was even considering it surprised her, so she guessed it was Taylor's personality and air of confidence that had kept her from giving him a definite no.

Still, she wasn't sure she really wanted to see her grandmother again. What was the point? Even if they discovered some sort of bond, a fondness for each other, they would only have to go through another painful parting. She recalled the dream of several nights ago, and she remembered how sad she had felt when she first arrived in India. It might be better if they didn't see each other.

But then...she thought of the man upstairs, of his eloquent description of Eleanor Cameron and her desperate desire to see her only granddaughter one more time. It wouldn't be easy to say no to Taylor. Something told her he wouldn't take it for an answer, and he was persuasive. Too, there was the book. It was hard to know what to do.

Ivy sighed and stood up. She supposed she would do what she had always done—let someone else make the decision for her. Erik would tell her whether or not to go to America.

WHEN TAYLOR WOKE the following morning, Ivy was already up. He could hear muted sounds coming from the kitchen. He slid out of bed, showered and shaved quickly, dressed in fresh cotton trousers and a short-sleeved polo shirt, then went downstairs.

"Good morning," she greeted him brightly when he came into the kitchen. She was wearing simple slacks and a bright print shirt tucked into the waist-band. She looked fresh and young and utterly lovely, and Taylor once again experienced a feeling of sad-ness over her plans for the future. "Sleep well?" she asked.

"Like the proverbial log."

"Good." She offered him fruit, coffee and some kind of coconut punch. "We have bicycles. If you know how to ride one, we could ride to Erik's plan-tation. It's a good way to see something of the is-land, and I know you'll be impressed by the plantation."

Taylor couldn't remember how long it had been since he'd been on a bicycle, but he discovered the truth of the old axiom—once one learned to ride, one never forgot.

He and Ivy set out down the two-lane dirt road that ran in front of the bungalow and headed away from the village. Occasionally they had to make way for ancient motorized vehicles, but mostly the people they encountered rode in carts or walked.

They pedaled for perhaps twenty minutes before coming to a massive masonry wall with a grillwork gate. The gate wasn't locked. Ivy pushed it open with her foot, and they proceeded up a narrow lane flanked by coconut trees. Taylor was treated to the sight of a young brown-skinned boy shinnying up the tall trunk of a coconut tree with the ease of a squirrel. In a minute, a shower of fruit tumbled to the ground.

They came to a curve, rounded it, and he gasped in surprise. Ahead of them stood one of the finest houses he had ever seen. It was about the same size as Eleanor Cameron's house in Rivercrest. Taylor had no idea what material it was constructed of—from this distance it looked like pale pink stucco. A covered veranda swept around three sides of the house. Flowers bloomed everywhere. And up ahead, as far as the eye could see, were orchards of some kind. Scores of bare-chested workers in shorts scurried about, tending to chores.

Ivy watched the expression on his face, smiling. "I knew you'd be impressed. My father liked to call this 'the house that nutmeg built.' Erik lives like a raja."

"I thought your parents disdained all the trappings of wealth. Yet they were friends of Erik's and wanted you to marry him."

"I know, it's odd. I think...I think they disdained *Cameron* wealth more than wealth per se. I won't pretend to understand that."

So, Taylor thought as he pedaled along beside her, she wasn't as entirely naive as she seemed.

A servant admitted them into the grand house and showed them into a large, sunny parlor. The Soewadji mansion stood in marked contrast to the thatch and bamboo houses Taylor had so far seen on the island. He wondered how the locals felt about the wealthy foreigner.

Erik entered the room. Actually he charged into it, dressed in crisp khakis and carrying a walking stick. "How nice," he boomed, stooping to kiss Ivy's cheek. Now that Taylor knew the nature of their relationship, the gesture that yesterday had seemed paternal now looked deliberately sensual.

He pumped Taylor's hand, then sat down.

"Taylor has proposed a plan, Erik," Ivy said, "and I want to ask what you think of it. He says if I go to America with him and visit my grandmother, he'll do whatever he can to see that my parents' book gets finished." She glanced at Erik uncertainly.

"Capital!" Erik said.

"You approve?" Ivy sounded surprised. It occurred to Taylor that she might have been hoping he would disapprove, thereby relieving her of the need to make a decision on her own.

"Oh, indeed," Erik said. "And it couldn't have come at a more opportune time. I received a letter yesterday that has me most upset. It was from my attorney in London. It seems my sisters and their dreadful husbands are making some sort of trouble over the disposition of my father's estate. I'm afraid I'm going to have to go to London. I dreaded leaving you here alone and had considered taking you to London with me, but I'm afraid it would be terribly boring for you. All that haggling. My family can be such a bother at times, and they seem to bring out the absolute worst in me. But if you go with Taylor, you can accomplish two missions, and I won't have to worry about you." He turned to Taylor. "You will see that she gets home safely, won't you?"

"Of course. You can count on it." It would ever amaze Taylor that these two people who had never laid eyes on him before yesterday trusted him completely. Erik was willing to send Ivy halfway around the world with him and seemed to have not a qualm about it. But this place did not belong in any world Taylor had ever known or even heard of.

"Capital!" Erik enthused. "How long do you think Ivy will be gone, Taylor?"

"I'm not sure. I think she should plan on a month, don't you? It hardly will be worth the effort if she doesn't give herself that much time."

"And I should be able to clear up the mess in London and be back before she gets home. Don't worry, my dear. I'll have someone check your house regularly."

"I'm not worried about the house," Ivy said. "But what if I hate it in America?"

The two men exchanged glances. Then Taylor said, "I don't for a minute think you'll hate it, Ivy, but if you do, if you're miserable...I'll bring you back here whenever you ask me to." *What am I saying?* he wondered.

Ivy still seemed to have her doubts. She looked around as if confused, then her shoulders rose and fell. "Well, I ... I guess that's it then. I have a lot to do."

"I'll help," Taylor promised. "You just tell me what to do."

"The first thing you can do is continue staying at my house." Ivy's eyes flew to Erik. "It was such fun having him yesterday. Do you mind?"

"Of course not, my dear," Erik assured her. "I'm sure he'll be a great deal of help to you." He got to his feet. "But first, I want Taylor to see the plantation."

Erik took Ivy by the arm and led her out of the room as Taylor followed. For the next hour or so, the trio strolled around the impressive compound, Erik acting as guide and narrator. Taylor found the tour more interesting than he had expected. All he'd known about spices was that they came in small jars or boxes, lined up alphabetically on shelves at the supermarket. It surprised him to learn the nutmeg was a fruit, the clove a red bud of a flower. They were harvested and sorted by hand, and the Spice Islands produced enough of them to supply the world. He was further surprised to learn the Indonesians themselves hardly ever cooked with them. Naturally he asked why and was told the crops simply were too valuable as exports for the locals to even consider consuming them themselves.

All in all, it was an enlightening tour, one he thoroughly enjoyed, but throughout it all he felt a certain uneasiness. Watching Ivy, he wondered what he was letting himself in for? She was a babe in the woods, a pure innocent in a purely non-innocent world, and she would have to be carefully escorted. He wouldn't be able to let her out of his sight until he had deposited her safely into Eleanor's care.

The realization was daunting.

CHAPTER FIVE

AT ERIK'S INSISTENCE, Ivy and Taylor had lunch at the plantation and the meal proved to be a banquet. First a large mound of rice was placed on each plate, then dish after dish was paraded by for the diners' inspection by a seemingly endless procession of servants. Taylor took as much as he thought he could eat. He wondered if the plantation served such meals every day. Ivy had been right; Erik apparently lived like a raja, with dozens of servants. As his wife, Ivy certainly wouldn't suffer any deprivation in her life, at least not in material things.

But emotionally? He wondered. Erik, it seemed to Taylor, treated Ivy like a cherished child, not as the woman he planned to marry. But perhaps that was exactly the way she expected, even *wanted* to be treated.

After leaving the Soewadji plantation, Taylor and Ivy toured the island by bicycle. The exercise helped work off the food. She rode ahead of him, her hair flying behind her. Occasionally she would twist and look over her shoulder at him, then smile. She had what possibly was the loveliest smile he had ever seen.

It was the smile of an innocent, of someone untouched by life's harsher realities, and Taylor thought how comfortable it was to find a woman so pleasant to be with, so quietly appealing, so vastly interesting and so guileless, she had no knowledge of the effect she was having on him.

It only took a few hours to see all of the island. Most of it was rain forest, and its lushness was breathtaking. Some parts looked much the same as Taylor imagined it had on the day of creation. He supposed that once one got used to the peace and quiet, the rest of the world might seem hectic and nerve-racking. He, personally, preferred the more hectic pace.

They returned to the bungalow late that afternoon, and Ivy immediately poured fruit punch for them. Then she put on some music, a long-playing record on an old-fashioned record changer. It was classical, the kind of music Taylor knew little about. He could have done with a nap. All that cycling in the heat had zapped him of energy, but it hadn't affected Ivy in the least, so he forced himself not to think of the bed upstairs. Instead, he sat at the kitchen table and watched her work in the kitchen.

The music wafted through the rooms of the bungalow, accompanied by the whop-whop of Ivy's cleaver on the chopping block. A rare sort of contentment washed over Taylor. Normally his idea of an enjoyable late afternoon would have been country music he could tap his foot to, either a cold beer or cold Scotch, and something slowly barbecuing in the smoker. But on this humid afternoon, in a place he hadn't known existed until a few weeks ago, the music, the aroma of roasting spices and the sweet fruit punch seemed an ideal combination.

"What will the weather be like in Texas?" Ivy asked.

"Hot."

"Will my clothes be suitable?"

"Wear anything you like. Slacks, if you prefer. Or those long skirts. You'll see every kind of attire in the airports and on the planes."

"Will I be able to eat American food?" she asked as she busied herself with preparing their dinner.

"Well, Ivy, all I can tell you is that I've only encountered one rather...er, strange meal since coming to Indonesia, and that was at the hotel in Djakarta. So if Indonesian food doesn't seem odd to me, American food should suit you. You'll be able to get all the fish, rice and vegetables you want."

"How will I get airline tickets?" she then asked.

She was getting more and more apprehensive, he could tell, and he was turning himself inside out to reassure her. Until they were safely on that plane, he'd know no peace. She could change her mind any time. "I have tickets for you," he explained.

"You were that sure I would go to America with you?"

"I got them when I made my own reservations. It seemed prudent. If you had decided not to go, I could have cashed them in."

His concerns were more practical. Did she have a current passport and what was her citizenship?

"Oh, I'm sure my passport is up-to-date," she told him. "My parents made absolutely sure of that since they never knew when they might be invited to lecture somewhere. I went with them quite often."

"And your citizenship?"

Although she'd been born in Brazil, she had a certificate registering the birth abroad of a citizen of the United States.

"It's what I've always used, and I've never had any problems with it."

"Then everything should go smooth as glass."

"Isn't all this awfully expensive, Taylor?"

"Oh, yes, but you and I don't have to worry about the cost, thank God."

"My grandmother?"

"Yes."

"Is she really so terribly rich?"

"She's rich enough to pay for all this and not miss the money."

"Amazing. Simply amazing."

Their only real problem was packaging her parents' work for shipment, which they did the following day. There was a mountain of it, and it had to be kept in perfect order if a stranger was to make any sense of it. But the Drs. Loving had owned a lot of

luggage, for they never traveled light. By the time
Taylor and Ivy were finished, four of the larger cases
contained nothing but papers and were unbelievably
heavy. So Eleanor would get to pay for overweight
baggage, too.

At last the five days were up and there was nothing
to do but go. Taylor breathed a sigh of self-satis-
faction when the DC-9 lifted off the runway, but it
wasn't until they had departed Djakarta that he allowed himself to believe he was bringing her home.
Ivy stuck to him like glue and looked panic-stricken
when he left her long enough to go to the rest room.
The only time she seemed to relax at all was when they
were seated side by side on the plane and she knew he
couldn't go anywhere.

He noticed how heads turned in her direction everywhere they went. For the trip she wore the saronglike skirt she'd worn that first day and a lipstick-
red top that hugged those beautiful curves. Somehow she managed to look ingenuous and exotic at the
same time. Taylor could only wonder at the impact
she would have on all the Camerons.

All in all, the trip went far more smoothly than he'd
dared hope...until they got to California. Just when
he was feeling relief that they were at last on the final
leg of their journey, the first major glitch occurred.
Their flight to Dallas-Fort Worth was canceled due to
mechanical difficulties. A chorus of groans rose up in
the waiting room when the announcement was made,
and a surge of passengers advanced on the ticket

agent. The man prudently picked up his microphone.

"Ladies and gentlemen, the next flight to DFW departs at 5:30, but it is overbooked. If you want to leave your name and wait for cancellations, I'll be happy to take them. The flight after that departs at 12:05 a.m. and arrives in Dallas at 5:05 a.m. central daylight time. Thank you for your patience, and we apologize for the inconvenience."

Taylor muttered a swear word under his breath. "What's the matter?" Ivy asked anxiously.

"Our plane cratered."

"Cratered?"

"It's broken, and the next flight is overbooked, and the one after that is the red-eye."

"Red-eye?"

"It leaves after midnight, and you arrive in Dallas bleary-eyed before dawn. Damn!" He thought a minute, then turned to Ivy. "I'm tired. Are you?"

"A little."

"I don't want to sit here three more hours hoping for no-shows, and for sure I don't want to wait until midnight. Would it be all right with you if I booked us on something tomorrow?"

Ivy looked bewildered. "Taylor, whatever arrangements you make are fine with me, but...what do we do until tomorrow?"

"That's the easy part. I'll get us rooms somewhere close by. We can have a nice dinner and a good night's sleep. I notice you don't have any better luck sleeping on a plane than I do."

"I . . . I guess it would be nice to lie down."

"Good. But first, let me find out what's available tomorrow." He got to his feet to head for the ticket agent. Ivy jumped up, grabbed his arm and went with him.

After a lengthy wait in line, Taylor was able to secure seats for them on a flight that would get them to DFW by midafternoon the following day. That done, he stowed most of their luggage in a locker, then headed for the information desk to inquire about hotels.

Ivy was in a daze. The entire venture—in and out of airports, on and off planes—had her head spinning. She didn't think she had ever seen so many people, and everyone was in a hurry. It was all she could do to stay out of everyone's way. She'd been gone from home less than forty-eight hours, and already she longed for the island's pace. Her feet hurt and so did her head. Her stomach felt queasy from eating so much unfamiliar food.

She watched Taylor put some coins into a slot on a phone, then heard him talking to someone about two rooms for the night. His energy and efficiency amazed her. He always knew just what had to be done and how to go about doing it. He had to be at least as tired as she was because he'd done all the work, but one would never know it to look at him. He seemed to manufacture energy out of thin air. Since she had undertaken what now seemed an unwise journey, at least she could be grateful she had him with her.

He hung up the phone, turned to her with a smile and took her arm. "All set. The hotel's sending a courtesy van for us. It'll pick us up at Gate 24. Now all we have to do is find Gate 24." And once again he strode off with Ivy almost skipping to keep up with him.

IT WAS JUST ANOTHER HOTEL to Taylor, but to Ivy it was a castle. She'd never been in such a place ... or if she had she didn't remember it. As grand as Erik's house was, it was nothing compared to the hotel. She gawked around the lobby, while Taylor checked them in, trying to take in everything at once. Bright lights blinked; plants cascaded down walls. Someone seemed to have attempted to create an indoor forest.

The lobby was crawling with people, and Ivy noticed something unusual. Most of them wore tags just below the left shoulder, and all of them were laughing loudly and calling to one another. They were very exuberant and a little rude, Ivy thought. Amazingly, there were as many women wearing the tags as men, and they were right in the center of the exuberance.

When Taylor turned back to her, she asked, "Why are all these people wearing tags on their clothes?"

He glanced around to see what she was talking about. "Oh, those are name tags. You know ... Hi, I'm So-and-So." He pointed to a banner draped over the entrance to a dining room. It read Welcome Petroleum Distributors of North America, Inc. "They're having a convention. It's a social phenomenon that allows people to get together, exchange ideas and party for a few days. Let's go to our rooms. We're both on the fourth floor."

The room Taylor led her to made Ivy gasp. "This is the prettiest room I've ever seen!"

Taylor chuckled. Ivy tended to speak in superlatives. Every new encounter was the most something she had ever seen. He crossed the room to draw back the drapes. "It's a pretty nice place, I'll grant you. Not bad for buying a pig in a poke."

"A what?"

"Er...I didn't know anything about the hotel when I made reservations."

Ivy walked into the bathroom, looked around admiringly, then opened the closet and all the dresser drawers. "Are all the rooms in the hotel as nice as this one?"

"Oh, I'm sure there are some that are even nicer."

"This must cost a fortune."

"Like I said, you don't have to worry about that. I think you'll be comfortable. You seem to have everything you need. Now, I've got some phone calls to make, then I want to take a quick nap. I advise you to do the same. After that, we'll go down to dinner about...oh, say, seven. How's that? Too early, too late?"

She shook her head and shrugged. "I guess that's fine. My inner clock is completely off. What time is it now?"

He looked at his watch. "It's three-thirty."

Her eyes widened. "I won't see you for almost four hours?"

"You'll be fine, Ivy. You have everything you need, and we both should get some rest. Seven will be here before you know it." He gave her his most reassuring smile. "I know this has been grueling for you, but it's almost over. A few hours on a plane tomorrow, and we'll be at your grandmother's." He placed the room key on the dresser, took another look around, then headed for the door. Opening it, he slipped the Do Not Disturb sign on the knob. "Don't leave this room unless I'm with you. I'm in 418, four doors down. Call me if you need me." Another smile and he was gone.

Ivy stared at the closed door, then looked around the beautiful room that suddenly felt like a prison. *What am I doing here? I must have been out of my mind to go along with this.* She felt chilled, and then she actually shivered. She would have gladly given all she owned to see Erik's familiar face at that moment.

She looked at the phone, frowning. Taylor had said she could call him . . . but how? She had become so accustomed to living without telephones that the instrument looked foreign to her. After carefully reading the instructions that were on the phone, she lifted the receiver and punched some buttons. It was with great relief that she heard his voice say, "Hello."

"Taylor?"

"Ivy? Is something wrong?"

"No, no…I just wanted to make sure I could reach you."

She heard his throaty chuckle. "I'm right here, two seconds away."

"Good."

"Now get some rest. I'll see you in a bit."

Ivy replaced the receiver, then threw herself across the bed. It felt wonderful. Within seconds she had fallen into a deep slumber.

Ivy slept for two hours and woke feeling rested and refreshed, but when she glanced at the clock she realized there was still an hour and a half before Taylor would come for her. The feeling of aloneness, of disorientation came back, stronger than before.

Rolling off the bed, she chided herself. If she was on Baksra tonight, she would be just as alone. Her parents were gone and Erik was in England. At least here she had Taylor, who was becoming a friend. And tomorrow she would see her grandmother for the first time in eighteen years. She should have been looking at it as a great adventure instead of feeling like a lost child.

She went into the bathroom to draw a tub of water. A complimentary bottle of bath salts stood on the ledge. She dumped them in under the running water

and sniffed the resulting aroma. Stepping out of her
clothes, she climbed in and sat down, letting the fragrant water caress her skin.

Every minute of the past forty or so hours had been
a revelation to her, but the biggest surprise of all was
Taylor. She had been sure they wouldn't have much
to say to each other. After all, they were the same
generation. But their conversations had flowed
smoothly, without uncomfortable silences.

He's so nice, she thought. Always solicitous, forever inquiring about her comfort, if she wanted this
or that. Of course, she realized he was doing it pri-
marily for her grandmother; still, it was nice. He
managed to convey the impression that nothing was
too much trouble, and she knew that couldn't be so.
She wondered what kind of background could have
instilled so much poise and self-confidence in him. A
far cry from her own, she'd daresay.

Ivy wasn't sophisticated about much of anything,
but even she knew her life had been unusual, and not
altogether in ways that had been desirable. Taylor had
once asked if she wouldn't like to get a conventional
education and perhaps work somewhere, and a part
of her knew she would never do anything of the kind.
Getting an education that would help her get a real
job would mean going back to a place like the university, and she had been so miserable there she had
wanted to die. After living where men and women
were segregated, she had found herself in a place
where they not only weren't segregated, they were fa-

miliar in ways she couldn't relate to. No one had
known what to make of her, so for the most part, they
had left her alone.

No, it was far better that she live on Baksra with
customs she was familiar with, where she would be
taken care of.

The water had cooled. She got out of the tub,
briskly dried herself and went into the room to dress.
She chose a sapphire-blue sarong and a matching
blouse. Viewing herself in the mirror, she saw that
from a distance the two pieces looked like a long
dress. She hoped it was appropriate for dinner in a
hotel dining room. She would have felt less conspicuous in a shorter Western-style skirt, but she didn't
own any. The sarong would have to do.

Slipping her feet into sandals, she crossed the room
to look out of the window. It was so strange for it still
to be bright daylight at this time of day. At home, the
sun would be very low in the sky by now.

She glanced at the bedside clock. There were still
thirty minutes until Taylor came for her. Boredom
and restlessness replaced loneliness and uncertainty.
Hunger, too. It had been a long time since that meal
on the plane. She strolled around the room, feeling
like a tiger in a cage. Pausing in front of the television set, she read the card propped atop it. If she
wanted to do this, she pressed such and such a but-
ton; if she wanted to do that, she pressed another. It
looked very complicated to her, and since she wasn't
sure what she wanted to do, she moved away from the

set. Then she spotted a cabinet she hadn't noticed before. Opening it, she discovered it was stocked with all manner of bottled drinks. Perhaps some juice would ease her gnawing hunger pangs.

The juice was at room temperature, and the ice bucket was empty. Ivy seemed to recall seeing a machine at the end of the hall. Going to the door, she opened it and peered out into the hallway. There it was, about four doors down from her room. Taylor told her not to leave without him, but he'd meant *leave*. Surely he wouldn't mind her getting some ice. Turning, she went back for the bucket and carried it to the machine, being careful to leave the door to her room open.

Ivy filled the bucket and was returning to her room when a door flew open and half-a-dozen people spilled out into the corridor, laughing and making a general racket. Ivy quickened her step, but just then a portly man with a gray mustache reached out and grabbed her arm. She was so startled she dropped the bucket. Ice cubes littered the carpet.

"Hey, darlin'. Where ya been?"

"I beg your pardon."

"You're Martha from Atlanta, aren't you?"

"Atlanta? I . . ."

"I thought so. Hey, Chuck, come over here! I want you to meet the little Georgia gal I was telling you about."

Another man came up to Ivy, grinning foolishly, and she smelled the distinct odor of liquor. Oh, Lord, were they drunk? She wondered if the big man had any idea how tightly he was grasping her arm. Struggling to free herself, she only succeeded in making him hold her tighter.

"Hi, hon. I'm Chuck Spencer from Minneapolis. You're right as rain, Merv. She's a pretty little thing."

"Say, Martha, did you lose your name tag?" the big man asked.

"I'm not Mar—"

"That's okay. You can get another one in the hospitality suite. It's on down at the end of the hall in 430. Let's go. Lotsa good booze and eats."

To her horror, the men named Merv and Chuck took her arms, and with the ease they would have used in picking up a rag doll, they swept her along the hall, her feet skimming the floor. The other men with them formed a band, and they marched resolutely toward the hospitality suite, talking in loud voices.

"Taylor!" Ivy cried as they passed Room 418, but it was useless. The men were setting up a frightful din, and Taylor could have been in the shower, watching television, on the phone, anything. Borne helplessly aloft, with her arms pinioned and her eyes widened in stark terror, she couldn't do a thing but allow herself to be taken to the hospitality suite.

Ivy had never seen so many people jammed into such a small space. All she could see was a sea of heads, but thankfully many of them were women. Somehow that made her feel better. Merv and Chuck charged into the throng, then set her on her feet.

"There you go, darlin'," Merv said. "It's a help-yourself bar so...help yourself. Hey, everybody, this is Martha from Atlanta."

"Hi, Martha from Atlanta," Ivy heard someone say. It was with a great sigh of relief that she watched Merv and Chuck become swallowed up in the crowd. She turned toward the door and began trying to inch her way to it.

"Excuse me, please...please, let me pass..." Someone stepped on her foot, and she let out a little squeal. "Please...may I get through...please..." An elbow caught her in the ribs. Her stomach churned, and tears filled her eyes as she realized she wasn't making any progress toward the door. Every time she took a step forward, she was pushed back two. Everyone was laughing and talking loudly, but no one seemed to be paying any attention to what anyone else was saying, least of all her. Were these people really having that much fun?

Tentatively she touched the arm of a man standing nearby. "Excuse me, sir, but..."

"Hi, there. Don't tell me. Your name's right on the tip of my tongue. Great convention, right? Best we've had in some time." Another man captured his attention, and he turned from her.

Ivy ruefully glanced toward the door. An eel couldn't have made it through the crush, but a woman in a green dress passed just then, and Ivy reached for her. The woman turned to her with bright eyes. "Oh, hi, there. Nice to see you again."

"Excuse me, but could you please..."

"Yeah. Girls on the right, boys on the left. Great convention, isn't it? A helluva lot better than Milwaukee, right? Be talking to you later." And she, too, moved off, heedless of the plea in Ivy's eyes.

Ivy had never felt so helpless in her life. In her mind she pictured being trapped with these idiots for hours, even days. Finally, in desperation, she stopped, took a deep breath, closed her eyes and began to scream ... over and over and over again.

The cacophony turned into an eerie silence as every head in the place swiveled toward her. Merv and Chuck were advancing on her, openmouthed and frowning. "Darlin', what is it?" the big man asked.

"I am not Martha from Atlanta!" she shouted. "I'm Ivy from Baksra!"

Merv and Chuck exchanged glances. "That must be one of the Canadian offices," Chuck suggested.

"Sorry, darlin', but you're a dead ringer for Martha. We had the best time in Detroit three years ago."

"All...I...want," Ivy said, speaking with considerable difficulty, *"is to get out of here!"*

"Well, sure, darlin', sure. You should have said something earlier." Merv waved his arm as if he were shooing flies. "Come on folks, make way. Let the little lady get through. Lordy, Lordy, let's show a little manners here."

Mutters rose up among the suddenly silent crowd, and people stepped back as best they could to make a path for her. All of them were staring at her as if she were some strange creature from another planet, but that was all right because that was precisely the way she felt.

"Thank you," she said more calmly, and squaring her shoulders and lifting her chin, she headed for the door.

CHAPTER SIX

TAYLOR WAS CLOSER to panic than he'd ever been in his life. The door to Ivy's room was open, but she was nowhere to be found. An ice bucket lay on the floor, its contents scattered about. Did that have some significance? He was sick to his stomach, and his mind was so rattled he couldn't think. He had telephoned Eleanor earlier to tell her he would deposit Ivy on her doorstep the next afternoon. The woman had uncharacteristically gushed her gratitude. Now he envisioned having to call her back to tell her he'd misplaced her granddaughter. His stomach made another revolution.

Where in hell could Ivy be? She wasn't the type to go off on her own. She looked like a cornered animal every time he left her side. There was absolutely no place in this hotel for her to go.

He stood in the hall outside her room, trying desperately to think what his next move should be, when a door at the other end of the corridor opened and a woman stepped out. He squinted, then his body sagged with relief. It was Ivy! Oh, thank God, thank God. He began loping toward her.

She didn't greet him, didn't say a word, just brushed past him and marched toward her room. Her mouth was set in a tight line, her face was flushed, and there were tears in her eyes. He spun around and followed her. "Ivy, where have you been? I was worried sick."

She stopped and faced him. If eyes could be teary and fiery at the same time, hers were. "I went to get some ice, and these men grabbed me...."

Taylor felt as though he'd been kicked in the stomach. "Oh, my God!"

Her chin trembled. "And then they took me down there to a room...."

"Oh, Ivy, *no!*" He crushed her to him, then held her at arm's length, studying her distraught face. Why had he ever let her out of his sight? "Are you... hurt?"

"Yes!"

Taylor felt faint. He could barely make himself ask. "How... did they hurt you?"

"There were all these people there, and they were laughing and drinking, having some kind of party, I guess, and someone stepped on my foot... and someone's elbow punched my ribs."

"Foot? Ribs? Party?"

"They were people from that... that convention. They thought I was Martha from Atlanta."

"That's... all?"

"Isn't it enough? They're maniacs, all of them! If that's the way people in America behave, I want to go home this instant!'' Whirling, she marched into her room and flung herself onto the bed.

Taylor was so weak with relief he couldn't move for a minute. Then he, too, went into the room and closed the door. He leaned against it for a minute, trying to think of a way to soothe her, before going to the bed, sitting on its edge and patting her shoulder. ''Ivy, I know it's strange to you, coming from the island and all, but...those people are only having a good time.''

''They're crazy!''

''Maybe, a little, but they never meant you any harm.''

She rolled over onto her back and looked at him. ''I was frightened half to death.''

He gave her a fond smile. Lord, she looked beautiful tonight. That color against that skin, that hair was...breathtaking. ''I'm sure you were. But remember I asked you not to leave the room unless I was with you?''

''Yes, I remember,'' she said contritely, sitting up. ''I should have obeyed you.''

The word ''obey'' sounded so quaint. ''Well, thank God no harm's been done.''

''Taylor, tell me something. Why would people pretend they know you when they've never seen you before?''

''I'm not sure I know what you mean.''

''In that room, a woman said it was nice seeing me again. We've never seen each other before. Surely she knows that.''

Taylor smiled. "Well, Ivy…that's just one of those social phrases that don't mean anything. For instance, when someone says 'How're you doing?' they don't really want to know how you are. Understand?"

"No."

"To tell you the truth, I'm not sure I do, either. It's just…superficial socializing. Now, dry your eyes, and we'll go down to dinner." He realized to his dismay that he was using the same tone of voice he would have used with a child. He'd have to watch that.

"All right." With a sigh, she got to her feet and went to look at herself in the mirror over the dresser. "I'm a mess."

"You look beautiful."

She turned to him with an expression of delight. "Do you really think so?"

"Absolutely. You're gorgeous. That color is perfect on you."

Ivy turned and looked in the mirror again, as if seeing herself in a new light. Did he really mean that, or was it more of that superficial socializing? Did it matter? "Thank you, Taylor. That's a nice thing to say."

THE RESTAURANT where they had dinner was located in a rotunda just off the main lobby. Diners had a clear view of all the activity, and that night there was plenty of it. The conventioneers were out in full force, making so much noise that Ivy was amazed the management put up with it. Some of the men even wore silly-looking hats. She had never seen even children behave in such an uninhibited, ridiculous manner. She had to focus on Taylor and remember that *he* wasn't rude and boisterous and silly, so perhaps more Americans would turn out to be like him than these people.

She ordered fish and rice and salad, while Taylor ate the biggest piece of meat she had ever seen. Her food looked delicious but turned out to be bland to the point of being tasteless. "Don't Americans season their food?" she asked.

Taylor glanced up from his steak. "Do you need the salt and pepper?"

"No, I need something hot and spicy."

Taylor summoned the waiter, gave him some instructions, and the man returned with a small bowl of something he said was jalapeño relish. It helped a little, though Ivy missed the fiery sting of Indonesian dishes.

It was almost nine when they left the dining room. Taylor solicitously inquired if there was anything she wanted to do.

"Like what?"

"Oh... go in the bar and have an after-dinner drink. Browse the shops in the esplanade. I don't know... anything."

Ivy shook her head. The food had made her so sleepy she wanted to drop, and she had another headache. It was so strange—she didn't think she'd ever had a headache in her life, and she'd had two that day. "I think not, Taylor, thank you. I just... want to go to bed."

He nodded understandingly. "It's been a bad day for you, and I'm very sorry about that. Tomorrow will be much better," he said, fervently hoping that would turn out to be the truth. Without thought, he took her hand, laced his fingers through hers and walked toward the elevators.

For Taylor, of course, taking her hand was the most natural gesture in the world, but Ivy was stunned by her reaction to the simple interlacing of fingers. His hand was warm, and his fingers were so much stronger and thicker than hers. She felt her cheeks flush. He didn't drop her hand when they entered the elevator, even though there were other people in it. Rather, he held it tightly until they reached her door, releasing it only to reach into his pocket for the key.

"I don't suppose it's necessary for me to tell you not to leave."

She shook her head. This time he didn't think he'd have to worry about her complying. He felt sympathy for her...and for Eleanor. Ivy's grandmother held such high hopes that the reunion would be a permanent one, but Taylor didn't see any way in the world for that to happen.

ONCE TAYLOR HAD LEFT, Ivy dressed for bed, but instead of immediately pulling down the covers and crawling in, she turned off the lights and stood at the window. The view was hardly inspiring. It seemed there were more lights in the city than there were stars in the sky. In front of the hotel was an elevated highway where vehicles of every description raced along at unbelievable speeds. She craned her neck, but she couldn't see the moon or even one star. The city's glare obscured the sky. How sad. At home the night sky looked like millions of diamonds against black velvet.

A sudden chill overtook her. The air-conditioning, she supposed. Her night wear, simple cotton gowns, were perfect for the island's climate, inadequate for here. Was everything in America artificially cooled? Why wouldn't people want to feel natural air on their skin? One tear fell, then another, then another. She turned from the window, crossed her arms under her breasts and let a silent torrent flow.

Her parents, her mother especially, had often told her how much she would hate America, and now she feared they had been right. If she had the slightest idea how to go about it, she would have been on the next plane back to Baksra, back to her own safe, cozy world.

ALL OF TAYLOR'S PRAYERS were answered the following day. Their flight to DFW Airport couldn't have gone more smoothly. Though never very talkative, Ivy seemed even quieter than usual, Taylor noticed, and she looked a little peaked, as though she hadn't slept well. However, she said nothing about having had a bad night. Maybe she simply was in a somber mood. As each day passed and she got farther and farther from the place she considered home, she probably was groping with emotions he could only wonder about.

As for himself, he was mighty relieved when the plane touched ground. It was over. The trip had been an arduous one, and it briefly crossed his mind that he was probably going to have to make it twice more, but for now all that mattered was that Ivy was in Texas, safe and sound. His mission was accomplished.

When they had claimed their luggage from the carousel, Taylor surveyed the pile. "Look, Ivy, we've got a bunch of stuff here. There's no way we can tote it across the street and down two flights of stairs to my car. Tell you what . . . I'll put it over there in that corner, and you watch it while I bring the car around. Okay?"

Her eyes widened. "You're not leaving me!"

"You'll be fine," Taylor assured her. "Just stand here, and I'll make a run for it. I can have the car here twice as fast if I'm alone."

"Oh, Taylor . . ."

"Nobody's going to bother you. Just stand here and *don't move*." With that, he sprinted away.

Ivy's wide, fearful eyes took in her surroundings. The crush of people was as bad as in California . . . maybe worse. Everyone seemed to be moving at a dead run. Why were Americans in such a hurry? She stood surrounded by the luggage for what seemed an hour but could only have been a few minutes before Taylor hurried up to her. She'd never been happier to see anyone.

"Here we go," he said, reaching for two suitcases. "I'm parked at the door with the trunk open, but we'll have to hurry. They don't give you much time to load."

Ivy picked up what she could carry and followed him outside. The heat assaulted her. It was like stepping into a blast furnace, a very different heat from what she was used to. Taylor deposited the suitcases in the trunk and reached for what she was carrying. He smiled at her. "Get into the car. I'll get the rest of the stuff." Again he ran off.

Ivy glanced uncertainly around, then opened the door on the passenger side and slid in. The motor was running. The automobile was far more luxurious than the one Erik owned, and she had thought that was the grandest vehicle imaginable. She rubbed the dashboard and stared at all the dials and gauges. Learning to drive a machine like this would be very complicated, she guessed. Erik had often mentioned teaching her to drive his car, but he probably wouldn't unless she pressed the issue. Now, as she admired Taylor's car, she thought she might press the issue.

She heard the trunk slam, then Taylor got behind the steering wheel. "Whew!" he said, smiling again. "All done."

"Is it absolutely necessary for you to do everything at a run?"

"It is if you don't want your car towed away." Reaching behind his left shoulder, he pulled a long strap across his chest and fastened it into a slot beside his hip. "Buckle up."

"I beg your pardon?"

"Your seat belt."

"Oh." She groped for the device. "Erik has these in his car, too, but he never uses them." She fiddled clumsily with the belt until Taylor released his, reached across her, secured hers, and rebuckled his own.

"Driving on Baksra is a bit different from driving here," he said. "Seat belts are the law here. If there's an accident, there's less chance you'll be hurt if you're wearing one." With a glance in the side mirror, he eased out into the traffic.

Within five minutes, Ivy understood why they had to take precautions against accidents. The number of vehicles on the road boggled her mind, and Taylor drove awfully fast. Erik drove like a madman on the island, but there he had to dodge little more than bicycles and chickens. Here Taylor was darting in and out of lanes of speeding automobiles. They were like ants. She shuddered and closed her eyes. It was all so big and fast and noisy... and ugly.

But Rivercrest wasn't ugly. It was quite lovely, in fact, an oasis of peace in a mad, mad world. And when Taylor pulled into the driveway of the Cameron house, Ivy gasped. She recognized it; it had hardly changed at all. The trees were taller, denser, but the house itself was the same. Suddenly she felt a little better. Not a lot but a little.

"Look familiar?" Taylor asked, braking and switching off the engine.

"Yes, yes . . . it does, and I wasn't at all sure it would."

"Let's go in. I'm sure Eleanor is on pins and needles. I'll bring our things in later."

Wilma answered Taylor's ring, and they stepped into the gleaming foyer. "I know you don't remember me, ma'am," the servant said to Ivy, "but I came to work for Mrs. Cameron when you were still living here." To Taylor she said, "She's waiting for you in the library. Goodness, I haven't seen her so excited in years."

Taylor took Ivy's arm and led her down the hall, but as they started to enter the library, Jethro put in an appearance, snarling his usual greeting. Ivy stepped back, grabbing for Taylor's arm.

"That's Jethro," he explained. "Don't mind him, and he won't pay any attention to you."

Ivy looked skeptical. "Are . . . you sure?"

"Positive. He doesn't have anything to do with people. Come on."

Eleanor was waiting for them on her thronelike chair, dressed to polished perfection, hands folded in her lap, legs crossed at the ankles. She looked regal, as usual, and yet there was something different. She was alive with anticipation.

"Eleanor," Taylor said, "this is Ivy." With a gentle pressure on the small of her back, he urged Ivy toward her grandmother.

She's not at all as I remembered, Ivy thought. *She's so old. But I have to remember how much time has passed.* She glided across the room, going to stand in front of Eleanor and smiled shyly. "Hello, Grandmother."

"Oh, Ivy... Ivy," Eleanor said, her voice choked with emotion. Reaching out, she took her granddaughter's hands in hers. "Let me look at you. Oh, my dear, you are a vision! Taylor, how can I ever thank you?"

HALF AN HOUR LATER, Taylor had brought in Ivy's luggage, and Wilma had taken the young woman to her room upstairs. Taylor and Eleanor were seated in the library with the door closed. It had been an emotional reunion, and Eleanor was only now recovering from it. "She's enchanting, isn't she?" she remarked. "There is nothing on earth I can say or do to adequately repay you for what you've done for me."

"You don't have to repay me, Eleanor, and I think you should save your thanks for later. There are some things you should know about your granddaughter. Ivy has led a rather strange life... or perhaps *strange* isn't the word. *Extraordinary* might be more accurate."

"I assumed she would have, considering those un-conventional parents of hers," Eleanor sniffed.

"It goes beyond that. She's told me a lot during the time we've been together. In India, she and her parents lived with a Hindu family who were strict vegetarians. Not even eggs were permitted. And the sexes were segregated to the point that a woman was never alone with her husband until their wedding night. We are talking here about something that sounds straight out of the eighteenth century. And those were the years when Ivy was coming of age."

Eleanor digested that but said nothing.

"Her education in India seems to have leaned heavily on classical literature, Latin, history, that sort of thing. Nothing that would help her with a career. She went to the University of Singapore for a while, but she felt so out of place she left."

"What could Claire have been thinking of to raise her that way? What is the island like?"

Taylor rolled his eyes. "There the customs are even more unconventional. They dictate that everyone has two spouses in a lifetime—first a much older one, then one much younger. Ivy plans to marry Erik Soewadji, the man who wrote the letter. He's in his sixties."

Eleanor gasped. "That adorable child? A man in his sixties? Oh, Taylor, we must do something to prevent it!"

"Eleanor, I . . . I know you plan to try to get Ivy to stay here with you, but . . . well, I'm not sure that's such a good idea. Nothing in Ivy's past has prepared her for living in America. Not only would she be out of place, I'm afraid she would be very unhappy. It would be like the university all over again.'' He then told her about Ivy's run-in with the conventioneers at the hotel. "She was absolutely terrified. Her reactions to things that you and I consider normal are . . . well, extreme to say the least.''

Eleanor's eyes narrowed. "If you think I am going to send that girl back to that island to marry a man older than her father was without putting up a fight . . . if you think that, you don't know me well.''

Taylor sighed, nodded and got to his feet. "I just wanted you to have an idea of what you're up against. Odd, isn't it? If one heard only the bare facts about her life—born in Brazil, lived in Texas, in India, attended the University of Singapore, lived on an Indonesian island—the picture of a world-weary sophisticate would emerge. But Ivy is a simple, innocent babe in the woods . . . and utterly delightful to be with because of the simplicity.''

Eleanor's incisive eyes bored into his. "There's a difference between sophistication and savvy, you know. It's the savvy I want to teach her.''

"Good luck. Now, if you'll excuse me, I'll leave the two of you to get acquainted. I've been gone from the office some time. There must be a small mountain of things to get caught up on.''

"Robert and Evelyn and Michael and Cheryl are coming for dinner tonight. I would love for you to join us. You might make the occasion easier for Ivy since she knows you. She seems very taken with you."

"That's nice of you, Eleanor, but I think Ivy needs to get used to my not being around all the time. I don't know if she's 'taken' with me, but she's certainly come to rely on me. It would be best if she got used to just family."

"Whatever you think, dear. And I do thank you so much."

Taylor smiled. "I'll show myself out. All of you have a nice evening. Give my regards to Robert and Michael and their wives...and tell Ivy I'll be by to see her soon." He left the room, crossed the foyer and opened the front door. But before leaving, he turned and glanced up the stairs to the second-floor landing. At this point he had expected to feel nothing but relief over a job well-done. Ivy was no longer his responsibility. Tonight all he had to do was pick up something delicious for dinner, go home, then sleep in his own bed.

But instead of the disburdening sensation he'd expected, a more curious one overtook him. Tonight would be the first one in a week that he wouldn't spend with Ivy. As strange as it seemed, he was going to miss her.

UPSTAIRS IN THE BEDROOM that had been hers as a child, Ivy inspected every inch of the place. It was beautifully furnished. A tester bed covered with an exquisite quilted spread was the room's focal point.

Small ornaments adorned the dresser and chest of drawers, and there was a television set in one corner. A bentwood rocker sat invitingly beside a large window that overlooked the backyard.

Behind Ivy, Wilma was bustling around. "I've hung your garment bag and put the suitcases in the closet. I'll be glad to put your things away for you."

"Oh, don't bother, please. Most of the cases contain papers."

"You have a private bath over there. Would you like me to draw water for you?"

"Wilma," Ivy said with a smile, "I'm quite capable of drawing my own bathwater. I'll require very little attention." Were there people who actually had others draw their bathwater for them? "Do you run this big house by yourself?"

"Mrs. Cameron runs the house."

"Well, of course, but I meant ..."

"You mean, do I have help? Consuelo is the cook, and there are the yardmen who double as handymen. And three times a year Mrs. Cameron has a cleaning service come in and go over the place from basement to attic. I, however, am in charge of daily upkeep." Wilma said it proudly.

"That's quite a job."

"I've been doing it for almost twenty years." The servant took another look around. "If that's all, ma'am."

"There is one other thing. Do you think you could call me 'Ivy?' 'Ma'am' sounds so formal."

"Very well." Wilma turned to leave, then stopped. "My word, would you look at that!"

Ivy glanced toward the door. The dog she had encountered downstairs filled up the doorway, his soulful eyes fastened intently on her. She swallowed hard. She knew it was ridiculous, but all the time she was in the library with Taylor and her grandmother, she had the feeling the dog was watching her.

"That dog hasn't been upstairs since the mister died," Wilma said, her voice incredulous.

"Is...is he dangerous?" Ivy asked.

"Jethro?" Wilma uttered a little laugh. "Oh, my, no. Useless, perhaps...and heartbroken. You see, he was devoted to your grandfather. I don't think he's ever gotten over his death."

Jethro made a move to enter the room, but Wilma shooed him. "Downstairs with you, Jethro. Get, now."

Jethro, however, stood his ground. He ambled over to Ivy and sat down at her feet. Tentatively she reached down and rubbed his head. The dog's tail wagged.

Wilma's mouth dropped. "That tail never wags, never. He certainly seems to have taken a shine to you, ma...Ivy. I'll get him out of here as best I can, but Jethro's pretty antisocial. No one can make him do what he doesn't want to do."

Ivy eyed the dog. "If he wants to stay up here, I don't see the harm, do you? He'll no doubt go downstairs when I do." Again she rubbed his head, and she was rewarded when he lifted one of his clumsy paws to her. Taking it, she murmured, "Good boy." She would have sworn he smiled.

Shaking her head, Wilma backed out of the room and closed the door behind her. Jethro, apparently realizing he was going to be left to do as he pleased, lay down on the floor beside the bed and closed his eyes.

Ivy glanced around. It was strange to think this room had been hers for the first nine years of her life. She remembered nothing about it, but of course it doubtless had been completely redecorated, maybe many times. She seemed to remember there had been a toy chest under the window, and it had been stacked with stuffed animals. If so, they were the last stuffed animals she had ever owned. How might her life have turned out if she had been left here?

She wondered if she should go back downstairs or wait a few minutes. Her grandmother had told her to take all the time she needed, so maybe she wanted to talk to Taylor about their trip.

She walked to the window and peered out. A tall brick wall enclosed the backyard, which contained a broad sweep of green lawn. Sprinklers were on, and two men worked in the garden at the rear. Slowly things were coming back to her. She seemed to recall a playhouse that she and her cousins had practically lived in when the weather was nice. And there had been a greenhouse that had always been filled with flowers, even in the winter. Both structures were gone now.

Turning, she reached over to flip on the television set, then sat on the edge of the bed and gazed raptly at the screen. She had seen very little TV in her life—only when she traveled with her parents.

The program was obviously some kind of discussion. The woman in the center seemed to be a moderator. She was talking to a group of very intense, earnest women. Ivy listened, trying to pick up the gist of the conversation.

After a few minutes, she frowned. The women, she realized, were discussing their respective marriages, and it seemed they were all married to men who had conducted multiple affairs with other women. Yet they all had elected to stay with their unfaithful husbands, and the woman in the middle was asking them to explain why they had made that decision. Furthermore, people in the audience were asking them the most unbelievably personal questions. Ivy listened more closely, puzzled by it all, but then the program was interrupted by an advertisement, and Ivy thought she really should get back downstairs. Switching off the set, she looked down at Jethro, peacefully asleep on the floor.

"I'm going downstairs, Jethro," she said. "Do you want to come with me?"

And as if he had responded to the sound of her voice every day of his life, the dog hopped up and followed her down the stairs.

Eleanor was alone in the library when Ivy returned. Her face broke into a radiant smile when she saw her granddaughter. "Ah, Ivy, come over here and sit down, dear. Wilma is bringing us some iced tea. I hope you like it."

Ivy crossed the room and sat down, and Jethro sat at her feet. "I don't know," she said. "I've drunk tea, of course."

"This is poured over ice and has lemon and sugar in it."

"It sounds delicious. Where's Taylor?"

"He left."

"Left?" Ivy's voice rose slightly. Of course she'd known he couldn't stay with her all the time, but she had thought he would be with her the rest of the day. A small quiver of panic rose up inside her. She realized she'd grown dependent on him, but she didn't suppose that was surprising. She'd always had someone looking after her. "Is he coming back?"

"Not today, dear. He's been gone from home quite a while and had things to catch up on."

Ivy did her best to mask her disappointment. She absently reached down and scratched Jethro behind an ear, eliciting a canine sound of contentment. Eleanor shot the dog a startled stare, then looked at Ivy. "This is incredible, dear. Jethro hasn't had a thing to do with anyone since Ben died."

Ivy smiled down at the animal. "That's what Wilma said. I think he's sweet. I never had a dog. Mom said they were too much trouble."

Wilma entered the library at that moment, carrying two tall glasses of tea. Ivy took a sip. It was good but not sweet enough for her. She smiled and thanked the servant, who slipped out of the room as silently as she had entered it.

"Robert and Michael and their wives will be having dinner with us tonight, Ivy," Eleanor said, carefully setting her glass on a coaster. "Do you remember your aunts and uncles?"

"Slightly. I remember the house being full of people. The adults would eat in the dining room, and there was a table on the porch for the children."

"Those were our Sunday dinners. We still have them."

"Will my cousins be here tonight?"

"No, I thought it best not to overwhelm you with family your first night with us."

Ivy sipped her tea. She couldn't stop thinking about those people on television. "Grandmother?"

"Yes, dear."

"Ah . . . while I was upstairs I turned on the television and I heard the strangest thing. There was a lady talking to some people, asking them questions . . . really personal things about their private lives."

Eleanor glanced at the clock and sighed. "Oprah," she said. "Or Sally Jessy."

"I beg your pardon."

"Those are what we call 'talk shows.' And how they do talk. Good heavens, there's no telling what you heard."

"All of the women were talking about their husbands, but it wasn't so much what they said as why they said it. Why would people go on television and talk about such things in front of strangers?"

"Why indeed?" Eleanor said with a little grunt. "The wonder of it is, why do so many people *watch* it? I feel like a naughty girl who's been eavesdropping at the keyhole when I watch them. Things are said on TV these days that weren't even whispered about behind closed doors in my day." Eleanor smoothed at her skirt. "Ivy, dear, do me a favor. I think it would be best if you didn't watch those things until after you've been here awhile and understand our customs a little better."

Ivy sat back. It was so bewildering. In fact, everything she had so far seen was bewildering. This was a peculiar country—those crazy people at the hotel last night and the ones on television a moment ago. Taylor seemed to think Baksra and its customs were strange, but after only two days in America, she was beginning to look on the island as the sanest spot on earth.

THAT EVENING, seated at the dining table and surrounded by her grandmother, her uncles and their wives, Ivy stared at the plate of food Wilma had placed before her. It held a very large piece of meat that Uncle Robert had oohed over. "Ah, Consuelo's roast beef!" he'd enthused. Next to the meat were potatoes that had been covered with some sort of brown sauce. Ivy, of course, recognized the green beans and wished there were more of them. A basket of hot bread was passed around the table, and everyone took some, often using their left hand. She fought back her revulsion. Having lived in the East for so long, she considered the left hand unclean, never meant to touch food. No such taboo was observed here. She carefully watched everyone else and did the best she could, but she staunchly refused to use her left hand. It soon became apparent, however, that she couldn't cut her meat unless she held her fork in her left hand, so her roast beef went largely untouched. Why on earth wasn't the meat cut into small pieces in the kitchen?

The talk that flowed around the dinner table had ceased focusing on her and had turned to business. Of course, all the men back home discussed business, too—everyone from the street vendors on their reed mats to Erik and his fellow planters. But there all similarity ended. Here the women were every bit as involved with Cameron Oil as the men were, something that was unheard of in any world Ivy had ever known. Amazingly, Aunt Cheryl was treasurer of the company. And her grandmother seemed to run the whole thing. Her adult sons even sought her opinion. That took some getting used to.

Ivy hated admitting she was bored, but she was. She couldn't understand half of what was said, and she contributed almost nothing. Her uncles were big, lusty men who resembled her mother to an astonishing degree, and her aunts were sweet, delightful women, she supposed, but they were as different from her as day was from night. Would she have enjoyed the evening more if Taylor had been there? Perhaps... but she had to remember that this was his world, too.

The dinner finally ended, and everyone left soon afterward in deference to Eleanor's early bedtime. After saying good-night to her grandmother, Ivy sought the privacy of her room where she could relax for the first time that night. Halfway up the stairs, she realized Jethro was following her.

"Are you supposed to be up here?" she whispered, stroking his head. He looked at her with dark, limpid eyes.

"Well, I suppose there's no harm," she decided, snapping her fingers and gesturing for him to follow. Inside her room, the dog claimed the spot in the corner he had occupied earlier.

At least she'd made her first friend in America, unless she could count Taylor, and she wasn't sure she could. He might have thought her more a bother than a friend. Shrugging out of her clothes, she slipped on a plain muslin gown, washed her face, brushed her teeth and crawled beneath the covers.

But once in bed, she discovered she couldn't sleep. Maybe there had been too much excitement for one day. After perhaps twenty minutes had passed and she still couldn't sleep, she realized she was hungry. There had been so much food, rich and heavy, so how could she be hungry again?

Then it dawned on her—she hadn't eaten any rice all day, and without a certain amount of rice, she simply didn't feel full. And without the burn of chili peppers, she didn't really feel she'd eaten. She wondered if it would be rude to tell her grandmother what she liked to eat.

Ivy rolled over and cradled her head in her arms. It was going to be very difficult to spend a whole month here. If only she had a little something to remind her of home—a letter from Erik—maybe she would feel better. But Erik wasn't on Baksra. He was in London, so it would be weeks before she heard from him, if she did at all.

She *knew* she would feel better if Taylor was here, not here in her room, of course, but here in the house, down the hall as he had been on the island.

But it was silly, and she knew it. He was back home now, where he had his work and his life and he had to be relieved. He was much too kind to give any indication that the trip to Baksra had been a bother, but he couldn't have actually enjoyed it. Now that he was home, he would have friends, people he enjoyed being with. Maybe there was a woman he liked better than others, someone he saw on a steady basis. As much as they'd talked while he was at her house, he'd never mentioned a woman, but maybe he wouldn't. Maybe he was with a special someone right now.

Ivy stared across the dark room. The thought saddened her, and she didn't even know why.

CHAPTER SEVEN

THE FOLLOWING MORNING, Ivy woke with a start, disoriented and wondering for a minute where she was. When she realized she was at her grandmother's house in Texas, thousands of miles away from her home and the people she knew, her eyes burned and she wiped at her tears, burying her face in her pillow. A feeling of the most abject loneliness overcame her.

Suddenly a very cold, wet object touched her cheek. "What on earth..." Then Jethro's face came into focus, abruptly altering Ivy's mood. "Well, good morning," she said. "I'll bet you need to go outside, don't you?" She threw back the covers and stood up. It did no good to mope. She was here, like it or not, and Erik was in England. It was only four weeks out of the rest of her life. In four weeks she would be back home, and her trip to Texas would be only a memory.

As if he could read her thoughts, Jethro gave a little growl. Ivy laughed. "I'll probably miss you and Grandmother, but that's all I'll miss." Opening the door, she shooed him out into the hall. "Go on now.

I'll see you in a little while." The dog reluctantly trotted out and headed for the stairs.

IVY ARRIVED in the dining room just as Eleanor was sitting down at the table. "Good morning, Grandmother."

Eleanor turned, noting that Ivy wore slacks and a short-sleeved cotton blouse, and she had pulled her hair back and secured it at the nape with a scarf. She wore almost no makeup. The effect was one of freshness and youth. She was so lovely, the elderly woman thought. Whatever else Claire and Gordon had done, they had raised a beautiful daughter. "Good morning, dear. Did you sleep well?"

"Yes, thank you," Ivy said, sliding into a chair. It wasn't a lie. Once she had fallen asleep, she had slept soundly. "Jethro slept in my room last night. I hope that's all right."

Eleanor chuckled. "How amazing that the dog took to you right off. Of course it's all right if you don't mind him. He's spent the last few years doing little but grieving."

At that moment, Wilma came out of the kitchen, carrying a teapot in one hand and a covered basket in the other. She immediately filled Eleanor's cup, then glanced at Ivy. "Would you prefer tea or coffee, Ivy?"

"I'll have tea, too, thank you."

Breakfast turned out to be fruit, fresh hot rolls and an omelet for Ivy. She was starved, but what she wouldn't have given for a bowl of the sweet, coconut-scented rice that was her favorite breakfast food, along with something, *anything* spicy.

"So, dear, what would you like to do today?" Eleanor inquired.

"I've been admiring your garden. I do quite a bit of gardening myself on the island. I thought I would like to study yours closer."

Eleanor's eyes brightened. "How splendid! I so used to love puttering in the garden. Perhaps there's something special you'd like to plant."

Ivy smiled. "Thank you, Grandmother, but that would be rather pointless, wouldn't it? Why plant something you won't be around to enjoy?"

Eleanor's bright look faded considerably. "Yes, of course," she said, and lifted her cup to her lips.

AFTER BREAKFAST, Eleanor went into the library to work on what she called "the books," and Ivy and Jethro went out onto a sun porch that opened onto the backyard. *Yard* really didn't do justice to the back of the big house. *Grounds* might have been more appropriate. The lawn looked like a green velvet carpet, and the gardens surrounding it on three sides were riots of color. Ivy knew enough about gardening to know that somebody, or several somebodies, spent long hours laboring to keep them looking so healthy and lovely.

"Good morning, miss," a man's voice called, and she jumped. She turned to see a man in faded denims and a work shirt emerging from the rose garden.

"Oh . . . you frightened me. I didn't see you."

"I'm sorry. I'm Clark, Mrs. Cameron's gardener. That young'un over there is my boy, Henry."

Henry, who looked to be in his late teens, smiled shyly and returned to his labors. "I'm pleased to meet both of you. I'm Mrs. Cameron's granddaughter, Ivy."

"Do tell," Clark said. "I thought I knew just about the whole bunch."

"I don't live here," she explained.

"You're up and about awfully early."

"My grandmother and I just finished breakfast, and I wanted to see the garden." Her appreciative eyes moved around. "It's so lovely."

"It takes a heap o' work, but the missus likes things nice."

"Tell me something, Clark. Did there used to be a greenhouse over there by that wall?"

"Yes. We tore it down about, oh, six years ago, I guess it was. Mrs. Cameron just couldn't work in it any longer. I offered to keep it up for her, but she missed the fun of doing it herself. Oh, what flowers she grew! A dahlia of hers once won first place at a garden show, and she'd carry her hothouse roses to nursing homes, just to brighten things up a bit. She had such a way with plants. Some people do and some don't, you know. It's like cooking. Some are good at it and some aren't. Mrs. Cameron used to make the best pies and cakes I ever put in my mouth.''

Ivy found it almost impossible to imagine her grandmother, who seemed such an authoritarian figure, as someone who liked puttering in a garden, who baked pies and cakes.

Why didn't Mom ever tell me that? she wondered.

TAYLOR WAS AT HIS DESK at ten-thirty that morning when the receptionist informed him he had a phone call. Lifting the receiver, he said, ''Taylor Edwards.''

''Good morning, Taylor. This is Eleanor.''

''Good morning, Eleanor. How did the evening go?''

''Oh, it was only mildly successful. Poor Ivy was absolutely mute all evening, not that it's easy getting a word in when Robert and Michael start yammering away. And she just picked at her food.''

Too late Taylor decided he should have told Eleanor something about the diet Ivy was accustomed to. ''What did you serve?''

''Roast beef, mashed potatoes, that sort of thing.''

''Well, Eleanor, that probably was much too heavy for Ivy. We have to remember that she ate a strict vegetarian diet for many years. And on the island the daily fare is fish, rice and vegetables. She's just not used to much meat.''

''Consuelo will, of course, prepare anything she wants. I'm glad you told me. We can't have the poor girl starving. But that's not why I called. There's something I want you to do for me.''

Taylor lifted his eyes to the ceiling, bracing himself for whatever she'd conjured up in her mind this time. "Yes, Eleanor.''

"Ivy acutely missed you last night, I could tell.''

"I'm the only person in America she feels she knows. That will change.''

"Perhaps, but until it does, I want you to make a practice of stopping by after work, just to let her know you're thinking about her, beginning with today. Can that be arranged?''

Taylor smiled. Anything Eleanor wanted could be arranged. Actually, he had planned to stop by later that day. He had thought of Ivy almost constantly since leaving the Cameron house yesterday, something that had surprised him no end. "Of course. As a matter of fact, I intended to stop by to see how she's doing, but I won't be able to stay long. I returned to a mountain of work, so I'm going to have to burn some midnight oil.''

"Come for a cocktail. I'm sure Ivy will adore seeing you.''

"By the way, what's she doing this morning?''

"She's outside in the garden. Would you believe Jethro has scarcely left her side? He even slept in her room last night. Isn't that amazing?''

"It's pretty unbelievable,'' Taylor agreed.

"She's so delightful, Taylor, and a month is such a short time. Already she's given my life new meaning. She is not going back to that island to marry a man in his sixties, not if I can help it.''

A sense of foreboding hit Taylor at that moment. If Eleanor felt that way after only one day, how would she feel if the month passed and Ivy still wanted to return to the island? He, too, thought her going back to Baksra would be a shame, but he had prepared himself for the very real possibility of that happening. Perhaps this was one of Eleanor's schemes he should have discouraged from the beginning.

AFTER TALKING to Taylor, Eleanor summoned Wilma into the library. ''When Ivy comes inside, ask her to come in here, please.''

''Yes, ma'am.''

''And, Wilma, I want you to tell Consuelo to keep plenty of fish, rice and vegetables on hand from now on. That's what Ivy's accustomed to eating, so we need to break her in to American food gradually.''

''Yes, ma'am. Anything else?''

Eleanor's eyes fell on the morning paper lying on her desk. Most of the headlines were, as usual, depressing. Shootings, robberies, threatened strikes, the president and Congress at loggerheads. She folded it and handed it to Wilma. ''As a matter of fact, there is. Keep these things out of sight for the next few weeks. I'll read them in my room.''

If Wilma thought that was a strange request, she showed no sign. ''Yes, ma'am,'' she said, tucking the paper beneath her arm. ''Is that all?''

"Yes, thank you." Eleanor was taking no chances. She would, to the best of her ability, keep the seamier side of American life from Ivy until she felt the girl could put it in its proper perspective.

When the servant had left the room, Eleanor turned her attention to the stack of photograph albums on the coffee table. There were over sixty years' worth of pictures, each one faithfully labeled by Eleanor herself with names, dates and occasions. If Ivy was ever to get a sense of being a part of the Cameron clan, this was the place to start. Eleanor opened to the pictures Ben had taken the day she arrived from Brazil with Ivy. How excited they had been to have an infant in the house again!

"You want to see me, Grandmother?"

Eleanor turned to see Ivy standing at the threshold. "Yes, dear, I do. Please come over here. I have some things I thought you might enjoy seeing."

Ivy crossed the room, and Eleanor handed one of the albums to her. "These are the pictures Ben took the day I brought you to this house," she said.

Ivy sat down and took the album, her eyes wide with wonder. A smile curved her mouth. The woman holding the infant was the grandmother she remembered. And the big, strong-looking man was her grandfather. Now she remembered him, too. He had, as she recalled, been a lot of fun.

Slowly she began turning the pages. Here was a picture of her taken the day she sat up for the first time; there was one of her first steps. Another was of

her on her first birthday. Still another commemo-
rated the day she entered kindergarten.

She was mesmerized. Her parents, naturally, hadn't
had photographs of her as a youngster, and they'd
had few of her in later years. Capturing life's little
milestones on film was simply something they'd never
done. They had always been too preoccupied with
their work; family life had taken a back seat. *This is
my history!* she thought in wonder.

For over an hour, grandmother and granddaughter pored over the albums, Ivy asking questions and
Eleanor supplying the answers. Wilma came in to
announce lunch, and Ivy carried an album into the
dining room. "I rarely have more than a bowl of soup
for lunch," Eleanor said, "but I'm sure Consuelo has
prepared something more substantial for you."

"I don't want to be a bother," Ivy protested.

"It's no bother. Consuelo gets rather bored with
my eating habits. She would be delighted if you made
requests, so please don't hesitate to tell her exactly
what you want to eat."

The door that led to the kitchen opened, and a
woman entered the room, carrying a plate. She had
coal-black hair, very dark eyes and the color of skin
Ivy was accustomed to seeing on the island. She was
rather plump and had a sweet face and smile.

"Consuelo, this is my granddaughter, Ivy,"
Eleanor said.

"*Mucho gusto,* Ivy. Wilma, she says you like rice."

"I love rice."

With a flourish, Consuelo placed a dish before her that held a heaping mound of rosy rice. "Mexican-style, like my mama made. I hope you like it." The cook stood back and waited.

Ivy assumed she was supposed to taste the rice in Consuelo's presence. She took a mouthful, chewed and swallowed. "It's delicious, Consuelo. Thank you."

"Not too hot with chili peppers?"

"Oh, no, I could stand it much hotter."

"*¿Verdad? Momento, por favor.*" Consuelo hurried out of the room and returned in seconds with a jar full of peppers. "Try one of these, but be careful. Just take a tiny taste at first."

Ivy gingerly bit off the end of a pepper, felt the familiar and welcome sting and smiled. "Perfect, just perfect." She proceeded to chop the pepper into bits with the edge of her fork and mix them into her rice.

Consuelo stood back, eyes wide and admiring. "*Dios, mio!* Never, never have I seen an Anglo eat a *pequin* and like it." Her voice was so approving that Ivy felt as though she'd just been initiated into a very exclusive club.

After lunch, Eleanor went to her room for a nap, and Ivy stayed in the library, studying the photographs, reading the labels when she couldn't figure out who was who. The pictures of her mother as a child, then as a teenager particularly intrigued her. She looked so happy and carefree. Ivy could only wonder at the forces that had changed Claire Loving into the mother she had known.

By the time her grandmother had wakened and come back downstairs, however, she had found one album that puzzled her. The pictures were very, very old.

"Who are these people, Grandmother? All you wrote beneath it was the place and the date."

"Your grandfather and myself when we first went out to West Texas."

Ivy stared at the picture, finding it impossible to equate that pretty young woman, who couldn't have been older than twenty, with the woman seated opposite her. "Look at that car!" She giggled at the vintage automobile.

"Oh, we thought it was quite luxurious," Eleanor said. "My parents had never been farther from home than their own legs or those of a horse could carry them, but Ben and I owned an automobile and could go anywhere our hearts desired."

"What's that building in the background?"

"That was our first house."

Ivy's mouth dropped. The building was little more than a shack. "You and Grandfather lived in *that?*"

"Yes. In 1928, we had that house, that car and each other, period, and we thought we were sitting on top of the world. The place where we lived was an oil boomtown, you see, very wild and woolly, probably dangerous, too, though I didn't know it. There were hundreds of people who slept in tents or rented cots for fifty cents a night, but we had a floor, a roof and four walls. Oh, I was quite smug with satisfaction.'' Eleanor smiled at the memories.

"But...how did you go from that to..." Ivy's gaze swept her surroundings "...to all this?"

"It took a lot of hard work and a lot of luck, and Ben Cameron was one of the luckiest men I've ever known. And a good thing he was since he was a gambler at heart.'' Eleanor began to reminisce, and Ivy looked up from the album to give her grandmother her full attention.

"He went out to West Texas bold as brass and presented himself as an oilman, though the only thing he knew about the oil business had come from watching some men drill a well near his old home. Oh, such days those were! We lived on pinto beans and corn bread for weeks at a time, and the sandstorms were just fierce. There were rattlesnakes and scorpions and I don't know what all. I won't tell you there weren't nights when I cried and longed for that old Oklahoma farm, but I wanted to be with Ben more than I wanted anything else in the world. So I just kept cooking beans, making corn bread and dusting furniture three times a day, waiting for something to happen.''

Ivy was fascinated. "What *did* happen?"

"Ben finally won a huge block of leases in a poker game, and he started to drill with a wooden rig held together with baling wire and prayer. His first well came in, and so did the second. Luck, pure and simple. There were some failures, too, but it was to Ben's credit that he never gloated over his successes or moaned over his defeats. If a well came up dry, he said, 'We'll have better luck next time,' and he always did.''

It amazed Ivy that her grandparents had come from such humble beginnings. In every society she had firsthand knowledge of, a person was born rich or poor and died the same way. To start out with almost nothing and end up with what appeared to be everything was inconceivable to her.

All day Ivy had tried—out of some sense of loyalty to her parents, she supposed—to be offended by what her mother had referred to as "a vulgar display of wealth and privilege," but she couldn't. She had seen less sign of overt luxury here than was displayed daily in Erik's house, for instance. And now that she knew something of her grandparents' past, she felt they deserved to enjoy the fruits of their labors.

And her grandmother was not the snob Ivy had half expected her to be. She definitely ran her household, but she wasn't domineering. She was a woman who obviously adored her family, something that touched a responsive chord. Ivy's own parents had been so distant that she'd sometimes wondered if they remembered she existed.

But what most impressed her was the way her grandmother treated Wilma and Consuelo. Eleanor always said "please" and "thank you" to them, very unlike Erik, who looked right through his servants and never noticed the nice things they did for him.

"You know, dear..." Eleanor's voice cut into her thoughts. "I have two automobiles that I no longer drive since I trust neither my eyesight nor my reflexes. Wilma and Consuelo use them occasionally for shopping and to take me where I need to go, but for the most part, the cars remain in the garage. You're more than welcome to use either of them whenever you want."

Ivy smiled. "Thank you, Grandmother, but I don't know how to drive a car."

"You don't? Good heavens, child, you must learn."

"There's really no need. I can get anywhere I need to go on the island by bicycle."

"Indeed. Well, this isn't the island, and you'll enjoy your stay here so much more if you can get around at will. I'm hoping there will be a lot you want to see and do. I'll arrange for driving lessons immediately."

Ivy started to protest but then remembered how Taylor's car had intrigued her. Learning to drive might be a good idea. She'd sometimes envied Erik his mobility, his ability to go wherever he wished no matter what the weather was like. It might be fun to go back home and surprise him by being able to drive. If she really did learn—and there was some doubt in her mind she would be able to—she might even buy a car. She didn't have much money, but she didn't need much of a car. "Is it very difficult to learn?"

"I really can't remember, but I shouldn't think so. Everybody does it."

"Then . . . thank you. I'll do my best."

"And you'll need a credit card. One simply can't move around without one these days. I'll call the bank first thing in the morning."

The two of them returned their attention to the albums, and the afternoon flew by. Jethro strayed from Ivy's side only when Wilma forced him to go outside. Eleanor had no idea it was anywhere near five o'clock until the dog suddenly jumped to his feet and growled. Ivy shushed him with a frown, then turned to see what had prompted that reaction. Then she, too, jumped to her feet and exclaimed, "Taylor!"

He strolled into the room, grinning at her fondly. "How was your first day in Texas?"

Ivy took him by the arm. "Grandmother and I have spent almost all of it looking at photographs. Come here, I want you to see some of me when I was a little girl."

Taylor didn't stay but an hour, pleading the necessity of work when asked to stay for dinner. But before leaving the house, he promised the disappointed Ivy he would find time for her the following day. Eleanor had carefully watched her granddaughter during the brief visit. Ivy was very shy and reserved, unusually so for a twenty-seven-year-old woman. That, of course, could be attributed to the odd life she had led . . . and to her finding herself in the midst of strange customs and unfamiliar people. But her reserve melted considerably when Taylor put in an appearance.

Ivy had been with her slightly more than twenty-four hours, and already Eleanor knew her heart would break if her granddaughter went back to the island. It mustn't happen. It couldn't!

So Eleanor determined that she would have to call on Taylor again. Perhaps she was asking too much, but it couldn't be helped. She'd make it up to him one of these days.

TAYLOR COULDN'T HAVE been more surprised the following afternoon when he returned from small claims court to find Eleanor waiting in his office. She so seldom left the house that it was something of a shock to see her outside her own domain.

"Eleanor, is something wrong?" he asked solicitously.

"No, nothing."

"If you wanted to see me, you should have called. I would have come right over."

"Oh, it's nice to get out once in a while. Wilma was taking Ivy to her first driving lesson, so I asked her to drop me off here."

Taylor took a seat behind his desk, picked up a pencil and tapped it against his smiling mouth. "So Ivy's taking driving lessons. How on earth did you ever talk her into that?"

"I merely suggested she would enjoy her stay more if she could get around. Poor dear looked frightened half to death when we left the house, but I'm sure she'll do fine. It's just one of the many hurdles she's going to have to clear, and that's why I'm here. There's something I want you to do for me."

It was such a simple phrase really, but Taylor's heart stilled. "What is it?"

"I'm sure you know that in her present state, Ivy is entirely unsuited to life here."

"Yes, of course. I believe I warned you she would be."

"And unless we do something about that, she'll never feel she fits in. I can't lose her, Taylor."

"Do something, Eleanor? Like what?"

"I'm afraid I'm going to have to ask for your help again. I want you to...oh, for want of a better word, Americanize her. Supervise her assimilation into our way of life."

Taylor's mind drew a blank. Just what did Americanizing Ivy involve? "I'm...not sure I understand what you're talking about."

"Well, I'm not sure I do, either. For one thing, she needs new clothes, a new hairdo, some makeup, just some general fixing up. She's such a beautiful girl, but right now she looks a bit like a waif...and foreign. I hate that. I desperately want her to feel she belongs. But I haven't the slightest idea what's in fashion for young women these days."

"Lord, neither do I!"

"Oh, come, come. You're a young man, and I'm sure you study young women."

"Well . . . I know when a woman looks great. But I don't have the slightest idea how she got that way. Hair, makeup, clothes are totally outside my realm of expertise."

Eleanor grew thoughtful. "Don't nice department stores employ people who do that sort of thing? Personal shoppers, or some such. I really don't care what it costs."

Taylor couldn't help chuckling. "This is important to you, isn't it?" he asked fondly.

"Very."

"Then I'll do the best I can."

"And afterward, do you think you could squire her around, take her to an expensive restaurant and teach her to enjoy herself. Take her to films. Take her dancing. Teach her about Western life in general. I'm convinced that when she learns those things, she'll want to stay."

The request caught him off guard. He was a rotten dancer. And if Eleanor had seen some of the movies he'd seen lately, she wouldn't want Ivy within a country mile of a theater. Of course he could take her to restaurants and to some of the nicer night spots, but would that do for Ivy what her grandmother wanted? He wasn't sure.

Eleanor saw the perplexed expression on his face. She was quite mindful of the enormity of the task she was assigning him. But who else could she turn to, and this was so important. "Taylor," she said gently, "if there was anyone else I could ask, I would. But Ivy trusts you. Did you see the look on her face when you showed up at the house yesterday? You're special to her."

Yes, he'd seen the look. Ivy had been overjoyed to see him. And, being honest with himself, he had been just as glad to see her. In fact, the sight of her had brought on a rash of emotions he couldn't give names to.

"That might be a problem itself. You're right—she does rely on me. She almost bruised my left arm by clutching it continuously for the two days of our trip. She'll probably at least try to do anything I ask of her."

"Then I don't see the problem."

"Think about it, Eleanor. We can fix her up, dress her to the nines, introduce her to half of Fort Worth, but a month is not much time for her to become assimilated into American society. In a month's time, we might succeed only in confusing her."

Eleanor looked down at her hands, then back up. "I have to try, Taylor... and you're the only one to whom I can turn for help."

How sad, he thought. She had two sons and four grandsons. She had two daughters-in-law. Yet she turned to him for almost everything. He didn't want to fault her family, they were busy people. But he wondered if Eleanor shouldn't drop that self-sufficient manner of hers and let them know she was an aging woman who sometimes needed her family's help.

"I'll do what I can," he said. "I'll give it my very best shot."

Eleanor smiled. "That's what I like about you. You give everything your very best shot."

"But please know there are no guarantees. We can turn ourselves inside out, and Ivy might very well still want to go back to Baksra when the month is up."

"I know," she said with a sigh. "But I have to try."

At that moment the buzzer on Taylor's intercom sounded, and the receptionist informed him that Mrs. Cameron's car had arrived for her. Eleanor pushed herself out of the chair. Taylor got to his feet and rounded the desk to give her a hand, but she gently patted it away. "I'm not doddering...yet. Ivy and I will expect you for cocktails shortly after five this afternoon. And I'd like to invite you to dinner tomorrow night. Kirk and Kevin...you know, Robert's boys, are coming to meet Ivy, and I think she would be more relaxed if you were there."

"Thank you, Eleanor. I'll be there."

"Good. Thank you, Taylor. Sometimes I wonder what I would do without you." With that, she regally swept out of the office.

As the door closed, Taylor's shoulders slumped. He returned to his chair to ponder the latest scheme he'd become involved in. Hair? Clothes? Makeup? He didn't have any idea where to start. He supposed he could do as Eleanor had suggested—take her to one

ing it to please my client. By the way, said client doesn't care how much it costs."

"Damned if you didn't just convince me. Okay, anything for a friend, especially one with money. Bring her by tomorrow afternoon, and I'll see what I can do with her."

"You're a sweetheart. Thanks. See you then."

Grinning, Taylor hung up the phone and spent a minute congratulating himself on overcoming yet another of the obstacles Eleanor threw his way at all-too-regular intervals. Then a picture of Marilee flashed through his mind. A mane of red hair, blue eyes, stunning figure. She had a laugh that sounded like church bells. She was fun, although he'd always thought her a little on the ditsy side. Marilee was almost exhaustingly energetic, and she held opinions on every conceivable subject, none of which she minded giving voice to. She was knowledgeable about the ways of the world, having been on her own since getting out of high school.

In short, she was the antithesis of Ivy. Watching the interplay between the two should prove entertaining indeed.

CHAPTER EIGHT

THE FOLLOWING AFTERNOON, Ivy timidly preceded
Taylor through the front door of Marilee's shop. The
tinkle of a bell sounded overhead. Last night when
Taylor had told her Eleanor wanted her to have some
new clothes, her first instinct had been to refuse. Her
parents would have been horrified at the way she was
accepting all this largess without protest.

Then she'd had second thoughts. If her grandmother thought she needed new clothes, she probably did. She'd had a feeling her island apparel wasn't
suitable, and she didn't want to be an embarrassment to anyone.

She looked around, trying to take in everything at
once. Hundreds of unfamiliar sights and aromas as-
sailed her senses. On her right, behind the display
windows, stood a long glass counter filled with jars
and bottles of cosmetics and perfumes. A similar
counter on her left held jewelry, scarves and hand-
bags. A sign at the foot of a spiral stairway read Bridal Salon Upstairs. Overhead, dozens of what she
would have called ball gowns hung from ceiling
hooks. Ahead, lining both walls and the rear of the

shop were cubbyholes where clothes hung. Ivy had never seen such a place. It was a visual delight no matter where she looked.

And out of it all emerged what was surely the most stunningly gorgeous woman in all the world. She almost loped toward them, arms outstretched. "Taylor!" she cried, and to Ivy's astonishment, the woman threw her arms around Taylor and planted a solid kiss right on his mouth. Ivy blinked. Public displays of affection were unknown to her, but Americans—if some of the spectacles she had seen in airports were any indication—had to be the huggingest and kissingest people on earth, and they didn't seem to care who was watching.

She looked at Taylor. If he had been startled by the woman's actions, he gave no sign. He merely grinned and said, "How are you, Marilee? You look great, as usual."

"You're a doll." The woman then focused on Ivy. She surveyed Taylor's charge and made some instant mental notes. Nice skin, good bone structure, beautiful eyes. Great coloring, so she wouldn't be hard to dress. Thick lustrous hair but a trifle lank. That would have to be fixed. What on earth was she wearing? An ankle-length sarong? Good grief!

"Marilee, this is Ivy Loving," Taylor said. "Ivy, this is Marilee Huntley."

"Hello, Ivy."

"How do you do, Marilee." Ivy felt overwhelmed by Taylor's friend. Marilee was several inches taller than she, and her hair was the thickest and the reddest Ivy had ever seen. It had been pulled behind her ear on one side and fastened with an ornate silver clasp. She wore tight black pants that clung to her legs like a second skin. Over the pants she wore a big, billowing shirt that was almost the same color as her hair. The shirt was belted with a colorful braided sash. More ornate silver hung around her neck and from her earlobes. Ivy hoped her grandmother didn't have such clothes in mind for *her*. She'd never muster the nerve to leave the house in such attire.

"Why don't you run along, Taylor?" Marilee suggested. "This is going to take some time, and you'll only be in the way."

"I didn't for a minute plan to stick around while you two talk about clothes," he said with a smile.

"You're leaving?" Ivy asked. She hated that little frantic note that crept into her voice every time he left.

"Yes, but I'll be back. I'm having dinner with you and your grandmother and your cousins."

"Oh, good!"

"Marilee, just give me a call at the office. I'll wait for it. Then I'll come and fetch Ivy."

"Oh, don't bother. I'll take Ivy home when we're finished. I'm sure we'll be busy until the shop closes. Give me the address. That way we won't have to worry that we're keeping you waiting."

Taylor gave Eleanor's address to Marilee, then turned to Ivy. His heart went out to her. She looked so bewildered and uncertain. How many new experiences could one person be expected to absorb in only a few days? He placed his hands on her shoulders and smiled down at her. "I'm leaving you in very good hands, Ivy. Marilee is an expert. And when you get home, I'll be there."

She clasped her hands in front of her and nodded. He gave her shoulder a pat before turning and leaving the shop. Sighing, she turned to Marilee, who already was rifling through some clothes hanging in the cubbyholes.

"What size do you wear, Ivy?"

"I don't know."

Marilee studied her a minute. "An eight, I think. Maybe a six. We'll see."

There was a chair nearby. Ivy took it and watched as Marilee pulled first one garment, then another, then another out and hung them on pegs. "Do you really own this shop?"

"Uh-huh. At least the bank and I own it."

"That's so amazing. Where I'm from, women don't own property. Their fathers or husbands or brothers or uncles do."

Marilee glanced over her shoulder. "But a woman inherits property when her husband dies, doesn't she?"

"Only if there aren't any men in the family, and that rarely happens. Even her son has precedence over her."

"Well, that's a load of crap!"

Ivy frowned. "That's just the way things are."

"If you women got together, the men wouldn't get away with that for long."

"I don't understand. What do you mean by 'got together'?"

"You know, have a meeting, decide what it is you want, then present your case to the men. Negotiate for what you want. Tell them you'll stop doing whatever it is they really want you to do until they consider your requests."

Ivy didn't understand. "What would we want?"

Marilee shrugged, studying a slinky black number. "Oh, equal opportunity in the workplace or something like that."

"There's no workplace for women on Baksra, nothing but being a servant or a sorter."

"A what?"

"A sorter. Nutmegs and cloves are harvested by hand. Then they're taken to the sorting sheds where dozens of women sort them according to size."

"Sounds like a hell of a way to make a living." Marilee triumphantly produced another garment, then gathered up everything she had chosen. "Come on, the dressing room is in the back. This is going to be fun."

TWO HOURS LATER, Ivy's head was swimming. She had lost count of the garments and shoes she had tried on. Then Marilee had scrubbed her face with some sort of grainy goo and begun what she called "gilding the lily." Ivy never knew there were so many things one could put on one's face—creams, powders, pencils. The only thing Marilee used that was familiar to her was lipstick.

But she had to admit the results were startling. Looking in the mirror, she could hardly recognize herself. Her eyes looked twice as big as they had before, and there was a faint blush to her cheeks. While all those pencils and brushes were being wielded, she had feared she would end up looking like a circus clown, but the effect was subtle. Taylor's friend, she realized, was something of an artist.

Now Marilee was doing something with her hair. "You're going to have to get a body wave and put some highlights in it," the shop owner said, "but for now I'll put it in a French braid. With those cheekbones, you ought to be able to get away with one. At last count, there are only about forty women in the whole world who can. I'll call my favorite salon tomorrow and make an appointment for you. Have you ever had a perm?"

"Ah . . . no."

"Oh, it'll do wonders for your hair. Give it some lift. You need to get a couple of inches cut off, too. You have split ends."

Most of what Marilee said went right over Ivy's head, but she supposed if she kept listening and did as she was told, things would fall into place eventually.

As her fingers flew, Marilee talked. "How long have you known Taylor?"

"About ten days," Ivy replied. It seemed much longer.

"Do you like him?"

"Oh, I think he's very nice."

"Yeah. Nice and Taylor seem to go together. He's pretty subdued compared to most of the characters I know. Every time I see him at a party he always seems to stand in a corner and watch the action over the rim of his glass. How's his love life these days?"

"Well, I . . . I have no idea."

"Yeah, figures. He doesn't talk about his women, but I'll bet there have been some, maybe a lot. There you go," Marilee announced, swiveling Ivy's chair and handing her a mirror. "What do you think?"

"It's . . . it's beautiful. How did you ever learn to do such work?"

"The way I've learned everything in this old life—by trial and error. Now for the final fillip. Are your ears pierced?"

"Yes."

"Then these little gems ought to put the icing on the cake." Marilee slipped out the gold studs Ivy usually wore and replaced them with dangling prisms. "Beautiful!" she exclaimed, clearly pleased with her own handiwork. "If I do say so myself, I'm a blinking genius. Go over there to that full-length mirror and tell me what you think."

The woman in the mirror bore little resemblance to Ivy Loving of Baksra. The flawless makeup and expert hairdo alone would have transformed her dramatically, but the clothes... such clothes as she had never dreamed of owning and would never be able to wear on the island. Made of some sort of lightweight silky fabric, the pants were fuchsia, the sash purple and the little top was gold. A lightweight unconstructed jacket completed the outfit; it, too, was fuchsia. The effect was electric. Odd how clothes could make one feel so different.

"Oh, Marilee, I don't know how to thank you."

"No thanks necessary. Your grandmother has made my day. My day? What am I saying? My month."

Ivy knew it was vain to stare at oneself in the mirror, but she didn't seem to be able to tear her eyes away. She was vaguely aware of Marilee bustling around the shop, locking the front door and turning off lights. Finally Ivy stepped back. "What about all these other things?" she asked, indicating the pile of clothes she had tried on.

"Most of them have to be altered. We'll get started on that tomorrow. Let me see your hands." Ivy dutifully offered them. "Hmm, not too bad," Marilee said. "I wish there was time for a manicure, but we'll do that tomorrow, too. How I envy you those nicely shaped nails."

Ivy looked at Marilee's ruby-tipped fingers. "But your nails are far prettier than mine."

"At a cost, sweetie. Five dollars a finger, to be exact. They're fake. They're also a lifetime commitment, like motherhood. I could no more do without Nails by Nanette than I could do without food and water. Come here."

Marilee beckoned her to the cosmetics display. She picked up a perfume bottle from a tray and gave Ivy two quick squirts of a heavenly fragrance. "Now, let me take you home where you can dazzle some relatives."

Ivy OPENED THE FRONT DOOR and stepped inside, pausing to listen. Voices came from the library so she headed in that direction. She stopped at the threshold and took in the scene. Eleanor was seated in her favorite chair, dressed in a long-sleeved, high-necked, ankle-length gown in a shade of blue that went beautifully with her silver hair.

Three men and a woman stood in a semicircle in front of her, giving her their full attention. One of the men was Taylor, and the other two had to be Uncle Robert's sons, Kirk and Kevin. Ivy had no idea who the woman was.

She felt nervous and exhilarated at the same time. Taking a deep breath, she stepped forward into the room. Letting out a roar of welcome, Jethro bounded toward the door. All eyes turned to the threshold. "Good evening," Ivy said, affectionately rubbing the dog's head. Meeting new people was never easy for her, but the most difficult part was being the center of attention when introductions were made.

Taylor's mouth dropped. *"Ivy?"*

"Oh, my dear, how marvelous you look," Eleanor enthused. "Come over here and meet everyone. What an elegant outfit that is. Taylor, your friend has superb taste."

Ivy joined the group, and introductions were made. "Hello, Ivy. I'm Kevin. I'm sorry my wife couldn't be here, but Alice is attending a friend's wedding. She's anxious to meet you."

"I'll be very glad to meet her, too."

"Mother showed us some photographs taken one Easter. You've certainly changed. You're very beautiful."

"Thank you, Kevin."

The other man put out his hand, which she briefly took. "Hi, Ivy, I'm Kirk, and this is my wife, Julie."

"It's very nice to meet all of you," Ivy said, and meant it. She was discovering that it was nice to have so much family.

"Grandmother tells me that when I was eight you could outrace me on a bicycle," Kirk informed her. "I find that most humiliating. Thanks for moving away. My ego couldn't have survived that for long."

"That's for sure," Julie said. Then she pointed to Jethro, who was clinging to Ivy's thigh. "I wish you would look at that!"

"Oh, Jethro's quite taken with Ivy," Eleanor said. "He sleeps in her room now."

There followed more of the relaxed chatter that everyone except Ivy seemed to enjoy. She still felt a little strange. After a few minutes, she realized that Taylor hadn't joined in, had not, in fact, said a word. That puzzled her, for he was normally quite talkative. So while her cousins continued to banter back and forth with Julie and their grandmother, Ivy turned to him. He still wore a bemused, rather stunned expression. "Ivy, I don't know what to say. You look so beautiful."

Her eyes radiated pleasure, and her smile broadened. Taylor had complimented her twice, once in the hotel room and now tonight. At that moment she felt like a princess. However, she suspected he was referring mainly to the clothes, which would have made anyone look lovely. Her hand snaked along the length of the jacket. "Oh, Taylor, I've never owned such clothes before. Do you really like them?"

Frankly, he wasn't sure if he did or not. Had he just seen her for the first time, he would have thought what a foxy lady she was. But this was Ivy, and she wasn't supposed to be a foxy lady. She was supposed to be . . . Ivy.

"They're really nice, but on anyone else they probably would look very ordinary."

Ivy felt her cheeks grow warm. "Taylor, you...you say such nice things."

He smiled at her fondly, and they both rejoined the talk swirling around them. But Taylor heard none of it. His thoughts were on something else entirely. He wondered if he ought to have a talk with Marilee and make her understand what he'd actually had in mind. Ivy had been able to turn heads before the make-over; now she was a knockout by any standard. He wasn't sure that was what he wanted. She didn't even smell like Ivy anymore. Whatever the perfume was, it didn't suit her.

Then he glanced at Eleanor and saw the obvious approval in her eyes. He reminded himself that this was *her* show, not his. His opinion was not the one that counted here. Still, Ivy's appearance tonight had an unsettling effect on him. He might not understand it, but it was there, nevertheless. Even Kevin and Kirk, he noticed, could hardly stop looking at her with obvious approval. They might be her cousins, but they were also men.

Taylor placed his hand on the small of her back and received another of her dazzling smiles in return. He felt a great rush of protectiveness toward her, though just what he wanted to protect her from would have to be analyzed later.

At that moment Wilma appeared to announce dinner. Kevin offered Eleanor his arm. Julie took her husband's, Taylor tucked Ivy's hand into the crook of his elbow, and they all filed into the dining room where the table had been resplendently set with white linen and gleaming china, crystal and silver. For reasons known only to herself, Eleanor obviously had decided to make tonight a festive occasion, and no one did that sort of thing better than she.

But it wasn't the elegance of the table appointments Taylor noticed as much as Eleanor herself. He didn't think he'd ever seen her looking so alive and animated. In the bosom of her family, she positively glowed with happiness.

MUCH LATER, after Kevin, Kirk and Julie had left and Eleanor had retired for the evening, Ivy and Taylor sat alone in the library, having coffee. She felt better than she had since leaving home. She had been twice as relaxed tonight as she had been the night her uncles came to dinner, and she wondered what had caused that. Perhaps it was because Kevin and Kirk, unlike their parents, didn't talk business. They, along with Julie and Grandmother and even Taylor, talked about people. All of them knew a lot of the same people. She, herself, had contributed nothing to the conversation, except when she was asked a question, but she had enjoyed listening. Americans, it seemed to her, were involved in so many things it was a wonder they weren't exhausted most of the time. By comparison, life on the island was simplicity itself.

Or perhaps she had been relaxed tonight because she'd felt good about herself. And the clothes had a lot to do with that. The sarongs had made her feel like a foreigner.

But probably she'd been relaxed because Taylor had been there. He had an amazing effect on her. She'd never dreamed she would ever have such a friend. When the day came that she had to say goodbye to him, it was going to be one of the hardest things she'd ever done.

"Jethro," Taylor said, frowning down at the dog, "I think I liked you better when you were antisocial."

The animal had his chin resting on Ivy's feet, leaving his rump to rest on Taylor's. Ivy laughed. "Isn't he the dearest thing?"

"*Dear* and *Jethro* were not words I had ever thought to use in conjunction with each other."

"I wish I knew something about his parentage. Grandmother says she thinks he has some bloodhound in him because my grandfather thought he was the best hunting dog he'd ever had." Reaching down, she scratched the dog behind his ears.

With some difficulty, Taylor managed to extricate his feet from beneath the dog, receiving a growl in the process. "What did you think of Marilee?" he asked.

"Oh, she's nice. I liked her."

"I wondered. I was afraid she might be a little too flashy for you."

"Flashy? Oh, no. She's just very... colorful."

"She can be that, all right... in more ways than one."

"I'm going back tomorrow after my driving lesson. Most of the clothes we picked out have to be altered, and Marilee's going to give me a manicure."

"Then I'll pick you up at the shop. Just give me a call when you're finished."

"It won't be too much trouble? Grandmother gave me some money so I can take taxis whenever I need to."

"It won't be too much trouble, Ivy, but even if it was, there's nothing wrong with asking a friend to go out of his way for you."

"Thanks. Maybe one of these days I really will learn to drive and then you won't have to carry me around so much." Ivy sighed. "It just astonished me that Marilee actually *owns* that beautiful shop. I told her that on Baksra, women couldn't own property, only men could."

"That's grossly unfair. What happens to Erik's property when he dies?"

"It would go to any sons we had."

"Well, just supposing there were no sons."

"I'd be well taken care of, Taylor. I just wouldn't own Erik's property."

"That's absurd."

Ivy sighed. "I think Marilee feels the same way. She said it's a load of crap."

"Ivy!" Taylor almost choked. He placed his coffee cup in a saucer, turned and took her hands in his. "For God's sake, don't repeat words like that."

She frowned, puzzled. "But, Taylor...you told me Marilee was an expert."

"Well...okay. But what I meant was for you to take her advice about clothes and hair and all that. I don't want you to be like her. I don't want you talking like her. She has a smart mouth and a lot of what she says doesn't sound right coming from you."

"All...right." Ivy glanced down at her hands. She had assumed that since Marilee had used the word, it must be okay. It was just so hard to know the right thing to do. On the way to the shop that afternoon, Taylor had told her how smart Marilee was. Now he was telling her not to be like the woman. How was one to know?

Seeing her downcast eyes, Taylor wanted to kick himself for being so sharp with her. "I'm sorry," he said contritely. "I shouldn't have barked. It was just a shock to hear you say that word."

"Then I'm sorry, too. I'll be careful from now on."

A few seconds of silence followed. Taylor sipped his coffee, and Ivy chewed her bottom lip. Finally she spoke. "Taylor?"

"Hmm."

"Is there a special woman in your life?"

He turned to her with a grin. "Right now? Yes, you."

"You know what I mean."

"Yes, I know what you mean, and the answer is no."

"Then I'm not a bother?"

"I promise you, Ivy, you're not a bother."

"Marilee says there might have been a lot of women in your life."

"By whose standards? I wouldn't say there have been a lot of women in my life compared to..." Ah, what the hell? He took one last sip of coffee, then got to his feet. "It's getting late. I'd better be off."

"Do you live far from here?"

"No, not far at all. Why?"

"No reason. I'd like to see where you live sometime."

"Then we'll do it. Good night, Ivy."

"Good night."

Bending, he meant to place a kiss on her cheek, but she raised her head just then, and he somehow missed his mark. His lips briefly closed over hers, and he thought how baby-soft they were. Then, against his mouth, he felt her gasp, and when he raised his head, he found himself staring at the most startled expression he had ever seen. Her beautiful eyes, now all penciled and shadowed and mascaraed, had widened, and her lips were parted. Seeing that expression, one would think he had slapped her. He was speechless until something incredible occurred to him. He *had* seen a similar expression before, on Betty Lou Sadler's face when he kissed her in the alley between their houses during the second grade. She'd looked at him exactly that way before turning and fleeing like a spooked rabbit. Could it be? "Ivy, haven't you ever been kissed before?"

She shook her head. "Who would have kissed me?"

"Good Lord." Taylor opened his mouth to say something, but no sound came out. He pressed his hand against the side of her neck, feeling its velvety texture. "I'll, ah, I'll see you tomorrow," he said, and beat a hasty retreat.

Good Lord, he thought. She was even more innocent than any of them had known. Who would have thought that any woman could live to be twenty-seven without once being kissed?

He was thoroughly shaken, and not only by the knowledge he'd just unwittingly given Ivy her first kiss. What was more unsettling to him was knowing the kiss, as soft as the brush of a butterfly's wings, had affected him, too.

CHAPTER NINE

WHEN IVY ARRIVED at the shop after her driving lesson the next afternoon, she found Marilee deep in conversation with a man. "Oh, hi, Ivy. Come over here and meet Glenn."

Glenn Fraser was a pleasant-looking man of medium build and height, possibly an inch or two taller than Marilee, and he had a shock of unruly sandy hair that he kept brushing off his forehead. He was charming and soft-spoken. Ivy didn't think he said more than a dozen words, but perhaps that was because it wasn't easy for anyone to do much talking with Marilee around.

After a few minutes, Glenn declared he had to go. Marilee gave him a sound kiss on his mouth before he left the shop, prompting Ivy to wonder if the woman kissed every man she came in contact with.

Right after Glenn left, two women came into the shop, one to buy perfume, the other to "just look." Ivy was forced to wait quite a while because the woman who was just looking ended up buying three garments. Finally Marilee was free.

"That man, Glenn, seems very nice. Is he a friend?" Ivy asked, as Marilee got all her manicure gear together.

"He's the man I live with."

Ivy laughed. "Why didn't you tell me? So he's your *husband*." She paused. "Then why don't you have the same last names?"

"He's not my husband yet."

"But you live with him."

"I know. I'm just not married to him. Okay, have a seat, Ivy, and we'll go to work on those nails."

Ivy sat down, again aware of the difference between American customs and those on Baksra. "Do all Americans live together before getting married?"

"Not all, but a lot do these days."

"Why?"

Marilee slipped Ivy's hands into bowls of soapy water. "Oh . . . to see how well you get along, for one thing. And just to be together. If you're crazy about each other, you want to be together all the time."

"If you were married, you'd be together all the time."

"Well, Ivy, marriage is a commitment not everyone is willing to make. A lot of people fight it, men especially."

Several seconds of silence ensued while Ivy tried to sort all this out in her mind. "You know, it's so different at home. There all men expect to get married, and the first time they marry very young, hardly out of their teens." She then explained the Baksrani marriage customs to Marilee, who listened, interested but disbelieving. "So then, when my first husband dies, I'll be older and will take a much younger husband."

"That last part doesn't sound half-bad," Marilee said. "But, Ivy, do you *want* to marry a man in his sixties?"

"Erik is very kind."

"That isn't what I asked you."

"I don't suppose I ever thought about whether I want to or not. I know that anyone I marry will be a great deal older than I am, and Erik is far and away the nicest man on the island. He's extremely knowledgeable. I'll learn so much from him. On Baksra, marriage is thought to be above all a learning experience."

Marilee snorted. "If you want to learn something, get yourself a good-looking guy somewhere near your own age. He'll teach you plenty."

Ivy was puzzled by her own reaction. All the new sights, people, experiences must have addled her mind. She couldn't understand why she wasn't defending the island's marriage customs more vehemently. But there was one thing she wasn't in the least confused about. "I can't imagine living with someone I wasn't married to. If you enjoy living with Glenn, why don't you marry him?"

Marilee dried Ivy's right hand and began working on her cuticles. "For one thing, he hasn't asked me, at least not in years, and the reason he hasn't is mainly my fault, I'm afraid. When I first met Glenn, I was in my upwardly-mobile-young-career-woman mode. What did I need with a piece of paper? Weddings were corny, and *wife* was the dullest word in the English language. Glenn would have liked to get married back then, but I brainwashed him. Now he's thinking like I was . . . and I've changed my mind.''

"Now you want to get married?"

Marilee nodded. "I want to have a baby, but I don't want to be a single mother."

"I should hope not!"

"There are a lot of them out there, Ivy, and I don't envy them."

"Have you told Glenn how you feel?"

"Yes, but he says marriage would ruin everything, that if I want to have a baby, have one and he'll be there for me. No, thanks." Marilee paused to sigh. "I guess there's still a lot of Brownfield left in me."

"A lot of what?"

"Brownfield, my hometown. But I've got enough smarts to know what's really behind my love's reluctance to make an honest woman out of me."

"What?"

"Fear of the word *we*. As long as we aren't married, it's 'you and me.' But once we got married, it would become 'we.' That scares the living daylights out of most men. It probably scares Taylor, too. Why else would a guy who looks like he does still be single at his age, I ask you?"

Ivy had thought about Taylor a lot that day, because of last night's kiss, she guessed. Oh, even she knew it hadn't been all that much of a kiss, not if the things she had read in stories could be believed, but it *had* been the touching of two pairs of lips. The sensation had been electrifying. Thinking about it had kept her awake a long time after she'd gone to bed.

"I'll tell you something else I've learned about men," Marilee was saying, busy with an emery board. "They're afraid of change, and they're afraid of no change. They don't want a woman to change them, but if they let one woman into their lives, they're afraid that'll be it, no change at all ever again. They also feel threatened by women in groups of more than two, and they have ever since the first steno turned to the one next to her and said, 'Hey, Shirley, does it seem to you that we're getting the short end of the stick around here?' So men get together and bang drums and beat their chests to reassert their manliness."

Ivy didn't have the slightest idea what she was talking about.

"You know," Marilee continued, "in some forms of lower animal life, if a male stops displaying aggressive behavior, his colors fade and his sex organs wither, so maybe men really do have something to worry about, who knows? What color polish do you want?"

Ivy, mesmerized by Marilee's dissertation while understanding none of it, came back to the business at hand. She surveyed the array of bottles. "That one, I guess," she said, indicating some pale pink polish.

Marilee pulled a face. "Dull, Ivy. Dull, dull. How about this? Crimson Passion."

"I . . . don't think so."

"What am I going to do with you? Okay, we'll compromise. A light coral." Without waiting for Ivy's assent, she began painting the nails.

Ivy watched, fascinated, for a minute before asking, "What are you going to do . . . about Glenn?"

"I'm not sure," Marilee said pensively. "I've got an awful lot of time invested in that man. But the old clock's ticking away, and I want some kids to fuss over me in my old age. If Glenn stays stubborn about marriage . . ." She sighed. "I don't know."

That surprised Ivy. To her, Marilee seemed the type who always knew what to do no matter what.

"My alterations lady was in this morning. She has some of your things done. And I got a new shipment in," Marilee said idly. "There are some things in it I want you to see."

"Oh, I can't buy more clothes. I already have so many."

"A woman can never have too many clothes. You have to dress up to your station in life. I've seen your grandmother's house, remember? Lord, to live like that, to be able to go anywhere you want, do anything you want. It must be nice. I don't know how you could consider going back to that island. You couldn't blast me out of that house with a cannon. By the way, you have an appointment with Edna tomorrow."

Ivy was having a hard time keeping up with Marilee's conversations. She skipped from subject to subject without a breath. "Who's Edna?"

"My hairstylist. Her salon's two doors down. She's fantastic. I can hardly wait to see you once she's finished with you. In the meantime, I'm going to take a curling iron to you, and then I want you to try on that little number over there."

Ivy sat patiently while Marilee worked with her hair, watching in a mirror while her straight, long hair was transformed into a mass of ringlets. Marilee chatted away about a hundred things that had no meaning for Ivy. "Now, I'm going to scrunch it and spritz it, and you're going to look like you have pounds of hair."

It was amazing, Ivy thought, staring at her reflection. If she went back to Baksra looking like this, Erik would order her to wash her face and comb out her hair. He would think she looked freakish.

And she really balked over the "little number" Marilee had picked out for her. After first making her put on a short slip, then panty hose, Marilee had her step into the dress. It was a simple sleeveless sheath with a mandarin collar made of jade silk. But it ended two inches above the knee.

"I can't go out in such a short skirt," she complained.

"Oh, of course you can. With legs like that?"

"I feel . . . naked."

"Well, you're not. You're stylish. And jade is a wonderful color for you. Ivy, you look absolutely marvelous."

The bell over the door jangled, and Taylor stepped into the shop. "Hi, Marilee. Where's . . ."

As Ivy turned from the mirror he did a double take. Could that really be Ivy? Last night was startling enough. Now she looked . . . incredible.

"Doesn't she look sensational, Taylor?" Marilee enthused.

Yes, she did. Or would have if she hadn't been Ivy. The woman standing before him belonged on the cover of *Glamour* or *Elle*. His Ivy was changing right before his eyes . . . way too much, way too fast.

"I . . . yes," he stammered. His eyes moved downward. He'd never seen Ivy's legs until now. She'd always worn pants or those sarongs. Was there anything about her that wasn't perfect?

"I think you should take her out to dinner tonight," Marilee said. "She needs to be seen by people other than family."

Taylor composed himself. "Yes, of course. Would you like to go to dinner, Ivy?"

"Yes, I would . . . if it's all right with Grandmother."

"It will be all right with Eleanor, I'm sure."

"Will it be a date?"

He smiled at her eagerness. "Yes, I'll take you to a nice place where you can show off your finery."

It occurred to Ivy that Taylor was responsible for several firsts in her life. He was the first man of her generation she'd gotten to know well enough to call a friend. He had given her her first kiss . . . and now he was taking her on her first date. Maybe others would follow. There wasn't time now, but tomorrow she would get Marilee to tell her exactly how a lady was supposed to behave on a date. She just hoped she didn't stumble and embarrass Taylor too many times tonight.

"Wait! Wait!" Marilee suddenly exclaimed. Rushing to the back of the shop, she returned carrying a shoe box. Opening it, she produced a pair of black pumps with two-inch heels. Ivy just stared at them. "How . . . how do you walk in those?"

"You don't know how to walk in heels?"

Ivy shook her head. Marilee rolled her eyes toward the ceiling, then disappeared into the back room again. When she returned she carried a pair of black pumps with just the suggestion of a heel. Ivy sighed her relief. "That's better," she said, slipping her feet into the dainty shoes.

"Tomorrow we start practicing walking in heels," Marilee declared. "They're so much dressier. You two have a great time tonight."

Bemused, Taylor helped Ivy gather up the other garments, and he followed her out of the shop. He wondered if he and Eleanor had gone too far. Ivy had been such pure delight from the first. Why should they try to change her? At the rate things were going, she wouldn't even be Ivy in another week's time.

Well, if she wasn't, she wouldn't want to go back to the island, and that would please Eleanor. He didn't know why the changes bothered him so much. Inside she was the same—innocent, unassuming, amazingly lacking in conceit. That, coupled with her beauty, would make any man in the world want her. The thought horrified him.

MARILEE CLOSED the shop at six o'clock, and twenty minutes later she was in her apartment, taking lasagna out of the freezer and turning on the oven to pre-heat. While she made a salad, she thought about her discussion with Ivy.

She was getting nowhere fast with Glenn, and that galled her. Usually when she set out to get something done, it got done. Glenn frustrated her. There had to be some sort of responsive chord inside that ador-able, maddening head of his she could touch, but she'd be damned if she knew what it was.

Promptly at ten after seven, he walked through the front door, just as he always did. Also, as he always did, he came into the kitchen, gave her a light kiss, took a beer out of the refrigerator, then went into the living room and turned on the television. A minute later, Marilee heard the unmistakable sounds of a baseball game in progress. *Why does he fight mar-riage so,* she wondered. *We already live like we've been married for years.* Sighing, she put the salad in the refrigerator and went in to sit beside him on the sofa.

"Are you going to watch baseball all evening?" she asked in a very wifely tone.

"It's the Rangers and Blue Jays," he answered, as if that explained everything.

Marilee sighed again. "I wanted to talk to you."

"We can talk at dinner."

"No, we can't, not if that's still on." She waited a minute. "Did you know that married men live longer than bachelors?"

He made an unintelligible sound and took a drink of beer.

"And they don't commit suicide as often or get sick as much."

"Hot damn, look at that! Now, that's heads-up ball! Did you say something, hon?"

Marilee's eyes flashed. "Not a thing. Not a thing." The buzzer on the oven sounded, bringing her to her feet. "Dinner will be on the table in fifteen minutes."

TAYLOR WAS ACUTELY AWARE of the curiosity he and Ivy aroused when they entered the restaurant. He patronized the place often enough to be considered a regular, so he was sure *he* wasn't the source of all the attention. Ordinarily, in a typically masculine way, it pleased him no end to find himself escorting the most beautiful woman in the place, but tonight he had mixed emotions about it. Some of the men cast looks in Ivy's direction that were downright lecherous.

"My goodness, it's crowded," she commented.

"It always is, but I was assured we would have a table. We might have to wait in the bar a bit, but the food's worth it."

The hostess approached them. "Good evening, Taylor."

"How are you, Brenda?" Though the hostess spoke to him, her curious eyes were on Ivy. "I'd like you to meet an out-of-town friend. This is Ivy Loving," he said.

"Hello, Ivy."

"How do you do, Brenda."

It was obvious Brenda's curiosity had not been satisfied, but she reluctantly returned her attention to Taylor. "I'm afraid there'll be a fifteen-to-twenty-minute wait."

"That's fine," Taylor said, slipping his arm to encircle Ivy's back. "We'll wait in the bar."

The little bar was even more crowded than the dining room. Holding her hand, Taylor led Ivy to the lone vacant table he could see—a small one in a secluded corner. Once they were seated, he gave the waitress an order for seltzer for Ivy. Then he settled back to watch her watch the crowd.

A minute passed while her eyes darted over the throng. "Everyone in America moves around so much," she finally said. "Stores and shops are crowded. Restaurants are crowded. On the island, once the sun goes down, everything becomes so quiet. It seems that here things just get started when the sun goes down. Are people like my grandmother the only ones who stay home?''

He smiled. ''No, of course not, but look around. This is a young crowd in their twenties and thirties. At night they're ready for some fun. They also don't want to go home and cook after working all day.''

She studied the people, finding it so strange to see huge groups of people the same age together. Then she turned back to Taylor. ''Did you know Marilee wants to get married?''

''Really?'' he said. ''That rather surprises me. Marilee never seemed the marrying kind.''

''She wants to have a baby, but she doesn't want to be a single mother.''

''Then she's not as ditsy as I gave her credit for.''

''Ditsy?''

''You know, flaky. Well...never mind. Apparently Marilee has a lot more common sense than she's previously displayed.''

Ivy studied her beautifully manicured nails before murmuring, ''Taylor?''

''Hmm?''

''Are you afraid of the word *we?*''

''Huh?''

''Marilee says most men are. She says you probably are, too, since you've never been married.''

Taylor made a scoffing sound. ''It seems to me Marilee has a lot to say about almost everything. Why didn't it occur to her that I'm not married because I never found anyone I wanted to marry?"

"Except once . . . the woman who got tired of waiting and married someone else."

"Well, I've thought about that over the years. I possibly used my sad financial state as an excuse. If I had wanted to marry her badly enough, I would have. Very few people wait to get married until they can afford to."

Ivy digested that, then sighed. "It's odd. On the island, the marriage customs are so simple. Here they're very complicated. I suppose I'm lucky to live where I do. I don't handle complicated matters very well."

It still pained Taylor to think of this lovely, winsome woman married to a man in his sixties, no matter what a sterling character Erik might be. And he didn't even want to think how Ivy's leaving would affect Eleanor. Earlier, while waiting for Ivy to come downstairs, the elderly woman had thanked him profusely. "I'm so glad you're taking her out to dinner, Taylor. Show her a good time. She looks lovely, doesn't she?"

Yes, almost too lovely. Could she actually spend a month wearing clothes like that, getting her hair and nails done whenever she wanted, and then put on her sandals and sarong and hie on back to Baksra to while away the years as an aging-planter's wife? Frankly, the idea made him sick. This was the damnedest thing he'd ever gotten involved in.

Suddenly a resonant male voice cut into his thoughts. "Taylor, you son of a gun, where've you been? Haven't seen you in a month of Sundays."

Taylor looked up into the face of Don McCall, one of his clients. Or rather, Don and his father were clients of Sheldon and Ernst. Taylor supposed the man could be described as handsome. Don wore the latest fashions, styled his hair and had the reputation as a womanizer in the first degree. Right now the man's eyes were all for Ivy.

Taylor started to rise, but Don put a restraining hand on his shoulder. "Don't get up. I'll just sit down for a minute." Looking around, he found an empty chair and pulled it up to the table. Taylor stifled a groan.

"Don, this is an out-of-town friend, Ivy Loving. Ivy, Don McCall."

"How do you do," Ivy murmured politely.

"Well, Ivy, I wondered why I hadn't seen you around. Where are you from?"

"Baksra."

Don frowned in thought. "I don't believe I know the place."

"It's an island in Indonesia," Taylor explained.

"Oh." A second passed before Don asked, "What brings you to Cowtown?"

"I came to visit my grandmother."

"Ivy is Eleanor Cameron's granddaughter," Taylor explained, knowing full well Don would recognize the name.

He did, and it was obvious he was impressed. Folding his arms on the table and focusing all his attention on Ivy, Don leaned forward. "Cameron, huh? Are you planning on staying in Fort Worth permanently, Ivy?"

She glanced quickly at Taylor, then back at Don, uncertain how to answer the question. "No, I . . . I'll stay about a month, I guess. Taylor is being kind enough to show me around."

"I'll bet it's no trouble." Don smirked, then turned to Taylor and winked. His gaze shifted back to Ivy. "However, if he finds himself tied up and there's somewhere you'd like to go, just give me a call. I'm at your service day or night. What do you enjoy doing? Do you golf?"

"No."

"Bowl?"

"No."

Don had never been one of Taylor's favorite people, and tonight the man irked him no end. The thought of Ivy spending five minutes alone with a man whose favorite topic of conversation was how irresistible he was to women was more than he could take.

It was with great relief he saw the hostess motioning to him with a wave. He jumped to his feet and took Ivy by the arm, almost bodily lifting her out of her chair. "Our table's ready, Don. Be talking to you soon."

"Well . . . sure." Don reluctantly stood up. "It was nice meeting you, Ivy."

"It was nice meeting you, too, Don."

"Remember—Donald C. McCall. I'm in the book."

Taylor cupped a hand under Ivy's elbow and spirited her away. "Don't ever call him, for anything, nothing, ever. Understand?" he muttered to her under his breath.

"But . . . isn't he a friend of yours?"

"Not really."

Ivy shook her head in bewilderment. Don McCall had greeted Taylor as if they were friends, but apparently they weren't. Taylor had gone to the trouble to seek out Marilee because she was knowledgeable, but he didn't want her, Ivy, to be like the woman. Americans were a mystery.

IVY HAD THOROUGHLY enjoyed her dinner, Taylor noticed. He also noticed she was a little more adventurous about food and had ordered a veal dish instead of fish and rice. His mind, however, was on anything but the food. The encounter with Don had made him aware of something he'd never really thought about before. McCall, unfortunately, was a fairly good representative of so many of the people he knew—either divorced and cynical about relationships, or totally focused on their careers to the exclusion of all else. Taylor knew only a handful of solidly married couples who were raising children, and most of them were two-career families. Ivy wouldn't be able to relate to any of them. He knew exactly the kind of role model Eleanor wanted for Ivy; he just didn't know where to find one.

It was relatively early when they left the restaurant, so he took her on an impromptu spin through Trinity Park. From the banks of the Trinity River, the lights of downtown Fort Worth looked close enough to reach out and touch.

"There are bicycle paths throughout the park," he told her.

"I don't have my bicycle with me," she reminded him.

"Well, I'll just bet if you mention wanting one, Eleanor will see that you have one. It might be fun to spend some early morning on the paths, or perhaps after dinner. It's much too hot from noon on. And picnics on the riverbank are popular. Or there are the Botanical Gardens. You ought to enjoy seeing them."

"It's lovely here," Ivy mused. "So different from what I'd imagined America would be like."

"Didn't I tell you so?"

The drive from the park back to Rivercrest took only a few minutes. Taylor parked his car in the Cameron driveway, got out and rounded the car to open the passenger's door.

"I had such a nice time, Taylor," Ivy remarked as she swung her legs around and stood up. "I'll always have wonderful memories of my first date."

"There'll be more. Eleanor and I want you to see everything, and I'm the logical escort."

They stepped up on the front porch. "You don't mind?"

"I don't mind. If I minded, I wouldn't do it."

She smiled. "Yes, you would," she said, "because of Grandmother. You'd do anything for her."

"You're right, I would. I owe your grandmother a lot, but more than that, she's my friend and I care about her welfare. I try to do whatever she asks of me, for her sake and for Ben's. So I suppose I should be grateful that what she's asked me to do now—squire you around town—has turned out to be such a delightful task."

"You say nice things, Taylor. I hope you mean them."

Her upturned face illuminated in the soft glow of the porch light was absolutely irresistible. Without giving too much thought to the wisdom of his actions, he bent and, deliberately, firmly pressed his mouth to hers, but he could tell from her wooden response that she didn't know what was expected of her.

"Ivy, you could relax your lips just a little. It won't hurt. It might even feel good."

She let her mouth go slack, and he bent his head again. This time his mouth lingered over hers for a heart-palpitating moment before he lifted his head and smiled down at her. But he didn't release her. Instead, he held her against him for a minute, and she felt his hand tracing small circles on her back. Shivers ran up her arms, and she wished she knew what to do with her own hands. They felt silly hanging at her side. Hesitantly she raised them and lightly placed them on his upper arms. She felt him drop a kiss on the top of her head, then heard him sigh.

Ivy didn't know what she expected to happen next, but it wasn't that he would gently push her away. Startled, she looked up at him and saw such a peculiar little smile on his face. Then he reached for the door and pushed it open. "I'll call tomorrow. We'll decide what we want to do. Lock up."

Ivy entered the house in a daze, and Taylor pulled the door shut. She clicked the lock into place, then stood in the foyer and listened to the sound of his car driving off. Jethro bounded out of nowhere, his tail wagging like an oscillating fan. A small lamp sitting on a console was on. She wondered if she should turn it off. She didn't know, so she left it on.

Slowly, as if sleepwalking, she climbed the stairs to her room, the dog right behind her. She saw that another lamp had been left on and her bed had been turned down. Wilma did so many thoughtful little things for her that she would have to do something nice for her before she left.

Before I leave. An eerie feeling came over her. She glanced around the room. Within the space of only a few days she had come to think of this as "her" room. It was becoming as familiar to her as the one in the island bungalow. It was always so spotlessly clean, and the sheets on the bed were as soft and smooth as silk. And because the house was air-conditioned, they were still smooth and cool when she awoke in the morning. Would she ever think about this room when she returned to the island?

"Oh, Jethro, I'm so confused," she said. At first she had been almost desperate for the month to pass quickly so she could return to Baksra, but now that didn't seem so urgent. Dare she consider extending the visit? She knew her grandmother would be pleased, but how would Taylor feel about it?

Taylor. She seemed to think about him almost constantly. Sinking to the edge of the bed, she stared across the room. When he had held her for that brief moment, she hadn't wanted him to let go ever. Placing her fingertips to her lips, she smiled. So that was what a kiss felt like, not the fire and passion of novels, but something warm and satisfying.

Try as she might, Ivy simply could not imagine Erik ever kissing her that way. The thought was almost ludicrous. But more than that, she couldn't imagine any kiss from Erik ever making her feel the way she did now.

TAYLOR MANEUVERED his car into his assigned spot, locked it, then crossed the sidewalk, climbed three steps and opened the door to his two-story town house. As he passed the kitchen, he flipped on the light switch and poured a glass of water. Then he carried it to his bedroom, placed it on the nightstand and threw back the bedspread. After a few minutes in the bathroom, he slid under the covers, placed his hands behind his head and stared at the ceiling.

Sweet Ivy. She tugged at him in some unfathomable way. Tonight when he'd kissed her, he'd meant it to be something warm and friendly, but it hadn't been that at all . . . not for him. How ridiculous! He was a man of the world . . . well, sort of . . . and the men in that world did not come undone by soulful eyes, winsome smiles and gentle kisses. He'd received more passionate kisses when he was fifteen.

But he'd never received one that had such a profound effect on him. By doing nothing but being Ivy, she had touched something inside him that no one else ever had. He tried to envision escorting her back to the island and handing her over to Erik, then saying goodbye forever. It was too painful to contemplate.

However, realistically, it probably would happen. For that reason, he had to keep Ivy at arm's length. He would do all Eleanor asked of him but somehow stay detached. No more kissing, no more dwelling on what a lovely woman she was. It was the only means he had of protecting himself.

CHAPTER TEN

"IVY DEAR, there's something you and I must discuss this morning," Eleanor said. "It's been preying on my mind."

Ivy and her grandmother were finishing breakfast, and Wilma was bustling around the table, removing plates and cups. Eleanor blotted her lips with her napkin, then placed it beside her plate. Ivy, having noticed her grandmother doing that at the end of every meal, did the same. Both women rose, left the dining room and went into the library, the younger woman a few respectful steps behind the older. Jethro, who was never allowed in the dining room, rose from his watchful vigil beside the doorway and followed them.

Eleanor took her customary seat, and Ivy sat down on the sofa, facing her. The dog lay down at her feet.

"Ivy, I'm sure by now you realize that I oversee a fortune of vast proportions," Eleanor began.

"I know you must have a lot of money," she said truthfully, wondering why her grandmother was bringing up the subject. Ivy had no idea what "a fortune of vast proportions" could be.

Eleanor smiled and, using one manicured finger-tip, scratched the side of her head, being careful not to disturb so much as a hair of her coiffure. "Well, it's difficult to say exactly how much we're worth—so much of it is on paper, you see, and fluctuates with the market—but *Texas Monthly* puts the Cameron fortune at something around two hundred fifty million. I'm not sure how those people arrive at their figures, but they have their system, I suppose."

Ivy sat stunned. If her grandmother had said ten million she would have been awed, though that at least was a figure she could conjure up. On the island it was said that Erik and a few others like him were millionaires, so to Ivy's mind that had always meant Erik had the equivalent of a million dollars. But two hundred fifty million was beyond the scope of her imagination. What did one do with that kind of money? How was it managed? Was it just piled in a vault somewhere?

"I see that surprises you," Eleanor said calmly.

"It's...unbelievable!"

"Yes, I know. Seventy years ago if someone in Checotah, Oklahoma, had told me that it was possi-ble to have more money than anybody wants, needs or can enjoy, I would have laughed uproariously. But it's almost come to that. That kind of money is a horrendous responsibility. Fortunately, Ben and I have had smart people managing it for us, but I'll confess to being frightened to death when I was told how much we were worth right after Ben died. I've since learned, Ivy dear, that money like that almost looks after itself.''

Ivy still had no idea why she was being told this. Was her grandmother going to offer her money? If so, should she take it? Her parents would be aghast, horrified, but she herself had come to believe there was nothing inherently wrong with having money. It hadn't corrupted her grandmother. She sat quietly and let Eleanor continue.

"Of course, much of that money is tied up in trusts for my sons and grandsons, and there are certain charities that would be in a hard fix without our annual donations. It's all very complicated, and there are times when my poor brain is taxed to keep up with it. The net estate, however, is sizable. As things stand now, it is divided six ways, among your uncles and cousins. I had never planned to cut Claire off entirely, but since she scorned the money, I had thought to leave her perhaps two hundred thousand dollars and be done with it." Eleanor paused to glance down at her hands. Then she looked up. "All that has changed now."

Ivy's hands went to her chest, as if that simple movement could calm her frantic heartbeat. She *was* going to be offered money, probably her mother's inheritance. What on earth would she do with two hundred thousand dollars?

"First of all, I'm going to ask Taylor to rewrite my will, naming you as one of my heirs. Naturally, Robert and Michael will inherit the company, but some time ago I established an eight-million dollar trust for each of my grandsons, and now I would like to establish a trust for you, dear—exactly like the ones your cousins have. It's only fair."

Ivy felt faint. Eight *million?* It was so incredible it was almost funny. "I . . . that's sweet of you, Grandmother, but I have so little use for money. I have *no* use for that kind of money."

"Ivy. . ." Eleanor paused to smile, realizing her granddaughter had no conception of what was being offered her. "The money I'm talking about will force you to reassess your entire life. You will be able to have *anything* your heart desires—clothes, jewelry, rare paintings, travel. You can own a very fine home, a luxury car, anything. And let me tell you something about owning a fortune. No doors will be closed to you. People will envy you and look up to you."

Ivy shook her head in bewilderment. In a very short time, her simple life had become complicated. She found herself questioning what she wanted, and she'd always thought she knew exactly what she wanted. Questioning wasn't a good feeling. It was a burden, and she was almost sure having a lot of money would be a burden, too.

"What if I just say no, thank you?" she quietly asked.

"I don't think you would, and I don't think you should."

"Why?"

"Because the money is rightfully yours, and I want you to have it."

"What about the rest of the family? Won't they resent having an interloper arrive and skim off part of their inheritances?"

Eleanor smiled. As unsophisticated as she was, Ivy could be surprisingly astute. "My darling girl, they all have more money than they know what to do with as it is. And they aren't that kind of people. Kevin once told me he hoped I didn't die until I'd spent my last dollar, and I have not the slightest doubt that he was sincere. When you get to know your cousins better, I rather imagine you'll like them all very much."

Her grandmother, Ivy noticed, had conveniently forgotten the existence of the island and the very different life her granddaughter led far away from this place. Then something occurred to her, something she was sure would put an end to her inheritance once and for all. "Grandmother, there's something I should tell you. On Baksra, when I marry, everything I have will become my husband's."

Eleanor's eyes narrowed and her brow furrowed as she considered that. Then she sighed. "I'm sure you realize I can't allow that to happen."

"I know."

"I suppose I'll have to ask Taylor about this. He might want to put in a teeny clause or something. Obviously I can't have a sizable portion of the family's money in the possession of an Indonesian nutmeg farmer."

Ivy couldn't stifle a chuckle. What she wouldn't give to watch the expression on Erik's face if he heard himself referred to as a "nutmeg farmer." He was so proud and proper.

Eleanor continued. "As I told you, dear, the money will force you to reassess your priorities. Life in America can be very easy with that kind of money. You might even decide you would like to become involved in the family corporation in some way."

"I'm afraid my education didn't prepare me for the business world."

"Oh, pooh, all it takes is common sense. I learned and so can you. Ben never discussed the business with me when he was alive, so when he died I had to learn it all very quickly."

"Why? You had your sons."

"A woman has to stand on her own two feet. I trust my sons implicitly... but not half as much as I trust myself. Remember that, dear. Don't ever depend on a man to take care of you. Learn to take care of yourself. Now, about the trust. I think I'll telephone Taylor and have him get started on that right away."

So there it was. Ivy was an heiress whether she wanted to be or not... but not if she became Erik's wife. What a dilemma. If she didn't return to the island, what would she do with the rest of her life? She thought of what Marilee had said—*to be able to go anywhere you wanted, to do anything you wanted.* The trouble was that she couldn't think of anywhere she wanted to go or anything she wanted to do. And she certainly didn't want to buy clothes, jewelry or rare paintings.

Eleanor had Taylor on the phone. Ivy sighed, stood and walked to the window to stare out at another bright, hot day. Everything that was happening to her was so...so daunting. She supposed there was a lot of good she could do with the money when...or if...it was hers. Money did not always have to be used to buy *things*.

But there was one thing she knew for sure—money like that would be of no use to her on Baksra...none whatsoever. But then, if she was on Baksra, the money wouldn't be hers, would it?

Ivy had never been forced to make an important decision in her life. Now she had come face-to-face with a monumental one.

"EXCUSE ME, but I'm in a bitchy mood," Marilee announced as Ivy entered the shop. "Oh, but I do love your hair. Edna did a superb job."

Ivy stared in the mirror over the cosmetics counter. Her hair looked much as it had after Marilee's stint with the curling iron, only more so. Now it was *permanent*...or at least it was for a few months. And the goo Edna had smeared over it after the perm was completed had lightened it several shades. "It's so hard to get used to."

"You'll love it when you do."

"She cut off two inches."

"It looks great, *très* chic. Come on in the back while there's a lull. I have some unpacking to do. How's the driving coming?"

Ivy shrugged. "Actually maneuvering the car is easier than I expected, but I'm frightened to death of the traffic. The instructor assures me I'll get over that."

"The traffic frightens me to death, too, and I've been driving since I was sixteen."

The back room of Marilee's shop was a clutter of boxes, garment racks and tables. A desk stood in one corner, its top littered with papers, and there was a tiny washroom just inside the delivery entrance. A small refrigerator occupied another corner. Marilee opened one large carton and began pulling garments out and placing them on hangers.

"Let me help," Ivy said.

"Would you, sweetie? That really would be a major help. I've been trying to get to this all day, but I've been swamped with customers. Not complaining, you understand, but I can't sell this stuff until it's out front."

At that moment, the bell over the entrance sounded. Marilee rolled her eyes and went to wait on another customer. Ivy worked industriously, taking exquisite garments out of the carton, hanging them and then using the hand-held steamer to take out the worst of the wrinkles. It was some time before Marilee returned. Seeing how much Ivy had accomplished, she let out a whistle. "Boy, you're fast. I ought to hire you."

"This is empty," Ivy said, indicating the carton. "What do I do with it?"

"Just stash it outside the back door. The trash collectors pick up tomorrow."

Ivy lugged the bulky carton out the door, and when she returned, Marilee was starting in on a new one. "You know, Ivy, this might be an idea worth looking into. I get so far behind in the little stuff—unpacking, pressing, stocking the cosmetics and accessories, to say nothing of cleaning up. Why don't you come to work for me? I might even turn you into a pretty fair salesperson."

"Is it allowed? I mean, can a person just come into this country and go to work?"

"Are you an American citizen?"

"Yes."

"Do you have a Social Security number?"

"I . . . don't know."

"You probably do. I'll bet your grandmother got you one when you were young. But if you don't, we'll get you one."

Ivy thought how much fun it would be to be surrounded by all these lovely things all day; there wasn't really much for her to do at the house. Save for the driving lessons, which would soon be over, she seemed to spend most of her time hoping Taylor would come by, and he was such a busy man.

Besides, she liked being around Marilee. Marilee had style, flair and vivacity, all the things Ivy considered sadly lacking in herself. "I have a better idea. If you need help, just let me help you, not work for you. I don't have much to do, and I love this shop."

"Are you serious?"

"Very."

"I don't pay much, but it would be something."

"I don't need money." It was on the tip of Ivy's tongue to tell Marilee about her inheritance, but she thought better of it. The money wasn't hers yet. It might never be.

"Then you're welcome anytime."

The two women worked until all the cartons were empty and the clothes had been hung and pressed. "Whew, thank God that's done," Marilee said. "Let's sit down and have a glass of tea."

"You look tired," Ivy observed as Marilee pulled the tea pitcher out of the refrigerator. "When I came in, you said you were in a bad mood. Is it because you've been so busy?"

"No, I love it when I'm busy. It's Glenn. He's on my list today."

"List?"

"I'm furious with him." Marilee collapsed into a chair across from Ivy. "I tried talking seriously to him about marriage last night, and I got a deaf ear in return. He was watching a ball game on the sports channel, so he just tuned me out. Ass! You know something, Ivy. There's no reason for me to even *like* the guy, much less love him. He's a sports freak, and

I love ballet. He guzzles beer, and I like wine. He eats the most vile food, and I'm something of a gourmet. He likes country music, the twangier the better, and I like show tunes. I mean, how did we ever do more than say 'hi' to each other? And yet, I love him. Go figure.''

Marilee's mouth was set in a pinched line, and her usually sparkling eyes were clouded. Ivy sipped her tea and thought...and thought. ''Marilee, do you remember the first day I was in here, when you told me how the women on the island could change things if they wanted to?''

''Sure.''

''Well, I was just thinking—why not negotiate with him? What is it about you that Glenn loves most of all?''

''Everything, simply everything.''

''What if you threatened to take everything away from him?''

Marilee was startled to hear Ivy say that. Another woman asking that question would have been suggesting employing womanly wiles, but Ivy's eyes were completely guileless, and Marilee suspected her new friend wouldn't know a womanly wile if she fell into a vat of them. Ivy was seriously asking ''what if.''

''I don't know, Ivy. I've heard that no one can accurately predict how a person will react to something, certainly not all the time. I know Glenn loves me to death, so it might work. But there's a big problem.''

"What's that?"

"If I threaten to break if off unless there's marriage in the offing, I have to mean it. If he sticks to his guns, I'll have to do it and be prepared to lose him."

"Well...I don't know much, but it seems to me that if you want to get married and have a baby, and he refuses...maybe you should pack and leave and find someone else."

Marilee smiled. "For someone who doesn't know much, you know a lot, but I can't pack and leave."

"Why not?"

"It's *my* apartment."

"Then he'd have to pack and leave."

Marilee nodded. "And I don't have to wonder what his reaction to that would be. I know Glenn's pride. If I ever asked him to leave, I'd never see him again."

Ivy digested that. It seemed to her that relationships between men and women in America were so complicated it was a wonder any marriages ever took place. An incredible number of considerations existed. "Marilee, I'd like to ask you something personal."

"Sure, sweetie. What is it?"

"What are you supposed to do when a man kisses you?"

Marilee looked surprised for a second, then laughed. "Well...step back or kiss back. Depends on the guy."

"What if you don't know how...to kiss back, I mean?"

Marilee simply stared at her a minute before saying, "Good grief, Ivy, I..."

"How do you learn?"

"Well...most girls start at about fourteen or fifteen, and over the years you just...learn. It actually ought to come naturally. Who's been kissing you?"

"Taylor kissed me good-night last night, and I just stood there like a statue. I didn't even know what to do with my hands."

Poor Ivy, Marilee thought with a sigh. She was so inexperienced, and yet no one would believe a woman her age, who looked like she did, could be so innocent. There were so many men out there who could easily take advantage of her. Marilee didn't think Taylor was one of them, but one never knew when it came to men. "I have an idea," she said, getting to her feet and crossing the room to the cluttered desk. Opening a bottom drawer, she withdrew a stack of magazines and carried them to Ivy. "Here you go. They'll teach you more than I ever could. Read 'em from cover to cover...and good luck."

DURING THE DAYS that followed, Ivy's indoctrination into American life continued, and as Taylor got to know her even better, a picture of the young Ivy Loving began to form. She had never given him anything but the barest facts about the years after she'd left Texas. Certainly she never gave voice to how she had felt back then, but he was a master of reading between the lines.

The years in India had been solitary ones, it seemed. Segregated from the Indian household by gender and religion, she apparently had spent her idle time with the various animals that populated the place. Perhaps that explained why a large, antisocial dog had taken one look at her and fallen in love.

Then had come the academy and the university, followed by the flight to Baksra with its laid-back atmosphere, its friendly citizens . . . and those marriage customs that dictated she would never have to attempt social intercourse with a man her own age. He could understand why the island had appealed to her.

But what he was having difficulty understanding was the blossoming friendship between Ivy and Marilee. The two had nothing in common, but Ivy was much taken with the older Marilee and took such personal interest in the shop one would have thought she owned a piece of the place.

And the bottom line was that Ivy was happy and busy. She had learned to drive and now had a license, an accomplishment she took great pride in, though so far she hadn't mustered the courage to drive anywhere but to Marilee's shop. Taylor tried to stop by the Cameron house every afternoon after work, and he continued to take her out to dinner to give her a chance to wear her new clothes, but he constantly cautioned himself to *keep it friendly*. No hugs and kisses. That was the hard part. With each passing day, she grew lovelier. She was such a delight to be with that he had to forcibly restrain himself from hugging her.

Eleanor was pleased with the way things were working out, something she mentioned every time she saw him. Her sons and grandsons and their wives filed in and out of the big house frequently enough to give Ivy a real sense of family. Eleanor had great-grandchildren, too, and they enchanted Ivy. She saw little of them, however, for they were much too young to be served to Eleanor in anything but small doses. But every time Taylor had seen Ivy with the babies, he'd noticed how she warmed to them.

As the days passed, he congratulated himself. Things had worked out better than he would have dreamed. Ivy was not the same woman she had been only weeks ago. She no longer reacted to new situations like a startled doe, and more importantly, it had been days since Taylor had heard her mention the island.

But the congratulations, he soon discovered, were a bit premature. A letter from Erik arrived. Eleanor always went through the mail the minute Wilma brought it to her, and when she saw the London postmark, her heart fluttered with trepidation. For a fleeting second she even considered throwing it away. Later, she almost wished she had. Whatever was in the letter plunged Ivy into such a peculiar mood. She seemed a million miles away, and Eleanor became really alarmed.

"We have to do something, Taylor," the matriarch said, the following day. "Ever since that letter arrived, Ivy has been acting so...strangely. The man apparently has considerable influence with her."

"Of course he does. She has spent several years thinking of him as the man she would someday marry."

It was late afternoon. Eleanor and Taylor were in the library waiting for Ivy to return home from work. Eleanor sipped a sherry while Taylor nursed a Scotch. The news about Erik's letter had upset him, too—far more than he wished it had. He had been going his merry way thinking that Baksra and Erik were no longer important to Ivy, but now he could see how foolish he'd been. Yes, she was happy here, but she doubtless felt an obligation to both Erik and her parents' wishes for her future.

How bewildered she must feel! Hadn't he feared this very thing would happen from the beginning?

"She can't go back to that island. It mustn't happen," Eleanor said for the dozenth time. "I thought...well, Ivy seemed to be acclimating herself to our way of life. She's looking so lovely these days, and I know how much she enjoys having you take her out. Has she met anyone she particularly admires?"

"There's Marilee."

"I believe you told me she isn't the kind of woman you want Ivy to emulate."

Taylor smiled. "Oh, there's nothing *wrong* with Marilee. I like her a lot, but she's...well, she's thoroughly modern, a self-made woman and all that. She doesn't take any guff from anyone. You'd probably like her a lot, but I doubt you would want Ivy to be like her. Am I making sense?''

Eleanor nodded, frowning. "I originally had hoped one of her married cousins would take her under his wing and show her what an American marriage can be like, but then I thought better of it and haven't encouraged it. They're all so busy, and their wives have careers of their own. All of them seem to go their own ways and meet at regular intervals. I'm afraid Ivy would find them a bit intimidating. But I do so wish she could see a really successful American marriage at work. Perhaps then she would give up all notion of going back to that island and marrying that man."

"I know," Taylor said. "I've been thinking about that, and I have just the person. Gloria."

Eleanor looked bewildered. "Gloria? Your sister?"

"Yes. She and Charles are the happiest married couple I've ever known. I thought of them the other day, and I know they would be ideal role models for Ivy."

"But don't they still live in Waco?"

He nodded. "Yes. And it's a nice Sunday drive away."

Eleanor sat back, sipped her sherry and smiled with satisfaction. "I knew you'd think of something, my boy. You always seem to."

Taylor tempered his enthusiasm a bit. "A visit with my sister guarantees nothing, Eleanor. I hope you know that."

"Yes, I know," she said with one of her little sighs. "If that doesn't work, perhaps the money will. I don't believe Ivy yet realizes just what that money can do for her."

"I have a feeling the last thing in the world that will keep Ivy here is the money."

One of Eleanor's eyebrows lifted slightly. "Then I'll have to come up with something else, won't I? An ace in the hole."

At that moment the front door opened and closed. Footsteps sounded in the hall, then Ivy rushed into the room. Although she went first to her grandmother to kiss her cheek, her brilliant smile was all for Taylor. Straightening, she went to him and took his hand. "I saw your car outside. I was so hoping you'd be here when I got home."

Eleanor watched the two of them over the rim of her glass, her eyes moving from Ivy to Taylor and back again. *Perhaps I already have my ace in the hole,* she thought with satisfaction. *I know I'm a meddling old woman, and I know I ask far too much of Taylor, but should it come to that, I won't hesitate to ask him to perform above and beyond the call of duty.* She had no intention of losing Ivy, and Eleanor Cameron was accustomed to getting exactly what she wanted.

"YOU'RE VERY PENSIVE tonight," Taylor said to Ivy as they sat in the library long after Eleanor had retired.

"Am I?"

"You hardly said a word at dinner."

"Sorry."

"It's nothing to be sorry about. Do you have something on your mind?"

"No, not really."

"Eleanor says you received a letter from Erik yesterday."

Did he imagine it, or did her expression alter in some subtle way? "Yes," she said quietly.

"How is he?"

"Fine."

"Still in England, I guess."

"Yes."

Dammit, she wasn't telling him a thing with those one-syllable answers. What he wouldn't have given to know what was going on in that pretty head of hers. He reached out and brushed at an errant strand of her hair, just grazing her cheek with the back of his hand. She turned and smiled.

"Now that I'm used to your hair, I'm crazy about it," Taylor told her.

"Are you? So am I." Ivy *loved* her hair. In the mornings after her shower she simply ran her fingers through the wet ringlets periodically until they dried into a wild amber riot that delighted her. Hearing Taylor say he liked her hair, too, filled her with delight. It seemed that pleasing him was topmost on her list of priorities.

Erik's letter had really shaken her. It had brushed away the silverdust in her head and brought her back to reality. What to do, what to do? She certainly couldn't imagine Erik ever telling her he liked her hair. The men on Baksra didn't do things like that. If a man kept a woman in his life, that was compliment enough.

And since when did you need compliments, Ivy? her inner voice nagged. *You've never received them before.*

"Ivy?"

She turned with a start. "Oh, I'm sorry, Taylor. Did you say something?"

"I asked if you're free Sunday. I'd like to take you someplace."

Her eyes lit up. "Some of the family is coming for Sunday dinner, but that's good because Grandmother won't mind my being gone."

"I'd like to take you to meet my sister and her family. They live about an hour and a half south of here. I'll tell Gloria we'll be there in time for lunch."

"You want to take me to meet some of your family?" She sounded incredulous.

"Yes. You seem surprised."

"Not surprised exactly. I'm more flattered than anything. You see…" Ivy paused. She had been about to say "back home" but for some reason didn't want to. She changed it. "On Baksra, being invited to meet one's family is the greatest form of acceptance and approval imaginable.''

He chuckled. ''Well, I'm afraid it doesn't carry quite that connotation here, but I think you'll like Gloria and Charlie.''

''I can hardly wait. What shall I wear?''

''My advice would be to keep it simple. It's a very casual, noisy household. My guess is we'll cook something on the grill. But wear whatever you want. You look sensational in everything.''

Marilee was forever telling her she looked great or sensational, but Ivy didn't place too much value on her friend's assessment of her appearance because Marilee tossed adjectives around with abandon.

But when Taylor told her she looked sensational, Ivy believed him. Maybe that was because she wanted him to think so.

Now he looked at his watch, so she knew he would be leaving soon. Ivy never could quite understand the bereft feeling she experienced every time he walked out the door. She knew he'd be back, if not tomorrow then Sunday. Her reactions to him sometimes were illogical.

Chief among them was her acute disappointment that he hadn't kissed her again since that first date. At first she had been puzzled, wondering if he simply hadn't enjoyed the kiss as she had. But then she'd begun reading Marilee's magazines and now she was sure she knew why there had been no more kisses. She was not a responsive recipient, and according to the magazine, men hated that. There was just so much to learn.

Taylor was getting to his feet. "Must you go?" she asked.

"Early tee-off time in the morning, and I can't keep the guys waiting."

Sighing, Ivy stood and walked with him to the front door. There he turned and placed his hands on her shoulders, as he always did. He smiled down, as he always did, but he made no move toward her. Ivy knew he wasn't going to kiss her, not unless she did something. She stepped closer to him, her insides flip-flopping wildly. Then, quickly before she lost her nerve, her arms crawled up his chest and locked behind his neck, forcing his head down. It happened in an instant, catching Taylor completely off guard. Her soft mouth closed over his, and when Ivy felt him begin to return the kiss, she allowed the tip of her tongue to slip between his lips. One of the magazine articles had presented that as a surefire guarantee to please a man.

Taylor jumped as though he'd been shot, staring at her with incredulous eyes. "Wh-what's the matter?" she cried.

"Where in the hell did you learn to do that?"

He sounded upset. Ivy's chin trembled. "From one of Marilee's magazines."

"You've been reading about kissing?"

"I thought...you see, you never kiss me anymore, and I thought it was because I don't do it right, so...I've been reading up on it."

"I see." Taylor looked down for a split second, fighting a smile. She looked so damned serious. Composing himself, he looked up, trying to match her seriousness. "I see. Well, Ivy, there's nothing wrong with reading for information, but practice is what makes perfect." He reached for her, drew her close and, throwing caution to the wind, began a lesson that no magazine article could ever match.

The kiss was like nothing Ivy had ever experienced. A slow, spreading warmth seeped into her pores. Remembering what the magazine had said, she leaned into it. Being crushed against him was another new sensation, pleasant and comforting. She discovered it was easy to press herself against him and feel the strength of his body. His arms tightened around her shoulders and suddenly she was in a warm cocoon, safe and protected.

Then Taylor delicately penetrated her mouth with the tip of his tongue. Ivy had wondered if she would like that and found to her surprise that she did, quite a lot. When he broke the kiss, he nuzzled his face in the gentle curve of her shoulder, then laid his cheek on top of her head. Ivy wondered if she was expected to say something. The magazine article had mentioned murmuring erotic phrases, but she didn't know why.

For his part, Taylor simply snuggled her close and thought how good she felt. She looked delicate, but there was a solidness to her body that surprised him. He was aware of her breasts crushed against his chest, a disturbing sensation. Somewhere in the back of his pleasure-drugged mind came the realization of just how vulnerable she was. She could be as easily hurt as a newborn kitten. With some difficulty, he broke the embrace and held her at arm's length. She stared at him, eyes wide and lips parted.

"Lesson One," he said in a husky voice that didn't sound like his own. "If I don't see you tomorrow, I'll call to make plans for Sunday." Giving her a little smile, he opened the door and left.

Ivy stared at the closed door for a minute. She had no idea if the kiss had been successful from Taylor's point of view, but it had left her absolutely stupefied. Never would she have believed another person's touch could turn her inside out.

Turning, she climbed the stairs and went into her room, with Jethro in his customary spot at her heels. She placed her hands on her cheeks; they felt very warm, almost hot. As usual, Wilma had turned down her bed and left the lamp on. As she walked to it, she saw Erik's letter on the dresser.

He hoped she was enjoying visiting her American family, he'd said, but he would be back on the island in two weeks and expected her to be there, too. They had to plan the future. It was time. Ivy's stomach stopped its dancing and dropped in a leaden heap.

It was time all right, time for her to decide what it was she wanted to do with the rest of her life. To be Erik's wife and enjoy all the privileges inherent in that? Or to be Eleanor Cameron's granddaughter, with privileges she wouldn't have dreamed of only a few weeks ago? To continue working with Marilee, who was the first female friend she had ever had? To stay in this wonderful house and enjoy the company of family? How odd that these people were becoming closer to her than her parents ever had.

To stay where Taylor was? Why, how had he become so important to her? He elicited feelings in her that she had never experienced in her life. She didn't even know what to call some of them.

The one option that never entered her mind was simply to be Ivy Loving, going her own way, doing as she pleased. Nothing in her life had prepared her for such a concept.

"Oh, Jethro," she moaned, "I've been playing Cinderella at the ball all this time, but I'm afraid midnight is fast approaching."

CHAPTER ELEVEN

SUNDAY WAS ANOTHER HOT day. The dog days of summer were upon them. By the time Taylor picked her up for the drive to Waco, Ivy had shaken off the gloomy mood Erik's letter had brought on and was in good spirits, anxious to meet Taylor's sister and more than happy to spend most of the day with him.

"Were you at the shop yesterday?" he asked idly as they left the city behind and headed south.

"Yes. We were very busy. Marilee really needed me, too. She was in a terrible mood."

"Marilee? Why?"

"Things aren't going well between her and Glenn, I'm afraid. That's a very complicated relationship."

And not the best one for Ivy to be around, Taylor thought. With Gloria and Charles, she would get a much better picture of what a marriage should be. Charlie was a sales rep for a business machines firm, and Gloria had quit teaching when the kids started coming along. Visiting them was like watching a "Leave It to Beaver" rerun, except Gloria wore jeans around the house, and Charlie didn't come to the supper table in a business suit. The word that most readily came to Taylor's mind when he thought of their marriage was *warm*.

But he and Ivy hadn't been in their house five minutes before he sensed that something was amiss. This afternoon, the house had all the warmth of an igloo. Gloria and Charlie had welcomed him with open arms and were gracious and cordial to Ivy, but they were barely civil to each other.

Sometimes Taylor thought he must have the world's worst luck. Gloria and Charlie probably didn't have more than one major argument a year, and this Sunday seemed to be the day for it. They stiffly sat across the room from each other, careful not to allow their eyes to meet. They directed most of their polite questions to Ivy. Taylor was accustomed to a lot of hearty camaraderie when he was with his sister and her husband, but today the atmosphere in the room definitely was strained.

Ivy, however, didn't seem to notice. She was bright and perky and so lovely it made him hurt to look at her, and she absolutely had Charlie eating out of her hand. Fascinated by her past, he bombarded her with questions, so when Gloria announced she was going to the kitchen to check on lunch, Taylor excused himself to follow her. He no longer worried that Ivy couldn't hold her own in a conversation with a stranger.

"Okay, what gives?" he asked Gloria when they were safely out of hearing range.

His sister slammed her fist on the counter, and her eyes flashed. "I'm so damned mad at Charlie I could kill him!"

"You could have fooled me. What's he done?"

"It's what he *wants* to do that has me looking up divorce lawyers in the phone book."

Taylor just grinned. Pigs would fly before Gloria left Charlie. "That bad, huh? Well, why don't you tell your big brother all about it?"

Gloria's mouth set grimly. "He got his bonus, and it's been a good year at the company. The bonus was larger than it's ever been, so I thought—hallelujah, we can finally do some things to this house that have needed doing forever. Oh, but no! Do you know what *he* wants to do with the money? Buy a new car! If that's not the silliest damned thing I ever heard. The car we have is only three years old and has less than twenty-five thousand miles on it. What in the devil do we need with a *new car?*"

Taylor was smart enough to know that, while the argument might seem insignificant to him, it wasn't to either Gloria or Charlie. He also knew they would work it out. But for the time being, their disagreement was spoiling his day.

"Look, sis, I know you guys will settle this eventually, but in the meantime...this afternoon is awfully important to me. You see..." As quickly as he could, he explained the situation with Ivy. "I badly wanted to give her a glimpse of a beautiful marriage at work, and you're giving me a war. Can't you *pretend* a little?''

"And let Charlie think I'm not serious about fixing up the house? No way, bro. Sorry. There have been too many unilateral decisions made in this family to suit me, and he's not getting away with it this time. I've waited a long time for new kitchen cabinets and carpet.''

Sighing, Taylor gave up. When he and Gloria returned to Ivy and Charlie, the kids had put in an appearance. David, Brian and Joy—nine, seven and five respectively—apparently had picked up on the family discord and were having their own squabble.

"Mom, the boys won't let me do *anything*," Joy complained.

"Aw, Mom, she's such a pest. She messes with all our stuff," Brian said.

"Yeah, and she doesn't show them any...respect," David added.

"They're being selfish and not sharing," Joy whined.

"Stop it this instant!" Charlie barked. "You three have exactly two minutes to settle this yourselves, or you're going to spend the rest of the day in separate rooms!" The kids skulked off with their chins on their chests.

Taylor recalled countless past episodes when he had so admired the seemingly endless patience his brother-in-law had displayed in settling childish disputes. All in all, this visit was a disaster. He had imagined he and Ivy would spend most of the day at his sister's, but under the circumstances, he thought it best if they got the hell out of there. They stayed a respectable time after lunch, then left to return to Fort Worth.

Though never a chatterbox, Ivy, he thought, was unusually quiet on the way back, and he was sure he knew the reason for that. His spirits plunged even further.

He had no way of knowing that Ivy actually had been impressed by the give-and-take between Gloria and Charlie. Now, staring out the window at the passing countryside, she thought of the few hours she had been in Taylor's sister's house. One didn't have to be too smart to know Gloria and Charlie had been on what Marilee called "the outs." Gloria had been very displeased about something, and she hadn't hesitated to let Charlie know it.

Ivy's thoughts strayed to the island and to Erik. If they were married, her role would be well-defined. A certain formality would exist between them, a code of conduct that could never be breached. If she was unhappy about something, she would have to quietly work it out herself. She certainly could never bother her husband with it. As his wife, she would have many servants, and her word would be law with them—but that word would have to be cleared with Erik first.

A tiny sigh escaped her lips. She was aware of Taylor's head turning toward her for a split second, but he said nothing. A thousand thoughts clouded her mind. She didn't for a minute think she belonged in America. A dozen things happened every day that reminded her of how different she was.

But she'd always been different—in India, at the university, on the island. She didn't feel any more different here than she had in those places. Maybe less so, as a matter of fact. It might be that her time in America was making her unsuitable for Baksra. She was growing to like all the things her parents had disdained, things like comfort and convenience. She also liked air-conditioning. How materalistic she had become!

Then her thoughts took a different turn and focused on her family. Now that she'd met her uncles and cousins and their families, she almost resented her parents for keeping her from them.

She thought of the grandmother she had grown so fond of. Once she returned to the island, she'd never see Eleanor again.

She thought of Marilee. On the island she would have no women friends, only acquaintances, for as a planter's wife, she would have few peers. Thinking of spending the rest of her life without another friend like Marilee saddened her enormously.

And she thought about Taylor. It always seemed to get back to Taylor. Even though she didn't understand all her feelings for him, she knew she liked being with him and liked having him kiss her. When she thought of him she felt all fuzzy inside. Once he escorted her safely back to Baksra, she'd never see him again—not ever. How was she going to say goodbye?

"Ivy?"

Her head turned with a jerk. "Yes?"

Concern was written on Taylor's face. "Is something troubling you?"

"No, nothing."

"I'm sorry about the visit. It didn't go exactly as I'd hoped."

"Don't be sorry. Gloria and Charlie are very nice."

"Yeah, and usually they're a lot of fun to be with, but today they were having a little spat."

"I know. Marilee's told me all about 'the outs.'"

Taylor imagined Marilee had told Ivy a whole bunch of stuff she might be better off not knowing. But that thought had no sooner formed than another arrived to take its place. Ivy needed to know the things she was learning from Marilee. That was the only way she would gain the savvy Eleanor wanted her to have, and without the savvy she would never adjust to life in America. He consoled himself by thinking that not even Marilee would ever turn Ivy into a cynic or sophisticate. She would always have something of the unspoiled innocent in her. "We'll be back in the city soon," he said. "Eleanor won't be expecting us for hours yet. You said you'd like to see where I live. Would you like to go there now?"

She brightened instantly. "Oh, yes, Taylor, I would."

MARILEE DROVE past the Cameron house three times before she mustered the courage to turn into the driveway. She rarely found herself in situations that made her nervous, but she was plenty nervous now. She hoped Mrs. Cameron wouldn't think she had her fair share of gall in coming here, but nothing ventured, nothing gained.

A servant answered her ring and looked at her with questioning eyes.

"I'd like to speak to Mrs. Cameron, please," Marilee said.

"May I ask your name?"

"My name won't mean anything to her, but I'm a friend of Ivy's."

"Oh?" Wilma offered her a small smile, opened the door wider and stepped back. "Come in. I'll see if Mrs. Cameron is up to a visitor. One of her grandsons and his family left a short while ago, and she usually takes a nap about now."

"Tell her I won't keep her long."

Marilee remained in the foyer while the servant went to announce her. Her eyes darted around. *Oh, this house!* It was to die for. What she wouldn't have given to make a grand tour of the place. How could Ivy even think about leaving?

The servant reappeared. "Mrs. Cameron will see you, ma'am. This way."

Marilee breathed a sigh of relief and followed the woman down a hall and through double doors. Mrs. Cameron was seated in a high-backed chair, looking very regal and a little forbidding. She was dressed in a stunning gray dress with long sleeves and a high neck. Marilee, with a trained eye for such things, recognized the designer.

"Come in, my dear, and sit over there where I can see you."

Marilee hurriedly crossed the room and took the chair facing Eleanor. "Mrs. Cameron, I'm Marilee Huntley. I own the shop where Ivy—"

"Of course, Marilee. I recognize the name. Ivy speaks often and highly of you. May I get you something to drink? A glass of wine perhaps?"

"No, thank you."

"You won't offend me. I'm not a teetotaler."

"It's just that alcohol during the day makes me sleepy. Thank you so much for seeing me. I apologize for coming without calling first, but I won't take much of your time. I had to come when I knew Ivy wouldn't be here."

"Take all the time you need. What can I do for you?"

"I'm not sure you—or anybody—can do anything, but...well, it's about Ivy. I absolutely adore her."

Eleanor smiled. "So do I."

"My customers do, too. Isn't it amazing? She's so shy, but people take to her right off."

"I think that's because she's so honest. In this day and age, that's so unusual it's appealing."

"It just kills me to think of her going back to that island where she'll hide her light under a bushel."

"I feel the same way, Marilee, exactly."

"Has she said anything, given any clue as to what she intends doing?"

"I'm not sure she knows yet. It doesn't seem to me that Ivy's had much control over her life. She's always done what she's been told to do. It's difficult to make decisions when one has never been given the opportunity to do so. For that I can thank my foolish daughter and her equally foolish husband. They considered themselves idealists, but they actually were fools."

Marilee was surprised by the elderly woman's chattiness. "You know, Mrs. Cameron, I think Ivy could have a real future in retail fashion. She loves being around pretty things and takes real delight in finding just the right thing for a customer. There's nothing for her on that island, nothing but a man older than her father was and a life that...well, I think I would prefer being in prison to living it. Surely there's something we can do to keep her from going back."

"I'm open to all suggestions," Eleanor said. "I personally have offered my granddaughter a fortune that most people would die for. My only stipulation was that in order to receive it, she must remain in America. Still, she hasn't made up her mind."

Marilee frowned. "Money probably doesn't mean as much to Ivy as it does to most people."

Eleanor nodded. "Refreshing in a way, isn't it? But it makes my task more difficult. My late husband used to say that the hardest person in the world to deal with was one who wasn't interested in money. So, if a fortune, a big loving family, an adoring pet, a chance to do work she enjoys aren't enough to make up her mind, I don't know what else could...unless..."

Two pairs of sage eyes met. "Can you possibly be thinking the same thing I am?" Marilee asked.

Eleanor's cheeks flamed slightly, and Marilee knew they were operating on the same wavelength. She found herself warming to the woman she had heard described as intimidating and formidable.

"I've suspected for some time that I might have to play my ace," Eleanor said.

"Taylor?"

Eleanor nodded, rather sheepishly, Marilee thought—like a child caught in an act of mischief. "Yes, Taylor. He's the obvious one, don't you think?"

Marilee laughed her delightful laugh and clapped her hands together. "I like you, Mrs. Cameron. You and I think alike. If Ivy was in love, she'd never leave here. I know about love."

Eleanor tapped her chin thoughtfully. "Has Ivy given you any insight into the nature of their relationship?"

"Oh, Ivy rarely talks about herself. But she feels close to him, I can tell that much. He's protective of her, and Ivy warms to that. And I know he once kissed her good-night..." Marilee paused to smile "...because she asked me what she was supposed to do with her hands when that happened."

Eleanor stifled a giggle. "That might mean a lot or it might mean nothing. It could have been simply a friendly gesture on Taylor's part. He comes to see her often...but then I asked him to. He takes her out to dinner and things of that nature. But again, I asked him to."

"If you asked him to court her, would he?"

"Oh, my dear, we really are unconscionable," Eleanor said, but her eyes twinkled merrily, and laughter bubbled up in her throat.

Marilee joined her laughter. "Yes, I suppose we are. I'm so glad I came, Mrs. Cameron."

"Marilee, I think you and I could be very good friends. I hope you'll come back often."

TAYLOR'S TOWN HOUSE was on the west side, not far from Rivercrest in distance but light years away from it in prestige. The compound consisted of eight "six-packs"—six two-story town houses to a unit. They all were red brick trimmed with white, nicely land-scaped, and they stood clustered around a fenced-in swimming pool that Taylor would have sworn no one had ever so much as dipped a toe in. It seemed to be more for sitting around than anything. To his knowl-edge all the residents worked away from home. On the few occasions he'd had to stay at home during the day, the place had been as quiet as a ghost town.

Opening the front door, he stood back to allow Ivy to enter. Though he wasn't a slob like a lot of bachelors, he wasn't a neat freak, either, so he made a quick survey of the place over Ivy's shoulder. Not too bad, he decided. Except for the Sunday edition of the *Star-Telegram* scattered here and there, the living room was tidy enough for guests.

Ivy, however, made a more thorough inspection, not for neatness but to get a feeling of the way Taylor lived. The focal point of the room was a gray stone fireplace. Two floor-to-ceiling windows flanked it. There wasn't a lot of furniture, but what was there was tasteful—a plaid sofa and two recliners, a few occasional tables and lamps and the inevitable TV set. There weren't many accessories. It was an anonymous room, lived in by a man who wasn't there very often. "It's very nice, Taylor. Have you lived here long?"

"Five years. Since these places were built. Before that, I had a tiny apartment, and I do mean tiny. I had to be in Fort Worth a few years, make sure things were going right before tying myself down to this place. Sit down, Ivy. Let me get you something to drink."

"Just water, please."

He went into the kitchen and talked to her through a serving window. "Ice?"

"Please." Instead of sitting down, Ivy walked to one of the tall windows and looked out. There was a splendid view of the swimming pool, deserted on a hot Sunday afternoon. Strange. It seemed to her it should have been crowded with bathers.

Taylor came up behind her with her glass of water. She took it and smiled her thanks. "Do you think you'll stay here forever and ever?" she asked.

"In this house or in Fort Worth?"

"In Fort Worth."

"Probably. . . but forever is a long time. All sorts of things could happen."

"Like what?"

"Oh, a better job offer, I guess."

"You would crush Grandmother. She relies on you so."

"Frankly, Ivy, I doubt I would leave as long as Eleanor needs me."

"She's very fortunate to have you." Turning, she walked to the sofa, sat down and took a sip of water. Then she stared off into space.

Taylor waited a minute. "Ivy, what's wrong? You've been off in the wild blue yonder all day. What is it?"

She took another sip of water and set it down on a glass-topped coffee table. "You know I got that letter from Erik?"

Taylor tensed. "Yes."

"He said his business in England will be finished soon. He hopes to be back on the island in two weeks.

He wants me there, too. He says it's time we talked about the future. I know what he means. His wife died a year ago this month.''

Taylor felt as though he'd been kicked in the stomach. He'd thought himself prepared for this, but he wasn't. And Eleanor damned sure wouldn't be.

"That's not very far away," Ivy said pensively.

"No, it isn't."

"It seems like I just got here. Oh, I know a lot of things have happened to me, but they happened very quickly. Time is . . . just passing so fast."

Taylor's mind raced. He had to think of something, anything. But nothing came to him. "You realize, I hope, that by returning to the island you are relinquishing a fortune."

"I know." She almost whispered it. "But I would never stay simply for money." Her eyes came up to his. *Oh, Taylor, if only you would give me some sign. Should I go or not? Do you want me to go or stay? If I stay, will we remain close?*

Taylor stared at her, willing her to tell him something. He could read nothing in her expression. Did she want to marry Erik? Did she want to stay here? What? When seconds ticked by and she said nothing, he gave a little growl. "I'm going to fix myself a drink . . . and it's not going to be water."

Ivy heard him opening drawers and banging cabinets. Then he was lounging in the kitchen doorway, looking at her. He held a drink in his hand. Since he usually drank Scotch when he drank, she guessed that was what it was.

"Tell me something, Ivy...if your parents had lived, would you have stayed on Baksra the rest of your life?"

"Th-that's hard to say. If I married Erik, I guess I would have. He travels a lot, and I assume I would travel with him, but...who knows? If his wife had lived another year, and if my parents had finished their book, I..." She stopped, her eyes widening.

The realization hit Taylor at the same time. Setting his drink on the kitchen counter, he raced across the room and lifted her to her feet. "Ivy! The book! That big, wonderful, beautiful book! You can't leave. We haven't done a thing about the book."

"Good heavens, we haven't. I'd forgotten all about it, and it was the reason I came here in the first place." She couldn't believe she was so relieved.

Taylor gathered her to him, hugging her so ferociously she could scarcely breathe. They were as exuberant as a couple of schoolchildren. Then he held her at arm's length. "You have to write Erik immediately. Explain about the book. And tomorrow I'll get started on finding someone who will finish it. And whatever you do, don't give Erik a definite return date. Tell him everything's up in the air at the moment."

She nodded. "I dare not send it to the address in London. He might miss it altogether. So I'll have to send it to the plantation, and he'll receive it when he arrives. He might be angry.''

"He'll get over it," Taylor said. Personally, he doubted the man would be angry... or be anything, for that matter. His marriage to Ivy would be an arrangement, not the love affair of the century. Right now, all Taylor wanted to think about was that they'd bought some time. He was ecstatic. "Ivy, call your grandmother and tell her not to expect you for supper. Let's eat here. I'll cook something...or you cook something, it doesn't matter. I just...don't want you to leave yet."

A delighted smile crossed her face. "All right." And as naturally as if she had gone into a man's arms every day of her life, she went into his, raised her face and silently asked for a kiss.

As their mouths locked together, Taylor felt a strong surge of eagerness, and he recognized it for what it was. He couldn't remember ever fighting such an urge before, but to feel sexuality toward Ivy seemed almost lecherous. He'd learned quite a lot about women over the years, but he could scrap every bit of information he'd gleaned, because he'd never known a woman like Ivy. There was no question in his mind that she was a virgin, just as there was no question she would try to do anything he asked of her. And that was the problem.

As one kiss became another, he felt her tremble and knew she was aroused, too. She might not know what to call the feeling or what to do about it, but she was experiencing the excitement, too. But when he felt her instinctively arch her hips into his, he came to his senses. Not now, not until he'd heard her say she was staying for good. It took every bit of willpower he possessed to break the kiss and step back. Her eyes were wide, her lips parted, and she was breathing as if she'd been running uphill.

"Oh, Taylor," she gasped. "All these odd little feelings...was that Lesson Two?"

"I think it was. Do you love Erik?" he asked abruptly, perhaps too sharply.

"I...don't know. What's love? Is it...this?"

"This is part of it."

Ivy looked down, unable to meet his gaze. Never in a million years would Erik make her feel like this. Her heart was beating like a thousand drums. She wasn't even sure she wanted to feel this way. It was frightening. "I...don't think I've had an entirely lucid moment since I got to America. All these forces are pounding away at me like the monsoons, never letting up. I'm not even sure who I am anymore. I don't feel like the person I was three weeks ago, but..." she glanced in the mirror behind the dining table "...I'm not sure that's me, either."

She was right, and he'd let it happen. They had all been bombarding her. Eleanor offering her a fortune most people would kill for. Marilee turning her into a cover-girl type and feeding her slick fashion magazines without first cutting her teeth on something a little less sophisticated.

And he was the worst offender of all. He had introduced her to emotions she wasn't ready for. He drew her to him again, this time gently, as one would a child. He stroked her hair and rubbed her shoulders in a comforting gesture. "You're Ivy Loving. A new hairdo and clothes can't change that. And Ivy Loving is a pretty nice person to be. You might also be happy to learn that those 'odd little feelings' are perfectly normal, so don't question or analyze too much, okay?"

"Okay," she said uncertainly.

Releasing her, he smiled at her tenderly. "Now let's go see what we can find in the kitchen. I haven't done any grocery shopping in ages. A trip to the supermarket might be in order."

As docilely as a child, she followed him, but she felt as if everything inside her was in turmoil. Was she capable of coming to terms with that?

MUCH, MUCH LATER, after Taylor had brought her home and she had gone to her room, Ivy lay in bed, scratching Jethro's ears and thinking. Taylor had taken her on her first trip to an American supermarket, an establishment that had filled her with wonder. It seemed that everything consumable on earth was under that roof. Then they'd had a wonderful dinner that he had prepared, and afterward, they had watched a sad movie on television. At least she had thought it sad; he seemed to think it funny. On the surface things had been as they always had between them, but that had been illusion. She no longer felt the same about Taylor and never would again. Now she wanted him in a way that would have been unthinkable only weeks ago.

She was inexperienced but no longer as ignorant as she once had been, thanks to Marilee. She knew that men and women all over the world kissed the way she and Taylor had. She also knew it was that very lack of experience that had made it seem different and momentous. And thanks to those magazines, she now knew what the weak knees and hot feeling in the pit of her stomach signified.

Of course she'd always known about the physical act between husbands and wives, the "wifely duty" that had been spoken about when she was in her teens, the act that brought children into the world. But the words *wife* and *sex* had gone together. The women in those magazines jumped into bed at the drop of a hat and seemed to think it normal. It didn't always happen in the marriage bed.

She closed her eyes, and Taylor's face came into view. She tried to conjure up Erik, too, but nothing happened. It was Taylor who filled her vision, made her heart swell and her fingertips itch just for the feel of him.

And that was where it became even more complex.

Marilee often spoke of the game of love, and it did seem like a game—a lot of rules, some guessing, some feinting, a lot of playacting. And wondering. How did Taylor feel? Did he think of her as Eleanor's

granddaughter, an appealing woman, a strange creature from an island across the Banda Sea, what? She
wouldn't know unless he told her, and even then, according to Marilee, could she trust him? "A man in
the throes of passion will say anything, promise you
anything," was the way her friend had put it.

Ivy rolled over, tucked her arm beneath the pillow
and sighed. It was taking some time, but little by little, she was getting smarter.

CHAPTER TWELVE

IN THE BEGINNING it had all sounded so simple, Taylor thought as he drove into the driveway of the Cameron home the following morning. Just go see Eleanor's granddaughter and persuade her to pay the elderly woman a visit. It might mean two tiring journeys, but it couldn't possibly complicate his life in any way. As he switched off the engine, he shook his head. How wrong he'd been.

It had been a long time since he'd thought even briefly he was falling in love, but that's the way he felt now. Looking back, he guessed it had been coming on for some time. Had he been falling in love with anyone but Ivy, he probably would have been engulfed in the rushing eagerness love seemed to produce. As it was, he felt as confused as she must.

But at least he had some good news for Eleanor. He had waited until after ten, when he could be sure Ivy would have left for the shop, to call on her. Wilma answered the door and showed him into the library where Eleanor sat, not in her usual chair but at her desk.

"Taylor! What a nice surprise. Ivy isn't here. I wasn't feeling very well this morning, so I missed her at breakfast. When I came down, she had already left for the shop."

"I wanted to see you, Eleanor. I'm sorry you weren't feeling well. Nothing serious, I hope."

"Just my old joints acting up. I stayed in bed until the medication took effect. Please sit down."

He sat in a chair facing the desk. "Am I interrupting something important?"

"Nothing that can't be returned to later. Once a month Robert brings me a computer printout of all the corporation's transactions. It's the only way I can possibly stay on top of things. What did you want to see me about?"

"Did Ivy ever tell you what was in the letter she received from Erik?"

"No. I was very curious, but she volunteered no information."

"He wants her back on the island in two weeks. He said they need to plan the future."

Eleanor's hand went to her chest. "What did she say? Is she going to . . ."

"Not right away. Fortunately, Ivy and I remembered the book."

"Book?"

"The book her parents were working on. That was the main reason I was able to convince her to come to America in the first place. I promised to help her find someone who would finish it. We haven't done a thing about it, and it's going to take some time."

"Well, thank heavens for that." Eleanor seemed pleased, but not as pleased as Taylor had expected. "That's wonderful, of course, but it's only a stop-gap measure at best. We need to find something that will keep Ivy with us permanently."

"Anything we do is a stopgap measure until Ivy makes up her mind for sure, but I have a feeling that every day she spends with us will bring her one step closer to wanting to stay." He *hoped* that was true.

"I wonder." Eleanor lapsed into thoughtful silence for a minute before saying, "Marilee came to see me yesterday."

"Marilee?" Taylor couldn't have been more surprised. "Why?"

"She wanted to talk to me, and she knew you and Ivy were in Waco. She doesn't want Ivy to leave any more than you and I do. She's grown very fond of her, and she says her customers are enchanted with her."

Taylor smiled. "That young lady has certainly made an impact on a lot of people in a very short time."

"Yes." Eleanor glanced down at her hands, then back up. "You were right, Taylor. I like Marilee. She and I think the same way. One doesn't sit around and hope things work out as one wants. One *makes* them work out. We spent a long time discussing what might make Ivy want to stay with us, and we came up with what I believe is the perfect solution.''

"Oh? And that is?''

"If Ivy were in love with you, wild horses couldn't drag her away from here."

Taylor simply stared at her while that sank in. It wasn't what she said—he certainly hoped Ivy would fall in love with him. It was the fact that Eleanor would say it at all. He had often suspected Ivy's grandmother would go to any lengths to get what she wanted, and now he was sure of it. The woman had no idea of the turn his relationship with Ivy had taken. She couldn't have any idea how Ivy felt about him or how he felt about her. For all Eleanor knew, he was little more than Ivy's mentor, someone she felt comfortable with. Yet the matriarch apparently had no pangs of conscience over calmly asking him to toy with Ivy's affections.

"Are you asking me to make Ivy fall in love with me?''

"Oh, come, come, Taylor. That shouldn't be difficult. I see the way she looks at you. And she's so lovely. Surely you don't begrudge a minute you spend with her."

"Eleanor, that's not the point." He stood and raked his fingers through his hair while he paced the floor. "Stop and think what you're asking. You're talking about manipulating her emotions. Under no circumstances would I do that. She's very confused right now. She's literally torn between two worlds."

Taylor wondered if he wasn't saying these things as much for his own benefit as for Eleanor's.

The woman was unmoved. "Then I'm counting on you to end her confusion once and for all."

"I'm afraid this is one time I'm going to have to say no to you. Anything that happens between Ivy and myself will have to be natural and heartfelt. No games. Anything else would be playing with fire."

"All affairs of the heart are gambles, Taylor," Eleanor persisted stubbornly.

At that moment Wilma appeared in the doorway. "The mail, ma'am. Do you want it now or wait until later?"

"Bring it to me now, Wilma. Thank you."

Taylor continued his pacing while Eleanor quickly sifted through the mail Wilma placed on the table beside her chair. Then she made some sort of sound that caused Taylor to stop pacing and turn. She held a letter in her hand and was staring at it with a frown.

"It's another one from that man," she said tersely.

"Erik?"

"Yes. What I wouldn't give to just tear it up."

Taylor felt the same way, but he said, "But of course you can't do that."

"I don't want Ivy under his influence at this particular time."

"You forget. He's many thousands of miles away, and we're right here."

"She's so special to me, Taylor. So special, my final chance to have a daughter."

"And she's special to me, too. Keep the good thought, Eleanor. Maybe things will work out exactly as you want."

But he scowled at the letter once more before he left. It was a reminder of Ivy's other life, one she had lived far longer than she'd lived this one, and he couldn't shake the fear that its hold on her might be greater than any of them could overcome.

"WELL, TODAY'S THE DAY, sweetie," Marilee said as she collapsed into a chair in the shop's back room.

"The day for what?"

"I'm going to talk to Glenn once more about marriage. If I still don't get anywhere, I give him his walking papers."

"Oh, Marilee..." Her friend sounded nonchalant, but Ivy knew it was a facade. By now she was aware of just how deeply Marilee cared for Glenn and how big a void there would be in her life if he left. Ivy wished she could think of something uplifting and encouraging to say, but she couldn't even sort out her own feelings. How could she help anyone with theirs?

"Are you...scared?"

Marilee gave a toss of her head. "Well, I'm certainly not brimming over with confidence, if that's what you mean." She uttered a sound, part growl, part sigh. "Men! They're such irritating creatures. You have to play them like fine instruments. You don't dare try to change them. You mustn't try to refine them. You can't even talk to them...at least not until they're so wildly in love with you that they've forgotten they're supposed to be wary of you."

Whenever Marilee talked about men, Ivy listened, since her friend seemed to know so much and she knew nothing. She thought about Taylor. She wouldn't want to change one thing about him. He was perfect as far as she was concerned. As for refining him, *she* was the one needing refinement, not him. And she could talk to him about almost anything.

"I'm going to give you a good piece of advice, Ivy. Go with your heart. True, you run more of a risk of getting hurt, but it's the only way you can really live."

In the main part of the shop, the bell over the door jangled. Marilee glanced at the clock. It was a quarter to six. In another fifteen minutes the shop would be closed. She groaned and started to stand, but Ivy detained her with a hand. "I'll see to it. You look tired, and I know you have a lot on your mind. If it turns out to be something I can't handle, I'll come for you."

"Thanks, Ivy. I'm bushed . . . and not looking forward to tonight."

Ivy left the back room and threaded her way through the racks of clothes. In the front of the shop, a man was bent over the perfume counter. "May I help you?" she called gaily, imitating Marilee's usual way of greeting customers.

The man straightened and grinned at her. "Oh, Taylor," she said, feeling her cheeks flush. Was this the way it was with all women when one certain man came into view? she wondered. Blushes, somersaulting stomachs, tingles?

"You asked if you could help me," Taylor said. "The answer is yes. You can have dinner with me tonight."

"How will that help you?"

"Looking at your pretty face helps me digest my food." Her blushes delighted him. He couldn't remember the last time he'd known a woman who blushed. Maybe he never had. "But first we have to see a man about a book."

"Oh?"

"I found someone who's interested. I called a friend who's a computer whiz at Texas Christian, and he put me in touch with the head of the English department. And *he* put me in touch with a local writer who writes the kind of stuff your parents did—scholarly things. He said he'd love to talk to us about it."

"Oh, Taylor, that's wonderful!"

"He also said that if he takes on the project, you'll have to be available in case he has questions." Actually, the unvarnished truth was that Taylor had suggested that, and the writer, whose name was John LeMasters, had agreed that it might be a good idea.

"Available? For how long, I wonder?"

"I have no idea. First, we have to see if he's interested in taking it on. And then we'll have dinner. Where would you like to go?"

"I could cook for you."

"You're on."

"I'll have to take Grandmother's car home."

"I'll follow you. We have to pick up your parents' work, anyway." Taylor smiled at her, and she smiled back. He touched her arm, a simple gesture that meant so much. It seemed to Ivy that forces were at work, conspiring to keep her in America, and she was a great believer in allowing forces to do what they would. It astonished her that people she'd never laid eyes on a month ago had come to mean so much to her, especially Taylor. She gazed into his eyes, and for a moment they might have been the only two people on earth.

Marilee had come to the door of the back room to see what was keeping Ivy. When she saw her helper and Taylor staring at each other, she lounged against the doorjamb and smiled. So Eleanor had talked to him, and he was going along with their idea. Good. Taylor would do a masterful job, Marilee was sure of that. Tomorrow her own romantic life might lie in the pits, but she had a feeling it wouldn't be long before Ivy was hopelessly, wildly in love for the first time. Ah, the first time, Marilee thought. There was nothing on earth like it.

At that moment, Ivy turned, saw her in the doorway and called, "I'm leaving now, if that's all right."

Marilee threw her a jaunty little wave and watched as Ivy and Taylor left the shop arm in arm. Then she locked up, turned off the lights and went out to her car parked behind the building. Checking her watch, she saw that it was at least an hour before she could expect Glenn home, so that gave her plenty of time for a stop at the supermarket.

Glenn's absolutely favorite meal, as bourgeois as it seemed to her, was hamburger steak smothered with onions and a baked potato that weighed a pound. He declared there was no one on earth who made hamburger steak the way she did. Of course there wasn't, because she didn't buy hamburger or even ground round. She bought a piece of sirloin and hovered while the butcher trimmed it to her specifications, then ground it only once. For Glenn she needn't have bothered. A gourmet he wasn't. He would promptly drown his steak in Worcestershire sauce, but she had to eat the stuff, too, and she demanded a certain refinement in her food.

Oh, she hated herself for doing what she was doing. Preparing his very favorite dinner, buying a red velvet cake at a horribly expensive bakery just because he loved them, stocking the fridge with plenty of his favorite beer, doing all the things she had once said she wouldn't do even under penalty of death. But desperate times called for desperate measures. If she was going to go through with this, she needed all the help she could get.

By the time Glenn walked through the door a few minutes after seven, Marilee had dinner well under control, had rehearsed what she planned to say a half-dozen times and was convinced she was prepared for anything.

"Hi, sweetheart," he said, dropping a light kiss on her mouth. "How was today?"

"Passable. A lot of my regulars are buying for fall cruises, so sales are pretty good for August. How was your day?"

"I've had better." Opening the refrigerator, he took out a can of beer. Then he picked up the paper he never had time for in the morning, went into the living room and flopped down in an easy chair.

Great, she thought. *Blinking wonderful.* At least he hadn't turned on a ball game. She momentarily gave some thought to putting this off until an evening when he seemed more receptive, but then she thought better of it. Being honest, there probably never would be a perfect time, and she was tired of this wait-and-see. She wanted to know something *now*.

Dinner was perfection, according to Glenn, which was encouraging. As she served him a hefty slice of red velvet cake and poured coffee, she said, "Let's talk."

He eyed her warily. "About what?"

"I think you know."

"Aw, babe, do we have to start in on that again? You know how I feel. Why ruin a perfect romance with marriage?"

"It doesn't have to ruin it. Nothing will change. Look at the way we live. Unless we have somewhere in particular to go, I come home from work, then you come home from work. I fix dinner, you fix dinner, or we both fix dinner. Then we read or watch television. Sometimes, glory be, we even have meaningful conversations. What would change?''

Glenn laid his fork across his plate and looked her directly in the eye. "I seem to remember our having a similar conversation about four years ago. I also seem to recall your saying, 'I don't need a piece of paper.'"

"I was wrong, so sue me," Marilee said with a lift of her chin. "When a child is involved, I need a piece of paper."

"That's another thing. Why has this motherhood bit suddenly taken hold of you?"

"Maybe I want someone to be a problem to someday. Maybe I like the idea of my genes hanging around for the next ten generations. Maybe I don't have a reason. Maybe it's a primitive need. I want a baby, that's all."

Glenn sighed, picked up his fork and returned his attention to the cake, but Marilee had promised herself she wouldn't capitulate this time. Her heart was in her throat, but she wasn't going to back down. "I want a definite yes or no this time, Glenn. I mean it."

His mouth was full. He swallowed and took a sip of coffee. "No," he said. "I like everything just the way it is."

Silence lay over the room like a shroud. Then Marilee stood and gathered up her own plate and cup. "I see," she said, turning on her heel and going into the kitchen. She laid the dishes on the counter and gripped its edge for support. Her eyes stung, but she didn't know if the tears were brought on by sorrow or anger. Grabbing a tissue, she blotted her eyes, then squared her shoulders and returned to the dining room. Glenn was just getting up from the table.

"Then it's over," she announced in an amazingly controlled voice.

"Aw, for Pete's sake, Marilee..."

"I mean it. I'm not satisfied with things the way they are, and I'd like to think my wishes still count for something around here. I've worked hard all my life so I wouldn't have to depend on anyone for my welfare, but there are some things I can't do alone. I want a husband and a child, in that order, and since I'm not getting any younger, I can't afford to wait. I'll ask you to please sleep in the guest room tonight."

Ignoring his stunned, openmouthed expression, she went back into the kitchen and tearfully, angrily, began cleaning everything in sight.

JOHN LEMASTERS LIVED in a ranch-style house on the city's southwest side, not far from the university. The writer himself answered the door and invited Ivy and Taylor into his study, at the back of the house, a long narrow room that obviously had once been a sun porch.

LeMasters looked exactly the way Ivy tended to think "serious" writers looked. He did, in fact, remind her of her father. He had a narrow face and thinning salt-and-pepper hair. He wore dark-rimmed eyeglasses, and his expression was studious and thoughtful. Even when he smiled, he barely moved his mouth. His casual clothes were slightly rumpled and worn with the air of a man who gave little thought to what he wore.

Even his study reminded her of the one in the island bungalow. It was a mishmash of books, magazines, folders and stacks of paper, but in the middle of his large desk sat a computer and a laser printer, luxuries Gordon and Claire Loving had never known.

After inviting them to sit down and offering them something to drink, LeMasters briefly studied the formidable array of papers Ivy and Taylor had brought along. "This is an admirable amount of work," he commented.

"At least eight years' worth," Ivy said. "My parents did exhaustive research."

"Well, I'm a stickler for details myself. Did I understand you to say a publisher has expressed interest in the work?"

Ivy nodded. "My parents had planned to have something in an editor's hands by the end of the year. The name and phone number are on the front of that folder. There's an outline and maybe five or six chapters completed."

"That's good. I'm not interested in finishing someone else's work simply on speculation. I also understand, Miss Loving, that you'll be available in case I have questions."

"Yes. My phone number's there, too. And, please, call me Ivy."

LeMasters sat back in his chair and gave her what passed for a smile. "By the way, I've read *Coming of Age in Allahabad*. I found it an extremely interesting book. Are you the American girl in it?"

"To a large extent, yes."

LeMasters shifted his attention to Taylor. "Have you read the book, Mr. Edwards?"

"No, I haven't... and please call me Taylor."

"Interesting, very interesting." The writer looked back at Ivy, in particular studying her graceful hands. "Did you really spread fresh cow dung on the kitchen floor every morning?"

Taylor's head swung in Ivy's direction in time to see her nod her head. "Good Lord!" he exclaimed.

"I find that absolutely horrifying," LeMasters declared.

"Most Westerners do. All I remember is that the stuff dried in minutes to a surface almost as hard as cement, and once it dried, it was completely odorless. The Hindus thought it had antiseptic qualities."

Taylor stared at Ivy in shock. Those beautiful hands had spread *cow dung?*

"How old were you at the time?" LeMasters asked.

"Oh... about twelve, I guess. Not yet old enough to take my meals with the women."

"With the children then?"

"There were no small children, only two boys of thirteen and fifteen. I wasn't allowed to eat with them, so I took my meals alone."

"No playmates?"

"No. There was very little playing in the household. I had chores and the studies my parents gave me."

John LeMasters was vastly curious about Ivy's past, and he quizzed her for half an hour or more. Taylor listened, and a picture emerged—the picture of a girl child growing up in abject loneliness while her scholarly parents pursued their work. His heart went out to her, though she didn't seem to feel sorry for herself. It amazed him that a girl who had spent years like that had grown into such a lovely, delicate woman.

They finally took their leave of LeMasters, who promised to get in touch with Ivy as soon as he'd had time to go over the material.

"Are you satisfied with him, Ivy?" Taylor asked as they drove away. "If you aren't, we can keep looking."

"I think so. He seemed interested, and he'd read *Coming of Age*, so he knows what kind of book will be expected of him. His published credentials seemed impressive, but what do I know?" She glanced down at the book in her lap. "Perhaps after I've read this book of his I'll know more, but for now, he seems like just what we were looking for."

"Then if you're satisified, I am. Did you say you wanted to stop by the supermarket?"

"Please."

They drove in silence for a few minutes before Taylor shot a quick look at her. "Ivy, did you really..."

She giggled. "Yes, Taylor, I really spread cow dung."

"Good Lord!" he exclaimed again.

SOMETIME LATER, Ivy stood in Taylor's neat, efficient little kitchen and scraped vegetable parings into the sink where a disposer whisked them out of sight like magic. Taylor lounged in the doorway. "What are you fixing for dinner?"

"A feast," she told him with a smile.

"I'd really like to help. What can I do?"

"Nothing, thanks. Just prepare to be impressed."

Turning, he went back into the living room, and Ivy returned to her work, humming under her breath. She was feeling very good about the world and herself. She loved working at Marilee's. She was pleased that the book would be finished. And whenever she was with Taylor, she felt a rare sort of contentment that amazed her. Whatever hold he had on her was a strong one.

Then her thoughts turned to Marilee and tonight's confrontation with Glenn, and she prayed everything would go the way her friend wanted. But if it didn't, Marilee wouldn't be destroyed. She might be heartbroken for a time, but she wouldn't be devastated. The woman fascinated Ivy more with each passing day. She was a bundle of energy and so knowledgeable about so many things that Ivy could only stand on the sidelines and watch her, awestruck. That Marilee had become her friend was one of the nicest things that had ever happened to her.

As she put on a pot of water to boil for yellow rice, her thoughts took a different turn. The one disturbing note in her otherwise contented existence was the letter she'd written to Erik, and the one that had been waiting for her when she'd taken the car home. In hers, she hadn't been completely honest, and that wasn't like her. She'd made it sound as though she'd been looking for a writer all the time she'd been in Fort Worth and hadn't had any luck. She wasn't sure why she'd felt compelled to say that. She supposed she simply didn't want Erik to know she had been so caught up in this new world of hers that she had gone weeks without once thinking about the book.

Or that she often went days without thinking of him. His letter had disturbed her, for in it he'd left no doubt about what he expected to happen when she returned to the island. They would be married, and she would become mistress of the plantation. He'd made it sound like something any woman would covet, but the thought of spending her days overseeing servants and making certain her husband's days were as serene as possible no longer held appeal. *I would be bored to death.*

Ivy peered through the serving window. Taylor was seated in an easy chair, feet propped on an ottoman, reading the newspaper. So much had changed in such a short time. *She* had changed. Now when she was alone with Taylor she sensed an intimacy that didn't truly exist, except possibly in her own mind. She could no longer look at him without thinking of yesterday's kiss and her own response to it. Desire was something new to her, but it very swiftly had gotten a foothold.

Giving herself a shake, she got back to the business of preparing dinner, and very shortly she was summoning Taylor to the table.

"Wow, that looks like a masterpiece!" he exclaimed when he saw the stunning platter she set in the middle of the table. A cone-shaped mound of bright yellow rice had been surrounded by shrimp and half-a-dozen stir-fried vegetables. Atop the rice she had placed a red chili "flower." Because the vegetables had been cooked so quickly they had retained their vibrant colors. The platter looked like a still-life painting.

"In the islands, this is a dish served on festive occasions—weddings, births, birthdays and the like," she said.

"It looks almost too pretty to touch."

"You'd better touch it after all the trouble I went to."

It turned out to be as delicious as it was beautiful, and while they ate they talked. "What did you do today?" Ivy asked.

"Actually I went out on a mission for your uncles, to a ranch about thirty miles from here. Cameron Oil wants to lease a section of it."

Ivy had learned a little something about the oil business, mainly from listening to her grandmother and her uncles. "Why did they send you? Don't they employ people who do that sort of thing?"

"Sure, but the ranch is tied up in an estate, and there are three heirs. Robert and Michael thought I might be able to cut through the legalese more easily than a lease scout could. I couldn't, though. I ran up against a family feud, and it's going to take more than a battery of lawyers to settle it."

It seemed to Ivy that he was so polished, so eloquent that he could talk anybody into anything. "A feud?"

He nodded. "The ranch is jointly owned by two brothers and their sister. Seems the sister has always had to take a back seat where her brothers are concerned, but now she finds herself on an even par with them. She's enjoying the hell out of it, too. The brothers are dying for that oil lease, but she says no. She doesn't want to 'spoil' the land. She'll come around in time because it's in her best interests to, but for now, she just wants to make her brothers squirm." Taylor chuckled. "She's doing a good job of it. They are positively apoplectic."

It still amazed Ivy that a woman could get away with that—that she was even consulted in the first place, let alone that she had any influence over the final decision. The independence of American women was astonishing. Answering John LeMasters's questions earlier had taken her back to a place and time she didn't particularly care to remember. There had been nothing enviable about the lives of the women in Allahabad, and though customs were more lax on the island, women there still "knew their place." It was in the sorting sheds, the kitchen or in the parlor giving servants instructions—never by their husbands' sides for anything but decoration and, sometimes, companionship.

She looked across the table at Taylor, who was enjoying her dinner. Her heart filled her chest. She knew she was terribly ignorant about so many things, but not once had he shown that he thought she was, too. He treated her as an equal, as someone he enjoyed being around, even as the *one* person he wanted to be with to the exclusion of all others. Could that really be so? To leave and never see him again—a knot formed in her chest just thinking about it.

And then it hit her with the force of a typhoon. She loved him. Oh, she loved him so!

CHAPTER THIRTEEN

WHEN THEY FINISHED the meal, only one tired-looking heap of rice and a few tag ends of vegetables remained on the platter.

"That was wonderful, Ivy, just wonderful," Taylor enthused. "You are an excellent cook."

"Thank you. It's such a pleasure to cook in an American kitchen. A dishwasher must be the most marvelous invention ever." She stood up and began clearing the table, and over her protestations, Taylor helped her clean the kitchen. Having a man work beside her in the kitchen made her feel a little uncomfortable, but it was amazing how quickly the chore was finished when two pairs of hands were working.

She turned off the light and followed him into the living room. "I would so love to call Marilee," she commented, "but I guess I'd better not."

"Why?"

"She's giving Glenn an ultimatum tonight. Marriage or nothing. I might catch her at a bad time."

Taylor was only minimally interested in Marilee's love life, but Ivy was fascinated by it, as she was with everything else about Marilee. Strange. "Oh," was all he could think of to say.

"I received another letter from Erik today," she told him.

That got his interest. He turned. "I know. I was at Eleanor's house this morning when the mail arrived."

"He...expects me to marry him."

Taylor took a deep breath. "Did he say that in so many words?"

"Yes."

"Are you?"

Ivy looked down at the floor, chewed her bottom lip, then looked up again. "I don't see how I can."

He saw her swallow hard, and the gravity on her face touched him. She seemed to be struggling. He reached out and stroked her cheek. "Why not?"

Ivy would never know where the courage came from. Maybe it was from Marilee. *Go with your heart.* Amazingly she heard her own voice say, "I can't marry Erik because I...think I'm in love with you. I'm almost sure I am." The words came in a rush. "I've read about the symptoms, and I never felt any of them for Erik, but I have for you...all of them. Every single one."

Taylor wanted to laugh or sing or do a dance. Their embrace was immediate. He hugged her tightly, so tightly she gasped for breath, but moving away from her was impossible. "Oh, Ivy, sweet Ivy. I love you, too. I don't even have to think about it."

Now she stepped back, staring at him solemnly. "You don't have to say that just because I did."

"I know that."

"If I hadn't said it first, would you ever have said it to me?"

"Yes, eventually I would have. I'm sure of it. I never would have let you go back to that island." Cupping her face in his hands, he kissed her lingeringly. He straightened and they studied each other's eyes. Hers were wide, not fearful exactly, but expectant. His gaze traveled to the hollow of her throat; the pulse beat faster than normal. "Are you afraid of me, Ivy?"

She shook her head vigorously. "No, no. You're the nicest person I've ever known."

"Then you're afraid of what comes next." It wasn't a question.

"I don't know...maybe...a little. I don't know. I was always told it was something a woman had to do when she got married, but now...now that I've been reading, it sounds so wonderful...and I know not everyone waits for marriage."

He burrowed his face in her hair to conceal his smile. "Surely you don't think I would ravish you."

"I'm not sure I know what that means."

"You don't think I would...be rough or use force with you, do you?"

"Oh, no, Taylor. I'm sure you would never do that."

Lowering his head, he kissed her again, this time finding open lips and an eager tongue. When they broke apart, he nestled her head in the curve of his shoulder and ran a hand up and down her spine. Lord, what *should* the next move be? He hadn't been this nervous and unsure of himself with a woman since he was in his teens. He could botch it horribly or make it the most glorious experience of her life. It was all up to him, and that was scary as hell.

Then he felt her tremble and lean against him. She clutched him around the waist, as though for support. Her knees seem to give way, so he held on to her just as tightly. Why was he standing like an oaf, wondering what to do next? She wanted him, too, and if he was unsure, think how she must feel. He'd just let nature and instinct take over.

"It's going to be very nice, Ivy. I'll see to it that it is."

"It's already nice. Please kiss me again."

They kissed, again and again, until Taylor let out a groan. "Ivy…darling…a man is incapable of doing this while standing up for very long." His physical desire had become an excruciating ache.

"I can't get close enough to you," she complained. "I feel like I want to crawl up inside you."

That did it. He took her by the hand, gazing into eyes that were dark with emotion. "Do you trust me?"

"With all my heart. I've never trusted anyone the way I trust you."

Sliding a hand into the thick amber mass that framed her face, he brought his mouth down to hers. She melted into the kiss. When he lifted his head and said, "Then come with me," she followed without a shred of trepidation.

He led her down the hall to his bedroom. A massive bed covered in a thick blue-and-burgundy spread waited. *The marriage bed,* Ivy thought. The place a woman dreaded, or so her training had led her to believe. Only she and Taylor weren't married. She expected to feel awkward, but she didn't. How could she feel awkward with Taylor? He was the gentlest person on earth.

He bent over the bed and pulled down the spread, then the sheets. Straightening, he turned to her and reached for the buttons of her blouse. His fingers were deft, Ivy noticed, and quickly dispensed with the blouse. She silently blessed Marilee for insisting she have an entire new wardrobe of lingerie. The lacy bra did little more than lift and define her breasts. Certainly it didn't adequately cover them, but the sight of the swelling mounds of flesh seemed to have transfixed Taylor. He stared at them as though they were the first he'd ever seen, something she knew couldn't be true. Then his hand slipped under her arms and around her back to unclasp the bra and push it off her shoulders.

Surely it was only seconds, but it seemed to take forever for him to undress her and himself. From the articles she had read she knew the woman was supposed to help the process along, but she was unsure of how to proceed. She wasn't familiar enough with masculine clothing, and he was doing an expert job of dispensing with hers.

Then they were together, flesh to flesh, locked in a tight embrace, kissing feverishly. And somehow they were under the sheets, still kissing, their bodies molded. Ivy surprisingly didn't feel timid or embarrassed. It seemed natural to have him with her like this, so warm and strong, his body so much larger than hers. His very maleness fascinated her.

His hands were gentle but restless and seeking. Ivy wondered if she was supposed to match him gesture for gesture, but he had her in such a state of wonder and discovery she couldn't move, couldn't think. The newness of it! The excitement! The curiosity!

A hand slipped between her thighs, and she gasped in pleasure. "It's wonderful, isn't it?" he murmured.

"Oh, Taylor... it's like... nothing else on earth."

"You're right. It is." Rolling over onto her, tucking her firmly beneath him, he slowly introduced her to the rites and mysteries of love.

Naturally ignorant at first, she was neither shy nor ashamed, and her loving, spontaneous responses delighted him. There was so much love in her just waiting to be tapped. His hands stroked and petted and soothed and inflamed until he was certain she was ready for him, couldn't stand another minute without him. Entering her as gently as he could, he drowned in sensations never before experienced. It went beyond the physical to the spiritual, and Taylor discovered for the first time what it was like to give oneself completely to another human being.

And Ivy learned that there were indeed many things that two people of the same generation could teach each other.

"DID I HURT YOU?" Taylor asked much later.

Ivy's face was buried against his chest. "No."

"Not even in the beginning?"

"Maybe...a little. It was soon forgotten. It was wonderful. I feel so...so...I don't know. There aren't any words."

"How about 'I love you,'" he suggested.

She wound herself around him and hugged him ferociously. "Oh, I do, Taylor, I do. So much more than I would have thought possible."

"And I love you, Ivy. I surely do." In fact, the enormity of his feelings staggered him. She was like no one else, and he felt himself caught up in protectiveness, possessiveness, the sure knowledge that he would never, ever let her go. All of his doubts and worries had flown out the window, but only this morning they had swamped him. As he was driving away from Eleanor's house, knowing there was another letter from Erik, the thought that he might lose Ivy became the worst torment imaginable.

But now he could forget nagging doubts and enjoy, enjoy. Maybe he had been marching toward this since the day she'd walked out of the bungalow and down the rise to meet Erik's car.

"You are such a beautiful man."

"And you're a beautiful woman, so I'd say we've made a good match, right?"

Suddenly she bolted, startling him. "Oh, good heavens!" she exclaimed.

"What's wrong, sweetheart?"

"Taylor, that...that's the way babies are made." She said it in wide-eyed wonder, as though she were giving him a news bulletin.

He smiled at her fondly. "I took care of that."

"Oh." Collapsing against him again, she sighed. "I should have known. You think of everything, and I'm very stupid."

"Inexperienced. There's a difference."

"What time is it?"

Taylor partially rose on an elbow to glance at the bedside clock. "A little after ten."

"We must have slept."

"You did, I didn't."

"I suppose I should go home. Grandmother will be worried about me."

"She knows you're with me. She won't be worried."

Ivy nodded. "You're right. She trusts you the way I do."

Taylor stroked her hair, staring over the top of her head, his expression sobering. The one tarnished spot in all this was Eleanor's request of him. He wished she hadn't made it. The request hadn't had a thing to do with what was happening between Ivy and himself. They had been heading for tonight long before Eleanor had come up with her latest scheme, but he wondered if the elderly woman would now always think he had staged a deliberate seduction at her request.

Oh, why borrow doubts? *He* knew what had happened, and that was all that mattered. And no one else would ever know about the request, least of all the adorable woman by his side. "Ivy?"

"Hmm."

"You realize, of course, that you won't be returning to the island."

"Yes, I know."

"How do you feel about that? Does it trouble you at all?"

"No. Perhaps it should, but it doesn't. I could never marry Erik, and if I wasn't his wife, what would there be for me on Baksra? Life there for a woman is so structured. Here the possibilities are limitless. Oh, I know I'm still different, that I don't yet entirely fit in. I say things that make people laugh when I don't mean to be funny, and I ask stupid questions. Does that difference trouble you, Taylor?"

"Of course not. It's delightful. It's what makes you so special. I would hate it if you were just like everyone else. In fact, I don't want you changing anything anymore. Do what suits *you*. I love you just the way you are."

Smiling, Ivy rolled over and covered his body with hers. Touching his mouth with a beautifully manicured nail, she said, "You know, my parents staunchly believed that everyone controls their own destinies, but most of the islanders believe that we control little of our lives. Almost from the beginning, since I first arrived in Fort Worth, I've had the eeriest feeling that forces were at work, conspiring to keep me here, refusing to let me return to the island. Now I'm sure of it. I think love must be the greatest force of all."

He smiled back. "I think you might be right."

THE MINUTE ELEANOR SAW her granddaughter at breakfast the following morning she knew something about Ivy had changed. And if that dreamy sparkle in her eyes was any indication, she suspected she knew what the changes signified. So Taylor had given Marilee's ideas a second thought. Perhaps some hugs and kisses had been exchanged. How thrilling! She wasn't so old that she'd forgotten what it was like to be swept away on a tide of passion.

Taylor, bless him, was a fast worker. "You look especially pretty this morning, dear," she said.

"Why, thank you, Grandmother."

"Will you be going to the shop?"

"Yes. I do love it so. I'm learning a lot about retailing. Marilee knows everything, simply everything. You don't mind my being gone all day, do you?"

"Of course not. I like it that you're busy doing something you enjoy." Eleanor took a sip of tea and bit off a piece of toast. "You received another letter from that man on the island, right?"

Ivy had noticed that her grandmother never mentioned Erik by name, as though by not doing so she stripped him of an identity. Ah, Erik. The one sour note in her newfound happiness. She was going to have to write to him, and it would be a very difficult task. "Yes, I did. Why?"

"No particular reason. I simply wondered if he's putting any pressure on you to return to the island."

"He would like me to be there when he returns, but I've already written to explain why I can't. The book, you know."

"Ah, yes, the book." The blessed book, Eleanor thought.

Ivy dabbed at her lips with a napkin, then set it beside her plate. "If you'll excuse me, Grandmother, I'll go get ready for work."

"Of course, dear." Eleanor smiled fondly as she watched her granddaughter leave the dining room. Ivy spoke of going to work as though she were off to pursue a demanding career. Well, perhaps she was learning something valuable. If she really continued to enjoy retailing, she certainly would have enough money to set herself up in business someday... provided she stayed in America.

Please, dear boy, do your work well. I'm shameful, I know, she thought, *but in this case, the end justifies the means.*

IT WOULD NOT HAVE occurred to Ivy to discuss her personal relationship with Taylor with anyone, not even Marilee, who was her friend and contemporary. She wouldn't have dreamed of telling her grandmother that she was in love. She had, after all, spent most of her adult life on the island, and the islanders never spoke of personal matters or deep feelings to friends or even other family members. Perhaps husbands and wives conducted serious personal conversations, she didn't know. But beyond that, to give voice to one's innermost thoughts would have been in shockingly bad taste.

Marilee, however, had no such restraint. Ivy knew that, good or bad, she would hear virtually every detail of last night's confrontation with Glenn ... provided Marilee had actually gone through with it.

Ivy drove around to the back of the shop at her usual time, half an hour before opening. She was surprised that Marilee's car wasn't already there. The shop's proprietor always arrived a good hour before it was time to open the front door, but then there were any number of things that could have detained her.

Ivy unlocked the back door and turned on the light. Then she moved soundlessly through the shop, taking stock of everything before returning to the back room. She thought of Marilee's unvarying morning routine and put on the coffee. Her friend sipped the stuff all morning, then switched to tea in the afternoon. Ivy had read an article about the effects of large doses of caffeine and no longer wondered why Marilee reminded her of a bubbling kettle about to spill over.

The minutes ticked by, and still there was no sign of the shop's owner. As the minute hand inched toward ten, Ivy went out front, turned on the lights, unlocked the front door and turned the Closed sign around. A few minutes later a woman came in for bath powder, did some browsing and ended up buying a four-hundred-dollar dress. Marilee would be very pleased.

By ten forty-five, Ivy was getting worried. Nervously chewing her bottom lip, she went into the back room to call Marilee's apartment. She had just punched in the first digit when the back door opened and Marilee rushed in.

Ivy replaced the receiver. "I've been worried about you," she said, her voice slightly admonishing. "Where have you been?"

"Sorry, sweetie, I overslept, but I knew you'd handle everything. Oh, Ivy...*it worked!* It damn well worked! Standing before you is a woman engaged to be married!" Her smile was like a brilliant burst of sunshine.

Ivy burst into laughter. "Oh, Marilee...how wonderful. How fantastic!"

"Isn't it, though." Dumping her handbag onto the table, Marilee collapsed in a chair and stretched her arms high over her head. Ivy didn't have to ask what happened. She knew she would hear every single bit of it . . . and she was right.

"It was touch and go there for a while, I'll tell you. I was damned worried. At first he said no, absolutely not. He liked things the way they were. Oh, you would have been so proud of me. I was absolutely magnificent. So, says I with my little heart breaking into a million pieces, get out." Marilee paused for a minute to frown, but the exuberance was soon back. "I thought he was going to do it there for a minute, but then he came into the kitchen where I was cleaning the toaster, raving like a madman, telling me I was being stubborn and impractical. I didn't budge, not a centimeter. So finally he said, 'Okay, okay, if you feel so strongly about it, we'll get married.' And I said, 'Then ask me,' and he said, 'Marilee, will you marry me?'" She clapped her hands together with glee. "So I'm late because I spent half the night thanking him."

"I'm so happy for you," Ivy said, feeling oddly like crying. "When is the wedding?"

"In six weeks. I need some time to get ready. I'm going to throw myself a grand affair. God knows, I deserve it. And, Ivy, you'll be my maid of honor, of course."

"Me? But surely you have someone else who . . ."

Marilee shook her head. "I don't have any sisters, and all my former best friends have scattered to the four winds. You just have to do it."

"Then, thanks. I'm very flattered."

Business was slow this time of the year. No one was much interested in the lovely fall clothes that were arriving daily, not when the temperatures remained in the nineties, so Ivy and Marilee spent most of the day in the upstairs bridal salon. Marilee tried on dress after dress, all of them breathtakingly lovely to Ivy's notion, but she also noticed that not even demure bridal white could make Marilee look subdued.

The woman twisted and preened in front of a bank of mirrors. "I'll wear white, and you'll wear red. How I love blondes in red. Red and white all over the place. Red roses, white roses, red velvet ribbons, white satin ribbons. I wonder who I should get to walk me down the aisle. I haven't seen my father in years. He and Mom divorced when I was just a kid. What do you think of the veil? Yes or no? How about this little number? It's gorgeous from the back, and that's what everyone sees anyway. Oh, hell, I'll just walk myself down the aisle. Why do I need someone to give me away?"

By now Ivy had learned that a great many of Marilee's questions didn't require answers, just as much of what she said followed no logical conversational pattern. She just sat on the sidelines, smiling as gown after gown was modeled. But when Marilee brought out the one she wanted her maid of honor to wear, Ivy's eyes almost popped out of her head.

It was the single most beautiful garment she had ever seen, and she had seen plenty of lovely clothes since she'd been working at Marilee's. In vibrant red, the front was rather demure with a jewel neckline and nipped-in waist, but the demureness stopped at the knee where the dress exploded into row after row of ruffles.

"We'll get some pumps dyed to match the dress. Stark white pearls at the neck," Marilee decided. "Oh, Ivy, you'll be spectacular!" She hesitated and frowned. "Why am I doing this? I should put you in some plain little ice-blue thing that'll fade into the woodwork. I'm supposed to be the center of attention that day."

Ivy smiled. "Marilee, I can't imagine your ever not being the center of attention, wedding or not."

IVY AND TAYLOR WERE together every minute that could be arranged. Sometimes he took her to a charming French bistro he had discovered, where she learned to appreciate and enjoy all manner of food. Once he took her to a disco, a less successful venture. The music, she thought, was dreadful—loud and without melody. Fortunately she discovered that such places weren't his favorites, either. As the temperature dipped a bit, they took bicycles to Trinity Park. Those outings prompted Ivy to recall the first entire day she had spent with him on the island, and how much had transpired since.

But the best times were when they were alone in his apartment. There they spent hours talking, for Ivy was learning there was nothing wrong with talking about her feelings, that talking to the right person sometimes enabled her to sort out some of the more difficult aspects of her life. Taylor was wonderful to talk to because he really listened.

They were lying cuddled together in his bed one night when she responded to his inquiry about her parents. "I don't think Mom and Dad *meant* to be cold and distant. They certainly were very close to each other. I think it was more that I was a child, and they were intellectuals who never could bring themselves down to my level. I hate to say this, Taylor, but I think my birth was an accident. They simply weren't the kind of people who would deliberately plan to have a child. Discussions in our house were always so cerebral. I don't ever recall their talking about... trivia. When Grandmother tells me about my mother as a child—games, birthday parties, pep rallies in high school—it doesn't sound like Claire Loving at all. I've tried, but I simply can not picture my mother at a football game."

"Ivy, darling, tell me something," Taylor said after that particular revelation. "By the time you were, oh, say, eighteen, you must have remembered a lot about your grandparents. Why didn't you come back?"

She chewed her bottom lip thoughtfully. "I didn't know how to think for myself, to operate on my own. I wouldn't have had the slightest idea how to strike out for America. The most independent move of my life was to leave the university. My parents were very unhappy about that, but I was so miserable there I didn't care. The island became a refuge I was afraid to leave." Turning in his arms, she kissed the underside of his chin. "You never talk much about your own childhood."

"I guess that's because it was so ordinary. Dad had a drugstore, and Mom stayed home. She and Gloria were both artsy-craftsy types. There was stuff all over the house they'd made. Dad and I went fishing and hunting together, and he's the one who put the first golf club in my hand. In high school I was a pretty fair shortstop, and I don't think Mom and Dad ever missed a game. The year Gloria got Homecoming Queen, good grief, you'd have thought she'd won Miss America or something. Like I said, it was very ordinary."

Ordinary? To Ivy it sounded so extraordinary, so different from her own childhood. "It sounds wonderful to me."

"Did you ever know your father's family?"

"No, I never did. I asked a lot of questions about them, but all I ever got were vague, unsatisfying answers. They live in Virginia and raised horses. That sounded exciting, and I asked if we could visit them someday, but all Dad ever said was, 'Maybe.' It's so strange. He was obsessed with other cultures, other societies, the way people in other lands lived and their personal relationships with one another. But his own family was completely unimportant to him. So strange.''

''Perhaps someday you and I can find your father's parents.''

''I think I'd really like that.''

And at that moment, with her lying in the warm circle of his arms, Taylor vowed that the girl-woman who had never known love and closeness would never again know anything else.

IVY WOULD NOT HAVE dreamed life could be so full. John LeMasters sometimes called her three times a week to ask questions about the book. By now she had read his book and knew without question he was the man for the job. Marilee, having unearthed a sense of style that Ivy had never known she possessed, asked her opinion about store and window displays. After being alone for much of her life, Ivy now had a doting grandmother, a host of relatives, a devoted dog, a best friend, and...

A lover. Evenings meant being with Taylor. It seemed she lived for her hours with him. She was wildly in love, and that was a feeling so hot and intense she could only wonder at it. Every time he smiled at her or winked at her or touched her—especially then—happiness washed over her in waves. It was wonderful to feel so alive and free of the restrictions that had governed much of her life. Each morning she awoke overcome by an almost giddy sense of self. She felt like a princess in a fairy tale.

However, she conceded, this fairy tale had an ogre, and it was the letter she knew she had to write to Erik. She had received his answer to the one she'd written to him explaining about the book. In it he sounded rather like a stern father ordering a wayward child to return to the fold. If she needed any proof that she no longer was Ivy Loving of Baksra, she only had to recall her reaction to that. She had been furious at the letter's supercilious tone.

Still she put off writing Erik that she wouldn't be returning to the island at all. Taylor asked her almost daily if she'd done it, and she knew he was disappointed that she hadn't.

Tonight was no exception. "You've got to do it, sweetheart," he said.

She so loved that endearment. "I know. And I will, I promise. I've just been so busy with Marilee's wedding."

"That's a cop-out, and you know it."

"A cop-out?"

"A flimsy excuse."

"It's very difficult."

"I'm sure it is. All the more reason to get it over with."

Every day Ivy meant to write the letter, but she felt it had to be as diplomatic as possible. Erik, who had been her parents' friend and who had done her the

Baksrani honor of asking her to be his second wife, did not deserve what Marilee referred to as a "Dear John."

But Ivy's days were so full. She was with Taylor almost every evening and at the shop before it opened at ten. She tried to spend at least one private hour with her grandmother every day, and Jethro pouted if she was in such a rush she had no time for him.

Somehow the letter just didn't get written.

CHAPTER FOURTEEN

IN THE PAST, whenever Marilee had thought about the possibility of someday getting married, she had sworn she would do it quietly, privately. Perhaps it would be in someone's garden with only her mother and a few close friends in attendance. Though she herself had profited handsomely off generous parents who wanted their daughter to have the best they could afford, she privately had thought it was silly to spend so much money on something that lasted such a short time.

But now she had changed her mind. She wanted the works, every single thing. Flowers everywhere, an elaborate cake, engraved invitations and, of course, a stunning gown. The ceremony would take place in a church, someone would sing "Because," and it would be a ceremony that would make the editors of *Bride's* magazine weep with envy.

She could pull it off, too. She was a bridal consultant, wasn't she? Upstairs there was an entire salon of goodies to pick from, and she could have oodles more by picking up the phone. And she had a favorite florist, a favorite caterer, a favorite engraver and a favorite photographer, people to whom she had sent legions of blushing brides-to-be. They all owed her a lot, and she intended demanding a lot. She seemed to live with a phone stuck to her ear.

Ivy watched all the activity in awe. She couldn't believe there were so many details to be taken care of, and the wonder of it was, Marilee was planning three other weddings at the same time and not missing a beat on any of them.

"You know, Marilee, it isn't necessary for you to close the shop while you and Glenn are on your honeymoon. I can run it for you," Ivy said as she watched her friend dress a mannequin for the display window in front.

"No, I always close for a week every year anyway, so that will be as good a time as any. You could do with some time off, too. Pretty soon we'll be in our busiest time of the year, hip hip hooray, and your little hands are going to be mighty welcome around here."

"Where are the two of you going on your honeymoon?"

"It's a secret, even to me. Glenn's making all the arrangements, and I won't know our destination until we're at the airport. Isn't that romantic?" Suddenly Marilee's expression altered, and her hands stopped their work. "Oh, God, he wouldn't!"

"Wouldn't what?"

"Glenn is the world's biggest baseball fan. He wouldn't do something dreadful like...take me to the World Series, would he?"

"What's the World Series?" Ivy wanted to know.

Then Marilee's hand flew to her forehead. "No, no, it'll be too early for that. Whew! Thank God!"

"Where would *you* like to go?"

"Oh...someplace wonderfully elegant. A place where I have to change clothes four times a day. Maybe The Plaza in New York or the Mark Hopkins in San Francisco...or a posh resort somewhere. Vail, maybe. Aspen. Or Paris...or London. Those are places I was positively *meant* to be seen in." Giving the mannequin's derriere a pat, Marilee turned from her handiwork.

Ivy was completely caught up in the prewedding excitement. Except for falling in love with Taylor, she considered it the most thrilling thing she had ever been involved in. So it came as a surprise—and a disappointment—to learn he didn't even plan to attend.

"You aren't going to the wedding?" she asked in disbelief. "You aren't going to see me walk down the aisle in that beautiful red dress?"

"That's the part I regret, the *only* part I regret, I might add, but you can model it for me afterward. Sweetheart, that's the weekend of the club's biggest tournament of the year. I've already paid my entry fee, and David Ernst expects me to be there. A number of our clients are playing." Then he gave her the smile that made her heart melt, and she put her disappointment aside. She guessed weddings were more exciting for women than men anyway.

Basically Ivy was so happy she felt as though her feet were three inches off the ground, but sometimes when she was alone with her thoughts and Jethro for company, one nagging doubt troubled her.

What came next? She adored Taylor, and even with her limited experience, she could tell he adored her, too. But not once had he discussed the future beyond next week or next month.

Well . . . Christmas, a couple of times. He declared that Christmas at the Cameron house was an event not to be missed. It had been so long since Ivy had celebrated a real Christmas she could scarcely remember what it was like. The weather would have turned cold by then, and she wondered how she would react to that. She had to return to her grandmother's photograph albums to remember the enormous decorated tree in the living room with brightly wrapped gifts spilling over the floor. Taylor apparently felt that Christmas this year would be momentous.

But what about *them?* She did so wish she knew what his plans for the future were. Did he intend for things to just go on the way they were, or was he going to marry her?

Then an alarming thought crossed her mind. Taylor was thirty-seven and had never been married, and even he admitted that if he'd wanted to badly enough, he wouldn't have let money stand in the way. What if he was one of those men who couldn't make a commitment to marriage? Marilee insisted the woods were full of them. If that was true in Taylor's case, would she be content being his lover?

Ivy didn't have to brood on that long. The answer was no, definitely not. Like Marilee, she would want to be a mother, and mothers needed to be married.

So, could she do what Marilee did—issue an ultimatum? That was harder to answer. She wasn't much of an ultimatum giver. But she knew one thing—she loved him and wanted to be married to him. If he didn't ask her soon . . . well, she just might ask him what his intentions were. She'd go with her heart.

THE FINAL WEEKS before the wedding were hectic, so much so that Ivy hardly saw her grandmother or Taylor. She had to run the shop by herself most of the time since Marilee had to tend to dozens of other things. That meant Ivy opened, closed, unpacked new shipments, everything. She often worked late, and on those nights, Taylor came to the shop to give her a hand. And he declared that no one would be happier than he when Marilee was finally married. He wanted things back the way they were.

"Exactly the way they were?" Ivy asked.

"Exactly."

"No changes?"

"Why would I want to change anything?" he asked.

"Don't you think all the wedding to-do has been exciting?"

"No, it's been a huge pain in the butt. Half the time if I want to see you, I have to come down here to the store. You're too tired at the end of the day to talk. Why women get themselves involved in these things is a mystery."

Ivy sighed. She had hoped all the wedding talk would have put some ideas in his head. Maybe he really wasn't the marrying kind. The thought was so frightening, so depressing, that it made her quite miserable for the remainder of the day.

FOUR DAYS BEFORE the wedding, Marilee's mother arrived. Doris Huntley was a soft-spoken, sweet-faced woman in her fifties, so different from her vivacious daughter it was almost funny. And the woman's arrival necessitated a move to a motel for Glenn. "Poor baby," Marilee said to Ivy, "but my mother is from another century. She wouldn't approve."

"But won't she see all of Glenn's stuff around?" Ivy asked, surprised that her mother's approval was of such paramount importance to Marilee. That was a side of her friend she'd never seen.

"Oh, I'll just tell her he's been moving in little by little because we've decided to live in my apartment rather than his. She'll probably put two and two together, but she won't say anything. We'll both pretend I'm a virgin bride."

Then the big day finally arrived, and Ivy thought she was at least as nervous and excited as Marilee was. The walk down the aisle with all those eyes trained on her seemed a torturous mile to her. But it had to have been the most beautiful ceremony ever held, and Marilee was the most gorgeous bride imaginable. Glenn wore sort of a bemused expression and looked terribly uncomfortable in his tuxedo, but when they exchanged their vows, his expression changed to one of absolute adoration.

Ivy was enchanted with the whole affair. The reception in a nearby restaurant after the ceremony was lavish and well attended. Marilee, she noticed, drank a goodly amount of champagne, getting merrier as the party went on. Her friend was having the time of her life.

At last it was time for the bride and her maid of honor to go to the ladies' lounge to get Marilee dressed for going away. Ivy helped her out of her bridal gown.

"Wow, I'm buzzing!" Marilee exclaimed as they closed the door behind them. "Oh, Ivy, I adored every glorious minute of it! I loved the music and the walk down the aisle and the staid old minister and the flowers and cutting the cake. I'm still not too crazy about the word *wife,* but how much can a person change? Are you sure you don't mind taking care of all this stuff, sweetie?"

"I'll gather it all up and take it to your apartment," Ivy assured her.

"You've got the key?"

"Yes, it's in my bag. Don't worry about small details, Marilee. I'll take care of everything. You just concentrate on Glenn and being married." Sentimental tears formed in Ivy's eyes. She was thrilled for Marilee . . . and not just a little envious.

"You're a doll. Listen, I'll call tomorrow and tell you where we are. God, I hope it's someplace that just reeks with class and elegance. I have such gorgeous clothes."

"I know." Ivy carefully hung the bridal gown while Marilee slipped into the beautiful suit she had chosen as her going-away outfit. Just then there was a rap on the door. "Marilee," Glenn called. "Get a move on. We've got a plane to catch."

"Right," she called back. "Just a minute." She gave herself one last scrutiny in the mirror, then turned to hug Ivy. "Thanks so much for everything. The bridal bouquet is yours. That's tradition—whoever gets the bouquet will be the next one to get married, and I just know that's going to be you. I can tell by the look on your face every time Taylor's around."

"I must confess something. He hasn't said a word about marriage."

"He will. Eleanor and I are blinking geniuses to have even thought of it. We knew it would work, and it did. Oh, we'll have such a good time, Ivy. You really are the best friend I've ever had. We'll do all sorts of married-women things like . . . well, I don't know like what, but we'll learn."

Another rap on the door. "Marilee, for God's sakes!"

"Coming! Bye, sweetie. Much love and happiness. Give Taylor a big hug and kiss for me and tell him 'well done.'"

Marilee swept out of the door in a flurry, leaving a very stunned and disbelieving Ivy in her wake. When had her grandmother and Marilee even talked to each other? She didn't want to think what she was thinking, but how could Marilee be so sure Taylor would propose? Was there some sort of conspiracy afoot, something involving herself and Taylor? What had her grandmother and Marilee asked him to do? Make her fall in love with him? Her stomach made a sickening revolution as one thing occurred to her.

FOR THE NEXT HOUR OR SO, Ivy took care of everything that needed doing, but her movements were like those of a robot. She loaded all of Marilee's wedding paraphernalia into her car and drove to her friend's apartment, where she carefully put everything away, including the top of the cake in the freezer. Then she drove home. All very normal actions. But inside, her heart felt like lead, her eyes stung with unshed tears and her mind had not been at rest since she'd left the reception.

As she walked through the front door, she was accosted by Wilma. "Mrs. Cameron isn't feeling well and has retired for the evening, Ivy. May I get you something to eat?"

"No, I . . . there was a reception . . . a lot of food. Grandmother isn't seriously ill, is she?"

"I don't think so. She tires easily, which is to be expected at her age, I suppose, but she also has trouble sleeping sometimes. She's taken a sedative, so if she gets a good night's sleep, she should feel fine in the morning. Oh, my dear, you look absolutely worn-out, too. That's all those big weddings are good for. Are you sure I can't get you something?"

"I'm sure. I think I'll just go to my room."

"Of course. By the way, Mr. Edwards called. He said he's gotten tied up in some kind of social gathering tonight, but he'll see you tomorrow night."

"Thank you, Wilma. If . . . if he should happen to call again tonight, will you tell him I've gone to bed?"

"Of course. Good night."

Jethro followed Ivy up the stairs and into the room, taking his usual spot on the floor near the bed. In a daze, she took off the red dress, hung it in the closet and slipped on a robe. Then she went to sit on the bed and put herself through the painful ordeal of thinking.

Marilee had had too much champagne, hadn't she? She had been babbling, not even making sense half the time. She couldn't have actually meant that Eleanor Cameron had asked Taylor to make her granddaughter fall in love with him.

She wasn't that drunk. Everything else she said made perfect sense. And I've known for some time that Grandmother would do anything to keep me here.

Ivy couldn't believe Taylor would go along with such a thing, that he would do something like that to her. She had thought they were so close... tight, Marilee would have called it. She trusted him. He wouldn't do it.

Don't be ridiculous. Taylor would do anything Eleanor asked him to do, anything. He's admitted that much on more than one occasion.

Ivy tried to make sense of her jumbled thoughts. It now seemed that Taylor's behavior toward her had undergone a marked change right after Erik's first letter arrived. And she knew the letter had upset her grandmother. She could envision the scenario as clearly as if she had witnessed it herself. Her grandmother had done everything she could—had offered her a fortune, but only if she stayed in America. Ivy was sure it was her grandmother who had suggested Taylor take her to visit his sister and see her "perfect" marriage at work. Only that had backfired, hadn't it? What was left? Why a blazing love affair, of course.

But Americans took blazing love affairs lightly indeed, falling in and out of love, marrying and divorcing at will. For all she knew, Taylor had been in love dozens of times... and would be in love dozens more. Ivy felt sick to her stomach. So that's why there had been no planning for the future. There wasn't going to be one. How had he planned to handle that, just go on courting her until there was no way she could go back to the island, then break it off? Gradually, she was sure. Gently, of course. Taylor had too much finesse to ever be overtly severe or brutal.

Dear God, he was a good actor! The first sob caught in her throat, and she willed herself not to think about the hours she had lain in his arms, sated and so in love she thought she could fly.

She felt so *stupid,* so naive and ignorant. The veneer of sophistication she had acquired since coming to Texas had been thin indeed, and she certainly wasn't adept at playing the kind of games Marilee was forever telling her about. She never should have left the safe world of the island.

Jethro, as if sensing her unhappiness, came to rest his chin on her lap, looking up at her. "Oh, no, you don't," Ivy said, her voice breaking. "Don't look at me with those sad eyes. Go on back over there. Go on, now." And the dog obeyed...but still he watched her.

Ivy stood, hugging herself as she walked to the window to stare out at the dark night. Tears streamed down her cheeks. She brushed them away angrily. She couldn't think and cry at the same time, and she *had* to think.

Surprisingly, she wasn't the least angry at her grandmother. *She's guilty of nothing more than wanting me to stay.* But Taylor? That was something else. He had used her in the most despicable manner possible, and it had been pitifully easy for him. It seemed now that all he'd done was open his arms, and she'd fallen into them. Ignorant, gullible little Ivy.

You could still have a full life here, even without Taylor. You have your grandmother, your family, and you'll be a very wealthy woman.

But that was meaningless to her. Basically she still was a girl from an Indonesian island, and America was no place for her. At least on Baksra she would have Erik, who would take care of her because he wanted to, not because someone asked him to. Thank God she had never gotten around to writing that letter.

Of course, Erik might not want her now, either, but that was something she would face when the time came. She would be completely honest with him, tell him about Taylor and then ... what was the expression? Let the chips fall where they may.

She ached with pain and humiliation, but gradually her mind cleared. With a determination and sense of purpose that surprised her, she reached into her handbag and withdrew her wallet to inspect its contents. She had a credit card and almost three hundred dollars. It was enough, she decided. She didn't need much. Slowly she made her plans.

First she had to call the airline. Then she had to pack. She would take only the things she had brought from the island. All the lovely things she had acquired since coming to America would be of no use to her on Baksra. Most of them hadn't even been worn so perhaps Marilee could take them back and resell them. Then she would write her grandmother a note and put it at her place at the dining room table.

All of this would have to be done tonight, before anyone stirred in the morning. No matter what time her plane left, she would have to be out of the house before Wilma went out for the morning paper. She didn't think she could look her grandmother in the face and say, "I'm leaving." And certainly if she saw Taylor again, she would break down completely, the ultimate humiliation. So she would leave early, and once she got back to the island, she would write to Marilee and to John LeMasters. If he needed her help, it would have to be done by mail.

Ivy was amazed at how simple and logical it all sounded. She was astonished at how calm she was. Pivoting, she walked to the nightstand and took the phone directory out of the drawer. Then she met Jethro's gaze. If she hadn't known better, she would have sworn he looked at her accusingly.

"You'll be all right," she said in a shaky voice. "You got along just fine before I came, and you will after I'm gone. You've been a real pal and a buddy, but please understand, Jethro. I have to do this. I can't stay here."

Going back was not going to be as easy as getting here had been, Ivy discovered after a lengthy discussion with the reservations agent, chiefly because the direct flight to Sydney had been discontinued. She would not only have to change planes in Hawaii, she would have to change airlines. Her confidence faltered. "I've never done that before. Is it difficult?"

The agent sounded amused. "No, there'll be someone to help you. Just don't be afraid to ask."

"All right. Just get me to Djakarta."

"Will do, ma'am. How do you want to pay for this?"

She gave him her credit card number, he confirmed her reservations, and she hung up. She would have a depressingly long wait at the airport in the morning and another one in Hawaii. But at least it was done.

Now she could cry.

EVEN THOUGH IT WAS Sunday morning, Wilma rose at her usual time, six-thirty, and after dressing, she moved through the silent house to bring in the morning paper. But as she entered the foyer, she stopped and frowned. Jethro was lying on the floor at the door, whimpering. How odd. Normally the dog didn't come down until Ivy did.

When she opened the door, the dog was forced to move, but he didn't go upstairs, nor did he head for the side door to be let out. Wilma retrieved the newspaper from the porch, carried it to the dining table, then stopped and frowned again.

There was an envelope at Mrs. Cameron's place. The word *Grandmother* had been written on the outside. The maid stared at it a minute, her frown deepening. An uneasiness overtook her, which was probably silly. Turning, she went upstairs.

Ivy wasn't in her room. Of course that meant nothing. But she was so good about informing them of her plans. It seemed she would have told them if she had an early-morning engagement. She surely would have told her grandmother, and Mrs. Cameron hadn't said a word.

Oh, Wilma, you're getting to be an alarmist in your old age. Ivy no doubt changed her plans and simply left a note for her grandmother to inform Mrs. Cameron of her whereabouts.

Wilma crossed the room to straighten the bed. As she pulled up the top sheet, her eye fell on the wastebasket beside the bed. It was half-full of discarded tissues, as though Ivy had been blowing her nose a lot...or crying. Once more she glanced around the room. Something just didn't *feel* right. On an impulse, she went to the closet and opened the door.

Wilma took very good care of Ivy's lovely clothes, and she always hung them in precise order—skirts together, then slacks, blouses and dresses. They all were there, just as they had been yesterday, with the addition of the beautiful red dress Ivy had worn in the wedding. Still, the closet didn't look right somehow. Suddenly it dawned on her what it was. Ivy's garment bag was gone—along with the clothes she had with her when she first arrived. They had all hung at the very back of the closet, and not one was still there.

Wilma's eyes then fell to the floor. A dozen or more pairs of expensive shoes were lined up neatly on a rack. The only shoes missing were those dreadful sandals Ivy had been wearing the day she first came to this house.

Turning, Wilma went into the bathroom. She systematically went through all the drawers and cabinets, then did the same with the drawers in the chest in the bedroom. She wasn't imagining things. The only items missing were the ones Ivy had brought with her.

Alarm overtook the servant. She thought of the note downstairs, the missing clothes, and the dog whimpering at the front door. Yes, something was very wrong, very wrong indeed.

It couldn't be helped. She would have to wake up Mrs. Cameron.

CHAPTER FIFTEEN

TAYLOR HAD JUST FINISHED shaving when the phone rang. He left the bathroom and answered it. "Hello."

"Taylor, this is Eleanor. You must come right away. Ivy's gone."

"Gone? Oh, Eleanor, she probably had something to do early this morning." He couldn't imagine what it could be, but that was the only explanation that came to him.

"No, no! There's a note. Please come. I don't know what to do."

A note? In all the years he had known Eleanor, he'd never heard such distress in her voice. And she didn't panic easily. Something really was wrong. "I'm on my way," he said, and hung up, reaching for his shirt.

He had grabbed his keys and was heading out the door when he remembered the tournament. Reversing direction, he quickly called a member of his foursome, told the man he had been up all night with the stomach flu and couldn't possibly play today. Then he ran out the door and drove the short distance to the Cameron house, his heart hammering like crazy.

Wilma answered the door and motioned toward the library. The servant's face was twisted with worry. Taylor ran down the hall to the room and was astonished to find Eleanor in robe and slippers, wearing no makeup and her hair mussed. She was the picture of despair. "What on earth has happened?" he cried.

She thrust a piece of paper into his hand, then went to her chair and buried her face in her hands. He looked down at the paper. It was a note written in Ivy's neat, schoolgirlish handwriting.

Dear Grandmother,

I'm sorry, but I can not stay. I don't belong here and never will, but I'll always remember how much you wanted me to. I don't have enough money to get to the island, so I will have to use the credit card. I will mail it back to you the minute I can. All of the lovely clothes you bought for me are hanging in the closet. I'm sure Marilee will take back the ones that haven't been worn and give you credit for them. I can't thank you enough for all you've done for me, and please thank Wilma and Consuelo for their many kindnesses. I will write to you as soon as I get to Baksra.

I love you,
Ivy

Taylor had to read the note twice before he would let himself believe it. "What in the hell could have happened?" he asked in astonishment.

"I don't know. I've never been so upset. Wilma said Ivy looked terrible when she came in last night, but she attributed that to fatigue over the wedding."

"Does anybody have any idea how long she's been gone?"

"No, but Wilma went out for the paper at about six forty-five, and she had already left."

Taylor was completely perplexed. "I talked to her yesterday morning. She was fine, all excited about the wedding, and..." Could something have happened at the wedding? But what? She didn't know any of the people who were attending the thing.

"You've got to do something," Eleanor exclaimed.

"Well, I..." He snapped his fingers and headed for the desk. "Is there a phone directory here?"

"Yes, center drawer. What are you going to do?"

"Check on some airline schedules. Ivy isn't a seasoned traveler. She won't know any way to get to the island except the way we came. I want to find out what's going to L.A. this morning...or what's already gone."

"What will you do if she's already left?"

Taylor took a deep breath. "Go after her," he said. Finding the number he wanted, he called to check on flights to Los Angeles. "Has there been a flight out to L.A. this morning?'' he asked the man on the phone.

"Four-sixteen will be boarding in...in about thirty minutes."

"And that's the only one this morning?"

"So far."

"What gate will it be departing from?"

"Eighteen."

"Is there a passenger on that flight named Ivy Loving?"

Taylor heard a chuckle. "Oh, yes, I remember her well. She doesn't seem to have done a great deal of traveling."

"Good. I want you to do something for me. My name is Taylor Edwards. I'm a Fort Worth attorney, and you simply must detain Miss Loving until I can get to the airport."

"Well, I'm not sure anyone around here has the authority to do that, Mr. Edwards."

"It's very important that she not get on that plane. There's been a family emergency." Taylor looked across the room at Eleanor's stricken face. That was the truth if he'd ever told it.

"Gosh, that's too bad. Do you want me to say something to the lady?"

"No! Nothing, please. She's very sensitive, and this is something that's going to have to be handled delicately. I'm on my way."

Hanging up, he turned to Eleanor with a sigh of relief. "So far, so good. Her flight doesn't leave for half an hour."

"Wh-what if you can't make it in time?"

"I'll go after her, of course."

"I don't know what I would do without you, Taylor. Honestly, I don't."

"Don't worry, Eleanor. We'll get her back."

He hoped with all his heart.

IVY FELT as though she'd been in the waiting room half her life. She had left the house at six-fifteen. When she'd called for a taxi, she'd asked that they not honk; she would be waiting on the porch. Now she was starving, having arrived at the airport before seven, over two hours ago. Earlier, she had purchased a cup of coffee and a doughnut, all she would allow herself. Everything about traveling was so expensive, and she didn't want to spend any more of her grandmother's money than was absolutely necessary. She was going to have to watch every penny. It was a long, long way to Baksra. A sob caught in her throat at the thought of the island. Could she make herself fit back into her old life after all that had happened to her? She'd have to.

A headache was pounding at her temples. It was exhausting trying not to think of certain things—her grandmother, Jethro, Marilee, John LeMasters. And Taylor, of course. She couldn't think of him. He had broken her heart, but she still loved him. Would always love him. Being married to Erik wouldn't change that.

She glanced up to see the airline agent staring at her once more. When their eyes collided, he looked away, but he was making her nervous. Was it her clothes or her sandals? She had seen stranger-looking clothes during the past two hours. And there was some sort of policeman lounging against the far wall. Was it her imagination or was *he* watching her, too. If they didn't board that plane soon, she thought she might scream. Turning, she stared out the big window, then closed her eyes.

The agent chanced another look at her. Ever since that lawyer had called, he had been watching the woman, trying to think of some way to detain her. So far nothing had come to him. She had an expression of sadness or fear or a combination of both, and she had a death grip on her handbag. Man, he wished that lawyer would get here.

The agent glanced at his watch for the tenth time. He was going to have to give the boarding call for first-class passengers in five minutes, and not long after that the lawyer would just be out of luck.

TAYLOR WONDERED why he had never before noticed how far away the damned airport was. Thank God it was Sunday morning. The traffic was as sparse as it ever got, which wasn't saying a whole lot. The clock on the dashboard seemed to be twirling instead of ticking. And once he reached the terminal, he had to pray they hadn't changed gates on him, something they were famous for doing.

He sped through the entrance, stopping to collect his parking ticket from the machine. Then he forced himself to slow down to the speed limit. The airport police were an unforgiving lot.

Naturally the only parking place he could find was on the third level. He raced up the stairs and across the street, dodging automobiles and honking taxis, and sprinted through the entrance doors. Looking ahead, he saw that he was at Gate 10. Turning, he began to run.

"ATTENTION, Los Angeles passengers. Flight 416 is now boarding at Gate 18. Please have your boarding passes ready."

A sea of humanity uncurled from seats and began moving toward the exit. Ivy wearily stood and followed them, clutching her ticket.

"Miss Loving?"

Ivy turned to see the agent who had been staring at her. "Yes."

"May I see your ticket?"

"Why?"

"I have to double-check it against this list. You are traveling a great distance, you know."

Ivy knew so little about traveling that she didn't realize the request made absolutely no sense. She slipped out of line and handed him the ticket.

The agent didn't know why he was doing this, but that lawyer had sounded so desperate that he was going to buy as much time for him as possible. He thumbed through her tickets, pretending to check them against an imaginary list, until he heard her sigh impatiently. Shrugging, he smiled and said, "Thank you," and handed the tickets back to her. Ivy returned to the line inching its way down the ramp.

"*Ivy!*" A strong hand grabbed her arm and spun her around. "Ivy, what in the hell are you doing?" Taylor was so out of breath he could hardly get the words out. He took in the sight of her. She was wearing the blue sarong and top she wore that night in the hotel, but she didn't look the same because she wasn't the same. "What are you doing?" he repeated.

"I'm going home," she said, her chin trembling.

"Home? *This* is your home."

"I beg your pardon, sir," the agent said, clearing his throat. "Are you Mr. Edwards?"

"What? Oh . . . yes."

"Thank God," the man said, returning to his work with relief.

Taylor took Ivy by the arm and forced her back into the waiting area. "Leave me alone, Taylor. I'll miss my plane."

"You're damned right you'll miss it!" Gently pushing her down into a chair, he sat beside her, holding on to her arm. "You're not going anywhere till you tell me what's going on."

The waiting area had emptied out of all but perhaps a dozen people who were waiting for the next flight departing Gate 18. Several looked up from behind newspapers.

"I can't stay here!" she cried. "I don't belong. I'll never belong."

"What brought this on?"

Ivy set her jaw in a determined line and looked away from him.

"Did something happen at the wedding yesterday?"

She refused to answer.

He grabbed her shoulders and forced her to face him. "Dammit, I broke every traffic law in the book getting here on time, and now you're going to tell me what's going on."

"I'll miss my plane."

"You're not getting on that goddamned plane!" he roared. A few more heads came out from behind newspapers. A woman seated three seats away looked up from her knitting.

"Tell me what happened, Ivy!"

Ivy lifted her chin defiantly. "You've used me, betrayed me, made me think things that aren't so."

Taylor threw up his hands. "What are you talking about?"

She bit her bottom lip, then chanced a direct look at him. "Did my grandmother ask you to make me fall in love with you?"

So that was it! Taylor couldn't believe it. "Who told you that?" he asked, though he was sure he knew. Eleanor certainly would never say such a thing, so it had to have come from Marilee's mouth.

"Marilee. Well, she didn't say it in so many words, but I definitely got the impression . . ."

"Ah! No one who talks that much can be telling the truth all the time. There's not that much truth in the world!" He was almost yelling.

"Did Grandmother ask you to pretend to fall in love with me so I would fall in love with you?"

"As a matter of fact, she did, but—"

"Oh! How could you? I loved you with all my heart, and you were just playing a game." Ivy made a move to stand, but Taylor held her down.

"Why didn't you ask Eleanor what I said when she made that ridiculous request? Why? Why were you so sure I was guilty of . . . what you're accusing me of?"

"Because you would do anything for my grandmother, *anything* . . . and she would do anything to keep me here. I'm not very bright, Taylor. I know I'm not, but even stupid little Ivy can figure that one out."

Taylor took a deep breath. "Have I ever, ever once indicated to you that I thought you weren't bright? Have I ever, ever indicated that I thought you were anything but the most delightful woman I've ever met? Have I?"

Ivy looked away. He was so eloquent, so smooth. She had to keep her guard up. "How did you know I had left?"

"Eleanor phoned me."

"Ah! And told you to come and get me, right?"

"Yes! What did you expect her to do? She adores you. Did you honestly think she would let you just leave without trying to stop you? Ivy, listen to me, please...."

"No!"

Taking her by the shoulders again, he looked into her eyes. "You're going to listen to me. Do you know what I told Eleanor? I told her I wasn't going to manipulate your emotions, that anything that happened between us had to be honest. I was already in love with you when she made that request, so naturally I intended doing everything I could to make you love me back. But only because *I* wanted to, not because Eleanor asked me to. I love you so much. I want you to be my wife."

Ivy swallowed hard and looked at him skeptically. "If that's true, wh-why haven't you told me that before?"

"Well, I...you wouldn't write that letter to Erik, and that scared me. And I was waiting for the stupid wedding to be over, for things to get back to normal. We haven't really had time to talk lately. I guess I thought you *knew*."

"I...didn't. I thought you loved me, but I didn't know whether or not you wanted to marry me."

"What else would I want?"

"Marilee says the woods are full of men who can't commit to marriage."

"Don't always listen to Marilee!" he barked. "She doesn't know everything!"

"Don't shout at me!" Her eyes filled with tears.

"Ah, sweetheart, don't cry. I'm sorry. It's just that..." Taylor had never felt so at a loss in his life. He took a deep breath and tried again. "Think back over the past months. Think of all the time we've spent together. I have no social life except for you. Every minute I'm not working I spend with you. Now, no man does that unless he wants to."

Ivy didn't know what to think. He sounded sincere, he *looked* sincere. But did she really believe him down deep in her heart, or did she just want to believe him?

Taylor saw her falter, and he pressed his advantage. Sliding out of the chair, he knelt before her and took her hands in his. "You can't go back to the island, sweetheart. You have nothing there and everything here. If you go back, I'll just follow you. If you actually try to marry Erik, I'll throw myself over the goddamned incense pots. Spare me that, please. I love you, and more than anything in the world, I want to marry you. I don't have anywhere near the money you'll have, and I never will, but..."

"Oh, Taylor, the money has nothing to do with anything. Millions of dollars mean nothing to me. Would I have left, knowing I was giving up a fortune if it meant anything to me? All I care about is you, and it broke my heart to think you were making love to me only to please my grandmother."

"How could you think that, even for a minute?"

Neither of them noticed that everyone in the waiting area was staring at them, that the only sound was their voices, that the waiting passengers were as intent on them as they were on each other.

"How could you not know that I love you?" Taylor pleaded.

She looked at him fully, and then she saw it . . . the love. A quiet feeling of joy seeped into her veins. She was so tired her mind wasn't working well, but she believed he was telling her the truth. He could have fulfilled her grandmother's wishes with much less than he'd done, so Ivy had to believe he'd spent so much time with her because he'd wanted to...because he really did love her. "I guess because I was... scared."

"You don't have to be scared any longer. You and I are going to have a wonderful life together. You're the dearest person in the whole world." He stood and held out his hand. "Come on, let's go home."

She hesitated, then nodded and reached for his hand. "Yes, let's," she said, and stood up, slipping her arm around his waist. They stood locked together for a long, wordless minute.

"Sweetheart, I'm not ever going to let you go," Taylor vowed.

As they turned to leave, they both were startled when every one of the people in the waiting area broke into delighted applause. "I'm proud of you, boy," someone called. "Real proud."

Ivy smiled in embarrassment, and over her shoulders she saw Flight 416 taxiing away from the gate. "Good heavens," she said. "My luggage is on its way to California."

"We can have the airline get it and send it back."

Ivy thought about it. "No, don't bother. There's nothing in it...just the remnants of a life that no longer exists."

ELEANOR WAS CERTAIN she had never spent a more miserable two hours. Her composure, which she never allowed to slip—even under trying circumstances—had vanished completely. Wilma hovered worriedly over her. "Ma'am, you really need to eat something. Tea and toast, perhaps?"

"Thank you, Wilma, but until I hear something from Taylor, I can't eat a bite."

"What...what do you think Mr. Edwards will do if the plane has left?"

"If I know him, he'll follow her."

"All the way to that island?"

"I imagine so."

Wilma made a tsking sound in her throat. As she turned to leave the library, her eyes fell on Jethro lying by the hearth. "He won't eat, either," she said to no one in particular.

Just then Jethro's head came up; his ears stood at attention. Then he bounded to his feet and let out a roar as he ran from the room. Wilma turned to Eleanor, whose eyes had widened expectantly. In seconds, Taylor and Ivy entered the room.

"Oh, thank God," Eleanor said. "Thank God."

Ivy hurried across the room to kneel at her grandmother's feet. "I'm sorry I gave you a scare. I . . . I wasn't thinking properly."

Eleanor stroked her cheek. "It doesn't matter. All that matters is that you're here now." Her eyes strayed across the room. "I seem to spend a good deal of time thanking you, Taylor."

"Thanks aren't necessary this time, Eleanor. I would have forded snake-infested waters to get her back."

Ivy looked up at her grandmother. "I'm going to have to write to Erik immediately."

"Do you think he'll be heartbroken?"

"I don't think so. Nothing remotely romantic ever transpired between us. I rather imagine he'll wish me well. That's the kind of person he is. Oh, Grandmother, I have wonderful news. Taylor and I are going to be married."

"Oh, my dear, that *is* wonderful news. You know, I've never had the chance to plan a wedding for a bride. I've always been the mother or grandmother of the groom. I am going to give you a wedding that people will still be talking about years from now. I'll have the time of my life!"

Ivy glanced from her grandmother to Taylor, who was doing a poor job of disguising his dismay. Well, they'd talk about it. She doubted he would deny Eleanor "the time of her life."

Jethro's tail was slapping the side of Eleanor's chair. Ivy reached out and rubbed his ears. How could she have ever doubted? She had so much. At last she knew exactly what she wanted, and the miracle was, she had it all, every wonderful thing she could ever have dreamed of. At last she had come home.

CONSUELO PREPARED a gigantic breakfast, which they ate heartily. Even Eleanor appeared to be ravenous. Ivy had never seen her grandmother eat with such gusto.

And while they ate, they talked. Or rather Eleanor talked, mostly about the wedding. And the longer she talked the more elaborate the affair became. "It's been a long time, too long since this house has hosted a grand party, and this is the time for it. When the partition is removed between the parlor and Ben's old office, it makes one cavernous room that will easily accommodate a wedding. I can see it all now—a flower-decked canopy in front of the double windows, baskets of white roses, lots of white satin, and if you wait until after Thanksgiving, we can absolutely *fill* the house with white poinsettias.''

From time to time Ivy looked at Taylor, trying to gauge his reaction to the elaborate plans, but he had on his lawyer's face—impassive, unreadable except for once when their eyes met and he winked at her.

''We'll hire a string quartet, of course,'' Eleanor went on, spreading marmalade on toast. ''And then... oh, yes, Wilma, what is it?''

The maid stood in the doorway. ''I'm sorry to disturb you, but there's a phone call for Ivy.''

Ivy looked up. ''For me? Oh... it'll be Marilee telling me where they are.'' Her eyes were bright with expectation as she stood up. ''She so wanted it to be someplace romantic and elegant and... reeking with class. I'll be right back.''

As soon as she left the room, Eleanor leaned forward and spoke to Taylor in a hushed voice. ''Why did she run off? What was behind it all?''

''It's a very long story, and Ivy won't be gone long. Let's just say there was a breakdown in communication. She's back for good now, though. You don't have to worry that she'll ever leave.''

''There is no way I can ever possibly thank you for all you do for me, Taylor, but Ivy is the greatest gift of all.''

"She is, isn't she?"

Only minutes passed before Ivy was back in the dining room. "She sounds so happy," she said as she took her seat at the table.

"Well, where are they?" Taylor asked. "Did she get her classy, elegant place?"

"I don't know. What's Opryland?"

* * * * *

HARLEQUIN SUPERROMANCE®

COMING NEXT MONTH

#542 WORTH THE WAIT • Risa Kirk
Jack Stanton's dream was to buy the Gallagher family ranch and make
Margaret Gallagher his wife. But Margaret had her own plans . . . and
they didn't include Jack or a life on a Kentucky horse farm. She
belonged in New York. So why was she having such difficulty leaving
the farm?

#543 BUILT TO LAST • Leigh Roberts
Mary Ellen Saunderson had put her romance with Ramsey MacIver
behind her until her eccentric aunt decided it was time for them to
rekindle the flame. What Aunt Alma didn't realize was that her
scheme had put her niece's life in danger. Ramsey had enemies who
would stop at nothing to harm him—even if it meant hurting
Mary Ellen.

#544 JOE'S MIRACLE • Helen Conrad
Though Carly Stevens had just returned home to California to take a
breather and make some decisions, for Joe Matthews, Carly's arrival
was a miracle. His kids were crazy about her, and so was he. But then
she began asking questions about her family's past, and Joe knew he
had to keep her from learning the truth . . . for all their sakes.

#545 SNAP JUDGEMENT • Sandra Canfield
Women Who Dare, Book 4
There was no way Kelly Cooper was going to be a willing hostage.
Will Stone would rue the day he had broken into her apartment to
enlist her aid in clearing his name. He said she owed him—her
photograph had implicated him. Deep down Kelly was sure Will was
innocent, so maybe she'd help him. But not before she taught him
some manners.

AVAILABLE NOW:

Once upon a time...

There was the best romance series in all the land—Temptation

You loved the heroes of REBELS & ROGUES. Now discover the magic and fantasy of romance. *Pygmalion, Cinderella* and *Beauty and the Beast* have an enduring appeal—and are the inspiration for Temptation's exciting new yearlong miniseries, LOVERS & LEGENDS. Bestselling authors including Gina Wilkins, Glenda Sanders, JoAnn Ross and Tiffany White reweave these classic tales—with lots of sizzle! One book a month, LOVERS & LEGENDS continues in April 1993 with:

#437 DR. HUNK
Glenda Sanders
(The Frog Prince)

Live the fantasy....

LL4

HARLEQUIN®

Temptation

Where do you find hot Texas nights, smooth Texas charm and dangerously sexy cowboys?

COWBOYS AND CABERNET

Raise a glass—Texas style!

Tyler McKinney is out to prove a Texas ranch is the perfect place for a vineyard. Vintner Ruth Holden thinks Tyler is too stubborn, too impatient, too...Texas. And far too difficult to resist!

CRYSTAL CREEK reverberates with the exciting rhythm of Texas. Each story features the rugged individuals who live and love in the Lone Star State. And each one ends with the same invitation...

Y'ALL COME BACK...REAL SOON!

Don't miss *COWBOYS AND CABERNET* by Margot Dalton. Available in April wherever Harlequin books are sold.
